ADVANCE PRAISE FOR

THE DON CON

"A clever, fast-paced, and bittersweet caper. *The Don Con* is to Fan-Cons as *Galaxy Quest* is to *Star Trek* conventions."
—**Jonathan Frakes**, Commander William T. Riker on *Star Trek: The Next Generation*

"I loved this book! It could be my f*#%$@ autobiography!"
—**Joe Gannascoli**, Vito Spatafore on *The Sopranos*

"From its clever title to the crackling dialogue to the running gags that never get old, Richard Armstrong's *The Don Con* is a hilarious, fast-paced yarn in the tradition of Elmore Leonard and Carl Hiaasen."
—**Brian Rouff**, author of *Dice Angel* and *The House Always Wins*

"Marvelously entertaining, with witty dialogue, off-the-wall characters, and Shakespeare, *The Don Con* is clever, exceptionally well-written, and wildly funny."
—**Gretchen Archer**, bestselling author of the Davis Way Crime Capers

"A damn funny, fun, fast-paced caper story you won't want to put down."
—**Dan Kennedy**, coauthor of *Win, Place, or Die* and *Speaking of Murder*

"Sheer and unadulterated reading pleasure.'"
—**Beverly Swerling**, author of *Bristol House*

"You're in for a wild romp through pop culture peppered with mobsters and mayhem in Richard Armstrong's terrific new novel *The Don Con*. The book's smart, witty, and a joy to read from first page to last."
—**Donna Baier Stein**, author of *Sympathetic People* and *The Silver Baron's Wife*

"*The Don Con* lets loose on acting and stardom, Shakespeare, the mob, prison, revenge, redemption, and a dog named Gizmo. An amazing performance. Read it! You'll love it."
—**Deke Castleman**, author of *Whale Hunt in the Desert*

"Whether television bit player or Mafia big shot, every character in this book comes alive. Everyone who likes a good, suspenseful caper will be eager to keep reading."
—**David G. Schwartz**, Director of the Center for Gaming Research at University of Nevada, Las Vegas, and author of *Roll the Bones: The History of Gambling*

"Join hapless protagonist Joey Volpe on this romp through the hidden worlds of minimum-security jails, Fan-Cons and more. You couldn't possibly have more fun than I did."
—**Frank S. Joseph**, author of *To Love Mercy*

"Joey Volpe, bit actor on *The Sopranos*, rueful ladies' man, and involuntarily Mafioso, takes readers on a rollicking personal tour of pop culture, from *Star Trek* to aging child stars to Comic-Con, as he navigates the equally impossible systems of the Screen Actors Guild and organized crime. From the moment his dog, Gizmo, is kidnapped until he wages battle with the Philadelphia mob, you cannot help but root for Joey to come out on top."
—**Ann Bauer**, author of *Forgiveness 4 You*

"Here's your beach trip packing list. 1. Swimsuit. 2. Sunscreen. 3. Richard Armstrong's superb new caper novel *The Don Con*. It's a great summer read about ham actors, ham-handed gangsters, and inept con artists, all trying to survive the summer alive, and told with great humor and an insider's eye."
—**John Corcoran**, former KABC film & TV critic and author of *Doing Julia*

THE DON CON

Richard Armstrong

Pace Press
Fresno, California

Published by Pace Press
An imprint of Linden Publishing
2006 South Mary Street, Fresno, California 93721
(559) 233-6633 / (800) 345-4447
PacePress.com

Pace Press and Colophon are trademarks of
Linden Publishing, Inc.

ISBN 978-1-61035-336-6

135798642

Printed in the United States of America
on acid-free paper.

This is a work of fiction. The names, places, characters, and
incidents in this book are used fictitiously, and any resemblance
to actual people, places, or events is coincidental. Whenever real
celebrities, places, or businesses have been mentioned or appear
in this novel, they have been used fictitiously.

Library of Congress Cataloging-in-Publication Data

Names: Armstrong, Richard, 1952- author.
Title: The don con / Richard Armstrong.
Description: Fresno, California : Pace Press, [2019]
Identifiers: LCCN 2018052703 | ISBN 9781610353366 (pbk. :
alk. paper)
Subjects: LCSH: Swindlers and swindling--Fiction. | GSAFD:
Humorous fiction.
Classification: LCC PS3601.R577 D66 2019 | DDC 813/.6--dc23
LC record available at https://lccn.loc.gov/2018052703

Dedicated to the memory of my sister, Lydia K. Armstrong

"You've not experienced Shakespeare
until you've read it in the original Klingon."
—*Star Trek VI: The Undiscovered Country*

ACT ONE
THE SET-UP

1

Until the day they stole my dog Gizmo, I always thought my life would turn out to be a comedy. In other words, I thought it would have a happy ending.

That's what my Shakespeare professor in college taught me about the difference between comedy and tragedy. A comedy always has a happy ending, he said, even if a bunch of sad stuff happens along the way. A tragedy, on the other hand, could have you rolling in the aisles with laughter from the moment the curtain rises. By the time it falls, everybody onstage is lying in a pool of blood.

On the day they dognapped Gizmo, I was still betting on comedy. A lot of funny stuff had happened in my forty years on earth, that's for sure. But then a mobster stole my dog, and I realized he could kill me. Worse, he could kill my wife and daughter, too. I couldn't think of anything more tragic than that.

It all started with a silly argument between me and Caitlin about whose turn it was to walk the dog. It really was her turn to walk him. Honestly, it was. But I lost the argument. I was losing a lot of arguments in those days after she caught me cheating with another woman.

Wonder Woman, to be precise.

"It's not my turn to walk him," I said.

"I don't care if it's your turn or not," said Caitlin. "You've spent the last three days in Atlantic City screwing Wonder Woman while I've been taking care of the dog *and* your daughter. The least you can do to make things fair around here would be to take Gizmo for a walk around the block."

"Caitlin, please stop making jokes about me sleeping with some female superhero. It happened *one* time. Are you going to keep giving me shit about it for the rest of your life? Because if you are, I'm outta here."

"Good idea. Why don't you take Gizmo for a walk and just keep on going? But bring the dog back first."

"Gizmo, come." I put the harness and leash on our little white terrier and headed out the door.

It was the night before trash pickup on the Upper West Side of Manhattan, Gizmo's favorite night of the week. On most nights it would take me fifteen minutes to walk him around the block. This night, it took twice as long because Gizmo was a big believer in stopping to smell the roses. Only in his case the roses were old chicken wings, empty soup cans, and half-eaten bagels.

We were halfway around the block when a car ran up on the curb and screeched to a halt ten feet away from where Gizmo and I were standing, almost hitting the dog. There were two young black guys in the car and they threw open the doors and charged in my direction.

"What the hell are you doing? You almost hit my dog!"

They didn't answer.

Instead, one guy grabbed me by the throat and threw me against the brick wall of the nearest building. My head hit the wall hard and I could feel blood start to gush out. The other guy took the leash out of my hands and pulled Gizmo away from me. I could see him pick Gizmo up in his arms and carry him back to the car. A *dognapping*? That's strange, I thought. But I had more pressing things on my mind. The first guy shoved his forearm hard against my throat, almost choking me to death.

"Give me your money, motherfucker."

"All right, all right." I was in no position to fight back. He was bigger than me. Stronger. And there were two of them. All I could do was give them whatever they wanted.

"I don't have much money, but I'll give you everything I've got."

"Hand it over now, asshole."

So I gave him my wallet. My watch, too.

He looked over the meager haul. "That's it?"

"I'm just an actor," I said.

He slipped his foot behind mine and gave me a shove. I tripped and fell to the ground, scraping my arms and elbows as I tried to break my fall. The mugger ran back to the car. His partner was in the passenger seat, holding Gizmo in his lap. Gizmo struggled to break free and barked like crazy. I got to my feet as fast as I could and ran toward the car.

"Give me back my dog! You don't need the dog! Let me keep my dog!"

The car took off as fast as it had come. The driver laid a patch of rubber on both the sidewalk and the street as he floored the gas pedal. He ran a red light at the end of the block and took a hard right so fast that for a moment the car ran on two wheels. Then it vanished.

"Gizmo, come back! Come back, Gizmo!" I yelled, as if the dog could overcome his captors and drive the car back to me. I burst into tears.

A few minutes later, I stumbled back into the apartment and Caitlin could tell right away something was wrong.

"What happened to you? You're bleeding."

"I got mugged by two guys in a car."

"Mugged? Are you okay?"

"I don't know. I think so."

"Where's Gizmo?"

"Gizmo's gone."

"Gone? What do you mean gone?"

"They took him."

"Who took him?"

"The muggers."

"They stole Gizmo?"

"Yes."

"Oh my God. How could you let that happen?"

"How could I let it happen? There were two of them. One of them tried to kill me. He took my wallet. He took my watch. The other one took the dog."

"Why would they take a *dog*?"

"I don't know. Listen, Caitlin, we've got to call the cops right now."

I stumbled toward the telephone in the kitchen. As I was about to pick it up, it rang.

"This is Joey Volpe," I said. "I don't know who's calling but please hang up now. I need to make an emergency call to the police."

"Well, hello to you, too," said a familiar voice on the phone.

"Who is this?"

"Why don't we chat for a while and you'll figure out who it is. How does that sound?"

I knew who it was.

"Look, Mr. . . . Don . . . er, Godfather . . . sir . . . I'm serious. Please hang up. I need to call the police right away."

"What about?"

"Somebody robbed me on the street and stole my dog."

"Dognapping, huh? There's been a rash of that kind of crime recently. Disgusting. I bet it was a couple of *melanzane*, too, wasn't it? Animals stealing animals. You know, Joey, in my neighborhood people don't call the cops when something like this happens. They call me. The cops don't give a shit. But I can usually help out my friends in situations like this."

"What are you talking about?"

"Have you had time to think about my proposition, Joey?"

"Yes, I thought about. it. And I already told you my decision. Absolutely not. I don't want any part of it. I'm not a criminal. I'm just an actor."

"Well, think about it a little more, Joey. But first, I've got some good news for you."

"What?"

"I found your dog. He's with me now. What a sweet little guy. What do they call the breed of this dog? Some kind of terrier, right?"

"West Highland White Terrier."

"That's right. Westie. That's ironical. We used to do some work with a gang of Irish guys on the Upper West Side of Manhattan who called themselves Westies. They were mean bastards, though. Not like this little dog. He's a sweetie. What's his name?

"Gizmo."

"Cute name. I always liked this type of dog. Oh, I found your watch and your wallet, too. A Timex, Joey? Why don't you live a little and buy yourself a nice watch?"

"Well, I'm just an actor."

"You seem to say that a lot. Listen, Joey, here's the good news. In five minutes, you're going to hear a knock on the door. It's gonna be the same guy who stole your wallet and your dog. But don't be afraid. He's completely reformed now. He's turned his life around. He's in a twelve-step program. And his first step on the road to recovery is to give you back your dog. And your wallet. And your shitty little watch."

"That guy works for you?" I was slow to catch on. "How is that possible? He's a black guy, not Italian. Plus this is New York, and you're in Philadelphia."

"Well, Joey, we're an equal opportunity employer now. We have associates in New York who do favors for us, just like we do favors for them in Philly. We're like one big happy family, so to speak. So all's well that ends well, as you actors say, right?"

"I guess so."

"All I want in return for my generosity, Joey, is for you to think about something for the next few days."

"Think about what?"

"Think about this. If it was that easy for me to take your dog from you, think how easy it would be to take your daughter or your wife. In fact, think about how easy it would be for me to take your daughter *and* your wife. I could fuck your wife in front of your daughter. Then I could fuck your daughter in front of your wife. And then I could dump them both in the East River. I mean, if I *wanted* to. Which I don't. I simply want you to think about that possibility. Then I want you to think some more about what we discussed in Atlantic City."

I was silent for a long time. For all the problems Caitlin and I had been having in our marriage, I loved her more than anyone on earth. I suspected that half the reason I cheated on her was because I felt like I didn't deserve her. And our five-year-old daughter Bianca? Well, I loved her more than life itself.

"Joey? Are you still there?"

"I can't talk now. How can I reach you?"

"The nice young man who found your dog is going to give you a business card with a phone number on it. You can call that number any time day or night. Operators are standing by now," he added with a chuckle before hanging up.

Then there was a knock at the door.

Before I tell you what happened next, I should explain how an actor like me ran into a mob boss like Tony Rosetti. It happened two days earlier at the Taj Mahal Hotel & Casino in Atlantic City. I was signing autographs for fans of *The Sopranos*. You see, like Tony Rosetti, I too was a mobster.

Well, not really. But I played one on TV.

2

"What was James Gandolfini really like?" said the tall skinny guy looming over me as he handed me a photograph to sign.

The photograph was a picture of me. This guy had just paid thirty-five dollars for the privilege of having me sign it. That entitled him to fifteen seconds of conversation with me. Like many of the people who waited in line for my autograph, he wanted the inside scoop on James Gandolfini.

It was the most common question I heard in these autograph sessions. You'd think I'd have come up with a good answer by now. But it made me want to ask some questions of my own. For example: Do you want the truth? If so, do you want the *whole* truth? And if you don't want the truth, would you accept a stock answer that would let me move on to the next person?

The truth is I have no idea what James Gandolfini was like. We had one scene together in my three appearances on *The Sopranos*, and I had one line in that scene. The line wasn't even directed at Gandolfini, so he didn't have to wait for a reaction shot if he didn't want to. And he didn't. After he finished, he went to his dressing room to memorize his lines for the next day.

So the truth is that I didn't know him at all. But I thought he was an okay guy. I was the only actor in the scene who had never worked with him before. He was polite enough to introduce himself before we started rehearsing.

"Hi, I'm Jimmy Gandolfini," he said, holding out his hand.

"So nice to meet you," I stammered. "An honor, really. I admire your work. I'm a big fan of the show."

"And your name is?"

"Oh, I'm sorry. It's Joseph. Joseph Volpe. My friends call me Joey. I'm sorry, I'm a little nervous."

"Don't be nervous, Joey. This is a thirty-second scene that'll take three hours to shoot. Two hours from now you'll be so tired of doing it over and over again you won't be nervous anymore.

You'll just want to get it done and go home. So hang in there. Try to have fun if you can. You'll do fine."

It was good advice, so I smiled and nodded. But I didn't hear a word of it. Having a face-to-face conversation with Tony Soprano left me star struck.

So my impression of James Gandolfini? He was a decent guy.

But am I going to tell all this to some geek who waited in line for fifteen minutes to get an autograph? Of course not. First of all, it would reveal that I hardly knew James Gandolfini at all. That's the last thing I wanted to do in this situation. Secondly, it would take too much time. So I had a stock answer:

"He was a great man. A great actor. He was very helpful to me in my career. He gave me some advice about acting I'll never forget. But he was a troubled man. A complex man. I couldn't really get close to him. I wish I could, because maybe if I'd been a better friend I could've helped him."

The usual response to this was, "Wow!"

To which I would say, "Did you bring something for me to sign or did you want a photograph?"

This was the cue for my assistant at the convention to give his spiel, which went something like this: "If you brought something for Mr. Volpe to sign, the charge is thirty-five dollars. If not, you can buy a headshot for fifteen dollars. If you want me to take your picture with Mr. Volpe using your phone, that's an extra twenty-five dollars. Most people take the whole package, so that's seventy-five dollars. Cash only. Exact change would help."

My assistant's name was David. He was a nerd. And quite proud of it. He made no attempt to hide it. Crew cut, horned-rim glasses, white short-sleeved dress shirt. His skin was so pale that I thought he was wearing the shade of makeup referred to in the theater as clown white. Everybody here was a nerd or a geek and none of them seemed the least bit ashamed of it. This was the one place in the world where they could embrace their nerdiness. David was one of the hundreds of volunteers here at the 2014 Fan-a-Palooza Con in Atlantic City. He did this work for the sheer pleasure of rubbing shoulders with superstars like myself. He understood that at the end of the day, I would give him about 5 percent of the day's take for a tip. Some of my fellow celebrities were so cheap they refused to hire someone like David to help them. I tried that and regretted it.

It's demeaning enough signing eight-by-ten-inch photographs of yourself at a fan convention without managing hordes of autograph seekers. Keeping them in line. Asking them face-to-face for money. "Only cash, please, I can't take credit cards." Making change when necessary. Stuffing twenty-dollar bills until every pocket in your pants and your shirt is overflowing, and you're shoving money in your shoes and down your underpants.

(Nowadays, more and more actors take credit cards. Or so I'm told. But this was several years ago, and it was still an all-cash business.)

Meanwhile, each one of these fans wants to stop and chat with you about what James Gandolfini was really like. Or their secret theory that Carmela Soprano was an informant for the FBI. Or every now and then—and I must confess I had a soft spot for these fans—somebody would remember the other cable television series I was on, *Button Men*. I had a pretty big role on that show. Well, not big exactly, but big enough for my name to show up in the credits.

Even though I was a gangster on TV, it was David's job to play the bad guy in this little scene. I played the charming celebrity who wanted nothing more than to spend the day chatting with his fans. After I delivered my stock answer about Gandolfini, David took over. "As you can see, sir, Mr. Volpe is very busy. There are a lot of people waiting in line to get his autograph. Unless you want me to take a picture with you and Mr. Volpe—and that's an extra twenty-five dollars, cash please—I'm going to have to ask you to move along and give the next person in line a chance to meet him."

I smiled at the fan and shrugged my shoulders as if to say, "I'd love to talk to you all day. But alas, I must obey this geeky little nerd seated next to me because he's wearing an official volunteer badge around his neck."

"Naaah," said the fan. "No picture. I would like the autograph, though. And could you make it out to Barry, a real *pezzonovante*?"

I chuckled. Pezzonovante meant ninety caliber in Italian. I knew this for two reasons. My father was a professor of Italian literature at the University of Pennsylvania. He was born in Genoa and moved here with his parents, my grandparents, when he was five years old. So I'm second generation and I speak a little Italian. I also knew the word pezzonovante because it's used throughout the *Godfather* movies as a Sicilian expression meaning big shot. The characters always said it with a touch of sarcasm, implying the person in question was powerful but not trustworthy. In proper Italian the phrase would be *pezzo da novanta*. But I didn't bother to correct the guy.

Instead, I signed the autograph just the way he wanted it. David collected the cash. Before I knew it, I was face-to-face with the next fan in line. Who turned out to be a real pezzonovante. And who changed my life forever.

Not for the better.

3

I'd been watching the next fan in line out of the corner of my eye for the past fifteen minutes as he worked his way to the front. I noticed him because he looked like a gangster.

Not that this was unusual. In any given line of people waiting to get my autograph at a fan convention (sometimes known as a Fan-Con), at least two or three of them would dress like gangsters. Most of them wore 1930s-style zoot suits with spats on their shoes. They sported wide ties with a glittery diamond tie clasp fastened a few inches under the knot. The pinstripes on their suits were so wide you could no longer call them "pin" stripes. They were like chalk marks used to outline a dead body on the sidewalk. A Sinatra-style felt fedora topped it all off.

When considering the way most attendees at a Fan-Con dressed, the gangster-movie fans were the soul of sartorial understatement. There were Klingons from *Star Trek*, complete with the elaborate facial makeup that made their foreheads look like a turtle shell. There were a few Darth Vaders wandering around, dragging their light sabers behind them. Superman. Batman. Spiderman. Plus, dozens of caped crusaders of one kind or another that I didn't recognize. (I was never a big fan of superhero comics when I was a kid.) Then there was the whole contingent of fantasy, vampire, and zombie fans. Again, these are literary genres with which I am unfamiliar. I couldn't tell who was who and couldn't care less.

What was intriguing about the guy who looked like a gangster was that he did not dress like a movie gangster. He looked like a real gangster. No zoot suit. No chalky pinstripes. No diamond tie clasp. No tie at all.

So how does a real gangster dress?

It's *not* the fine tailored suits that John Gotti, the so-called dandy don, used to wear. He was the exception that proves the rule. A real gangster wears an ordinary white dress shirt with an open collar. The gold chains around the neck are a dead giveaway, especially the number of them. One necklace is not unusual on any man nowadays. Neither is an earring, come to think of it. Three or more gold chains tells you that you might be dealing with a mobster. One of these necklaces will have a crucifix attached with a small figurine of Jesus Christ in extremis. Inevitably, another necklace will contain an Italian teardrop-style heart. On a single neck you can not only witness the passion of Christ but also see someone shed a tear about it. A gangster's watch is almost always a fifty-thousand-dollar diamond-studded gold Rolex. For that kind of money you could buy a nice Patek Philippe from Switzerland or Breguet from France. These guys always think Rolex is the epitome of fine watchmaking. A diamond pinky ring? It goes without saying. The pants are ordinary gabardine black slacks. It's in their choice of shoes where they sometimes show a flash of good taste. Bruno Magli. Ferragamo. Gucci. Prada. Gangsters think nothing of spending a thousand bucks to decorate their feet.

How do I know all this? Two ways.

While killing time on the set of *Button Men*, I had a long conversation with a chatty woman who worked in the wardrobe department. She told me the producers hired consultants to tell them what real-life gangsters wear. How these consultants acquired such expertise, she couldn't say for sure. She suspected some of them were former undercover cops or gangsters themselves.

The other way I know what real gangsters wear is that every now and then I meet one of them. It's hard to tell for sure. For every hundred guys who come up to me and try to leave the impression they are in the Mafia, I'm sure ninety-nine of them are faking it. They're Italian. They've got the New York accent. They're dressed about right (except for the shoes and watch). But I'm sure the vast majority are insurance salesman, auto-body mechanics, or grocery store clerks who get a kick out of pretending to be Mafiosi—especially when they meet an actor who played a gangster on TV. If guys like this ever ran into a real gangster, they'd wet their pants.

Which may be why I felt a twinge in my bladder when I came face-to-face with the next guy in the autograph line. I had a feeling he wasn't faking it. Something about his hooded eyes. His bent nose. The nasty scar that extended from his left ear down to his chin. His old acne pockmarks looked like his face had caught on fire and someone tried to put it out with a chain saw. And his clothing? Well, it fit the pattern.

"How you doin'?" he said. "Nice to meet you."

The accent was *not* New York, which was unusual. Wannabe gangsters almost always spoke some version of Brooklynese. But this accent was 100 percent pure Philadelphia.

I was good with voices and accents as an actor. That was the big rap on me when I went to drama school and got my MFA at Yale. "He's just a voice and makeup actor," they'd say behind my back. Of course, I heard the gossip from my so-called friends.

"Yeah, well, Lawrence Olivier was a voice and makeup actor, too," I'd say. "And it worked out pretty well for him."

"You're no Olivier," they'd reply.

The criticism always stung. In part because I knew it was true. Whenever I approached a new role, I tried to come up with some exotic accent or strange voice that might fit the character. Lawrence Olivier notwithstanding, it's a superficial way to approach the craft of acting and it took me years to outgrow it.

I could never do the South Philly accent myself. Maybe I was too close to it. Like I said, my dad taught at Penn. I grew up in the Main Line suburban town of Gladwyne, where my mother had a private practice as an ob-gyn doc. And I went to college in Haverford, Pennsylvania, yet another Philadelphia suburb. I heard the accent my whole life on local television or whenever I ventured downtown to Center City ("Senner See").

But my father, who learned English the hard way as a five-year-old immigrant from Italy, was a stickler for correct pronunciation and grammar at home. So I grew up speaking a standard American dialect like a network radio announcer from the 1930s.

But I could recognize a South Philadelphia accent in a heart-beat. Like a latter-day Henry Higgins, I fancied myself something of an expert on it. I could tell you where a Philadelphian grew up within a radius of a hundred feet after hearing him say a single sentence.

So when the strange man in front of me said, "I came allzaway downashoor from Filelfia to seeyuz," I would've been willing to bet he was born no farther from Philadelphia's Little Italy than you could throw a strand of limp spaghetti.

Translated into English he said: "I came all the way down to the shore from Philadelphia to see you."

"Well, I sure appreciate it," I replied.

"Downashoor" could mean anywhere from Asbury Park at the northern tip of the Jersey shore to Cape May at the southern end. In this case, he was talking about Atlantic City, which was an hour from Philly. His weary tone implied that he had just made the pilgrimage of the Camino di Santiago, crawling on his hands and knees all the way from Paris to the coast of Spain.

"Yeah, I came allzaway downashoor to seeyuz," he said, as if his sacrifice had not made enough impact on me the first time.

"And I'm glad you did. What's your name?" I said while reaching for the Sharpie pen in the hope I could dispatch this guy as soon as possible.

"Tony Rosetti."

"Well, it's a pleasure to meet you, Mr. Rosetti. Should I make this out to you or to someone else?"

"My name don't mean nuthin' to you?"

(By the way, I'm going to stop trying to recreate the Philadelphia accent from this point forward. First, because it's not reproducible on paper, relying as it does on peculiar diphthongs, glottal stops, and other unpleasant noises that linguists haven't discovered yet, much less transcribed. Second, it's one of the ugliest accents in the world—like the Baltimore accent without the charm.)

"Should it mean something to me? Did we work together?"

"No, you've never worked for me, that's for sure," he said with a nasty smile.

"I mean were you on *Sopranos* or *Button Men* or in some other show with me?"

"I'm no actor," he said.

"Then how do we know each other?"

"We don't know each other. I thought you might recognize my name, that's all."

"Well, I'm sorry, Mr. Rosetti, but it doesn't ring a bell. We don't even have any Rosettis in my family. Sometimes I think I'm related to every Italian on the East Coast."

It was a lame attempt at humor, but I thought it might at least get him to crack a smile. Instead, he bored into me with those hooded eyes.

He said nothing for a long time. Like any actor, I abhorred the vacuum of silence and felt the need to fill it with the sound of my own voice. "So I'll make this out to Tony Rosetti, then, okay?"

"I don't want your autograph."

"Sir, you already paid for it."

I turned to David to confirm that this guy had purchased the eight-by-ten photo and paid for my signature. David was looking rather pale. Paler than usual, I should say. He'd been listening to this conversation. Maybe *he* recognized the name Tony Rosetti. I felt the need to wrap this up. I began writing without waiting for any further instruction from Mr. Rosetti.

"'To Tony Rosetti,'" I said aloud as I wrote the words in big block letters with a silver Sharpie that would show up against the dark background. "'*In bocca al lupo*! Sincerely, Joseph Volpe.' How does that sound?"

In bocca al lupo was an Italian expression that meant "Good luck." Literally, it meant "In the wolf's mouth." The traditional response was "*Crepi il lupo*," or "May the wolf die." (Failure to complete this non-rhyming couplet is bad luck indeed.) I always used this line whenever I ran into an autograph-seeker of Italian descent. But I usually had to translate it for them. Not Mr. Rosetti, though.

"*Crepi il lupo*," he said. "But I already told you I don't want your autograph. I want to talk to you."

"Mr. Rosetti, sir, we've got hundreds of people behind you in line."

I glanced at the line to confirm the accuracy of my estimate. There were about seven people standing around looking ready to go somewhere else.

"Well, I mean, we've got almost a dozen people in line waiting for an autograph. It wouldn't be fair to them if I talked much longer to you. They've been waiting a long time."

I turned to David for support. Dealing with problems like this was what he was there for, after all. To say he had a deer-in-the-headlights look on his face would be putting it mildly. It was more like the look you'd expect to see on the face of an American newspaper reporter threatened by a terrorist with decapitation.

"Not here. Not now. I want to take you to lunch. I know a nice Italian place on Baltic Avenue."

"I already have a luncheon engagement today, sir," I said like Miss Manners declining an unwanted invitation.

"Drink at the bar, then?"

"I'm not a big drinker."

I appealed to David again with a helpless glance. He couldn't speak.

"Wooder ice onna boorwawk?"

Sorry, I know I promised no more Philadelphia accents. Wooder ice was South Philly's way of saying water ice, which most Americans call Italian Ices and what Italians themselves call *granita*. The rest of the sentence you can figure out for yourself.

"I'm sorry, Mr. Rosetti. I have ninety minutes for lunch. As I said, I'm meeting a friend. Then I have a panel discussion. After that, there's another autograph session in the afternoon. So I'm booked solid all day."

"How about dinner, then? Look, Mr. Volpe, I want to talk to you about an acting job. There might be some money in it for you."

An acting job with money involved? He happened to mention the two things I wanted most at that moment. I had simple needs in life. Fame and fortune, that's all. What he had to say tempted me to listen. But there was still something suspicious—like a cat offering a mouse two pieces of cheese. So I said, "You'll need to talk to my agent about that."

"Naaah, you don't want get your agent involved in something like this."

Just as well, I thought. If my agent ever got a call from someone wanting to hire Joey Volpe, her first reaction would be to ask, "Who's Joey Volpe?"

"So what do you say? How about dinner? My treat," he said.

I thought mobsters got people to do their bidding by threatening them with guns. I was beginning to learn that unrelenting, dogged persistence was their weapon of choice. This time I could think of no more excuses.

"Uh, well, I . . ."

"I'll be back," said Rosetti and he walked away.

I turned to David and signaled him to hold up the autograph line for a moment so we could talk.

"'I'll be back?' Who does that guy think he is, The Terminator?"

"Worse."

"You know him?"

"I've seen his name in the papers. He's part of what's left of the Italian mob in Philadelphia."

"I know the names of all the big Philly mobsters," I said. "Scarfo. Testa. Bruno. I never heard of this guy."

"He's just below them," said David. "Or maybe he's on top by now. A lot of those guys you mentioned are in jail. On account of RICO. The good news is that there isn't much left of the Philadelphia mob anymore. Most of them are dead or in prison."

"What's the bad news?"

"It looks like Tony Rosetti isn't one of them."

"How do you know all this stuff?"

"There's a website."

I looked at David for a moment. Here was a guy who spent a lot of time in front of a computer screen. I had no doubt he knew what he was talking about.

"Who are you having lunch with, by the way?" he asked.

"Jeremiah Pennington."

"Whoa!"

For the first time since I met David that morning, he seemed impressed with my star power. Or at least my star power by proxy. "Can you get his autograph for me?"

"I can get you *my* autograph. Hand me a photo."

"No, seriously. If you got me his autograph, I'd be your slave forever."

"You're already my slave for the weekend, David."

"Seriously. Can you get it?"

"I'll see what I can do. Meanwhile, let's finish up with these people in line now. Then I've got to go meet Jerry."

"You call him Jerry? Holy shit!"

"I should've known you were a Trekkie, David."

"I sure am. All the way back to *TOS*."

TOS meant *The Original Series* in Trek-speak.

"By the way, Mr. Volpe, what are you going to do if Rosetti comes back later like he said?"

"I don't think he's coming back. But if he does, I'll come up with some act. I'll fake like I'm sick or something."

That's what actors do, after all, right?

4

You must be wondering how a B celebrity like myself—oh, let's face it, a D-minus celebrity like myself—makes a living selling autographs at pop-culture fan conventions.

The simple answer is I don't make a living at it. Not by a long shot. Which has caused some friction between my wife and me. But it helps keep me out of the poorhouse. I can make a thousand dollars a day at one of these Fan-Cons. Usually, there are two days of autograph sessions. I'll bring home about two thousand for the weekend. And it's all cash so I don't have to declare it.

If there were a Fan-Con every weekend, I'd be okay. But I can only book about ten or twelve of these conventions a year, so I'm flirting with the poverty line. My wife has been making noises about applying for food stamps. Every once in a while, sponsors invite me to do a panel discussion with other actors, and they give me an extra fee for that. Usually, another five hundred bucks or so.

The bigger stars, like Jeremiah Pennington, for example, make plenty more than I do. They not only make more in the autograph room, but they make more for panel discussions, too. The sponsors bend over backward to give them all sorts of free stuff—from fruit baskets in their hotel rooms to limousine rides from the airport. I, on the other hand, have to *apply* for the privilege of appearing at one of these conventions. To add insult to injury, I have to pay an application fee. I pay my own expenses to and from the airport and pay for my own hotel room, too. I usually can't afford to stay in the same hotel as the convention because it's so packed with nerds and geeks that the rack rate goes up. I have to find a Motel 6 (or a friend's couch) twenty miles away.

Which brings up the next question you're probably asking yourself right now. Why would someone pay for the autograph of an actor who hit the high watermark of his career when he had three walk-on roles in *The Sopranos* and a small recurring role on another cable television series that nobody ever saw?

My answer to that question is: Your guess is as good as mine! There doesn't seem to be a celebrity in the country who can't make money signing autographs at a Fan-Con. One time I was signing autographs next to the girl . . . well, the elderly lady who played Janet Leigh's body double in *Psycho*. Back in 1960, legitimate starlets like Janet Leigh wouldn't dream of appearing nude—even though you couldn't see anything other than the small of her back and maybe the crack of her ass. So they hired this woman to portray Janet Leigh's naked butt. Fifty years later the line to get her autograph at thirty-five bucks a pop stretched out the door and into the hall. Can you believe it?

Heck, can you believe that people pay thirty-five bucks for *my* autograph?

I got into this whole acting thing by accident. I wanted to be a college professor like my dad. Not Italian literature, though. I wanted to be an English professor. I grew up a skinny kid who couldn't play sports so I spent most of my childhood reading. My parents let me read anything I wanted on the theory that reading would be better for me than watching TV. Even at the age of twelve or thirteen, they'd let me read "adult" novels, true-crime stories, and all sorts of trashy stuff. But my father would urge me to elevate my taste.

Dad would catch me reading some soft-core porn novel and say, "You like titillating novels, Joey? Try *Lolita* by Nabokov. Or *Tropic of Cancer* by Henry Miller. You like crime stories? Try Dostoevsky. That's the good stuff."

And so I did.

By the time I was ready for college, I'd read everything worth reading in the canon of English literature from Chaucer to Cheever. Maybe that's why I scored a perfect 800 on the verbal part of my SATs. I got 540 on the math part, though. Which is probably why I didn't get into my first-choice school, Swarthmore, and had to settle for Haverford, my second choice. Living in the Philadelphia area, both were commuter schools for me.

Haverford was an all-boys school at the time. Having graduated from an all-boys prep school, I yearned to socialize with members of the opposite sex. The only way to do that at Haverford was to take part in one of the extracurricular activities we shared with our sister school, Bryn Mawr. There was no better activity for that purpose than the theater.

Problem was, I didn't know diddly-squat about the theater and had no interest in it. I'd read all the classic plays, especially Shakespeare. But I knew nothing about acting, directing, lighting, makeup, or any of that stuff. When I was a kid, grown-ups (especially my mom's friends) gushed about how good-looking I was and said, "You should go to Hollywood when you grow up."

I thought I looked kind of weird. The strange combination of olive skin, pale blue eyes, and black curly hair was so different from any of my classmates I felt like a freak. I guess some people found it appealing.

In the fall of my freshman year, with nothing more on my mind than finding a way to meet girls, I showed up at the open auditions held by Haverford and Bryn Mawr to cast all the plays for the coming year. I arrived clutching a copy of *King Lear*, with Lear's mad scene on the heath highlighted in yellow ink. I knew so little about casting I thought it was appropriate for a seventten-year-old Italian kid with blue eyes and curly black hair to read for the part of King Lear.

Yet when I took the stage and began reading, I felt a powerful surge of energy take over my body. "Blow winds and crack your cheeks," I shouted in a voice that didn't sound like my own. "Rage, blow, you cataracts and hurricanoes . . ."

I felt like a demon had taken over me, expressing anger, bitterness, and self-pity I didn't know I had. It took me less than a minute to read the famous soliloquy. When it ended there was a stunned silence, with no one more stunned than myself.

Then came a burst of applause from the audience that struck me like a shotgun blast. Not just the sound of it, I could actually feel the wind on my face. I stumbled back to my seat in the theater, where the other actors about to give their audition were waiting nervously. One of them tapped me on the shoulder and said, "Awesome reading, dude."

Afterward, no fewer than a dozen good-looking Bryn Mawr girls came up to me to say how much they enjoyed my reading. They asked me where I was from. Where I went to high school. What other plays I'd done. They seemed amazed when I said the answer was none.

I could get used to this, I thought.

A few professors who were directing plays in the upcoming season stopped to say hello. "I'm directing *Othello* in the spring," said a man in a corduroy jacket with patches on the sleeves. "I think you might be right for Iago. Would you be willing to read for that part later on?"

Othello was set in Venice. Iago was a smooth-tongued, smarmy, Machiavellian villain. Here was a guy who knew something about casting.

So I did play Iago the following spring. It turned out to be a big success. Altogether, I must've been in five plays that year and in each succeeding year, too. Haverford didn't offer a degree in theater back then. It was strictly an extracurricular activity. So I wound up majoring in English after all, like I planned. But I fell in love with the theater at college. Soon it became much more than just a way to meet girls. By the time I graduated, I knew it was what I wanted to do for the rest of my life.

Then I made a terrible mistake.

Instead of heading for Hollywood, I allowed my father, a life-long academic, to convince me to get an MFA at Yale.

"With a graduate degree from a prestigious university, you can always teach if things don't work out," he said.

"Those who can't . . ." I almost replied. But I had to admit he had a point.

So I spent two years at Yale, where I learned such vital skills as how to position my hands and feet when acting in a Restoration comedy. How to practice my enunciation before a performance: *"What a to-do to die today at a minute or two to two."* And why I should never refer to Shakespeare's *Macbeth* by its proper name, but as "The Scottish Play." (Bad luck, you know.)

The only good thing that happened to me at Yale was that I met my wife there. I met her doing *Romeo and Juliet*. I played Romeo. She was Juliet. Can you believe it? Can you think of anything more romantic than that? Or anything more clichéd?

Funny thing is, I didn't think Caitlin was all that pretty at first. She was cute as hell. But she had the kind of face that was better suited for sitcoms—like Julia Louis-Dreyfuss or Amy Poehler. Not the drop-dead beauty you want to cast as Juliet.

I remember saying to a friend when the cast list appeared on the bulletin board in the drama department, "Is that the best-looking girl they could find at Yale? They should've opened the audition to the townies."

"What a great idea," said my friend. "A biracial *Romeo and Juliet!*"

He was referring to the fact that many of the townies in New Haven were African-American. (It wasn't such a bad idea at all. It would've given the Montagues and Capulets another reason to hate each other.) But we were doing a more traditional *Romeo and Juliet*, set in Verona, Italy. Which is probably why I got the role in the first place.

At any rate, I wasn't all that impressed with Caitlin until we started rehearsals. But it didn't take long for her to impress me. For one thing, she was a terrific actress. Charismatic. Charming. Captivating. She was one of those performers who lit up the stage as soon as she made an entrance. She could recite Shakespearean couplets as naturally as most people could chat with their best friend. The biggest challenge when it comes to performing Shakespeare is to help the audience understand what's being said. The language is so foreign to the modern ear. Caitlin could do that as well as anyone I'd ever seen—including Gielgud, Olivier, Branagh, and all the other Shakespearean *pezzonovanti*.

So Caitlin and I fell in love. We couldn't even wait until we graduated to get married. We held the ceremony right in New Haven in the chapel at Yale. Both the campus and the town were enchanted by the fact that Romeo and Juliet got married. The *Yale Daily News* and even the *New Haven Register* wrote our story. We were the toast of the town for a while. Then we graduated and we had to face the cold, cruel world of show business armed with nothing but two worthless MFA degrees. That's when we made our second big mistake:

We moved to New York City.

If there are any budding actors reading this, let me give you some advice. Please, please, please don't move to New York City. Move to Los Angeles. That's where the jobs are. There's hardly any work in New York for actors anymore. Not unless you're a good enough singer and dancer to work in a chorus line.

I couldn't dance to save my life. Even a simple two-step would get my feet so tangled up I'd trip and fall. And Caitlin? She was the worst singer I ever heard in my life. Her speaking voice was like a melody. But as soon as she tried to sing, she sounded like a stray cat in the alley.

So what's left for an actor in New York who can't sing or dance? Not much. A handful of legitimate dramas appear on Broadway and off-Broadway every year. Most of them close within a month or two. They tend to have small casts to save on production costs, and your chances of landing one of those roles are next to nil. There's almost no television production left in New York, except for news programs. And movies? Well, Hollywood directors love to *set* their movies in New York, but they do their casting out of Los Angeles. Hell, even most television commercials cast in Hollywood these days.

So most actors in New York spin their wheels by doing off-off-Broadway, or Equity Showcases. The idea is to *showcase* your talent in a nonsalaried production in the hope that an agent might wander in and sign you up. You've got a better chance of getting discovered hanging out at a drugstore like Lana Turner than doing an off-off-Broadway show.

Nothing was happening for either Caitlin or me in New York for year after year. We sent out our résumés to agents and casting directors asking them to see our showcases, but they never came.

I kept telling Caitlin that something would break for us. But she was more pessimistic than I was. She had two clocks running out on her.

Her biological clock was ticking because she wanted to have children someday. (She spent most of her thirtieth birthday crying in the bathroom.) And she had the female actor's clock running, too. If you're an actress who hasn't made it by the time you're thirty, your chances of becoming a star go from small to vanishingly small. But when things were looking their bleakest, something good happened . . .

The Sopranos.

HBO came up with a new television series about the modern-day Mafia and—guess what?—they decided to film it in New York City! At Silvercup Studios in Long Island City, Queens. The word went out to casting directors that they needed dozens, scores, no *hundreds* of New York actors of Italian descent to cast this new show.

The news triggered a veritable dragnet for Italian-American actors in New York City. I got calls from agents and casting directors I hadn't contacted in years. I could almost see them going through their files—probably their trash cans, too—looking for postcards and résumés from actors with names ending in a vowel.

I tried out for some of the big parts and most of the smaller roles. The casting director and associate producers must've liked me because they kept calling me back. Sometimes I'd get pretty far along in the process, two or three callbacks. But something was holding me back. You know what it was?

It was my goddamned blue eyes!

Every time I auditioned, some assistant casting director or associate producer would say, "So how does someone named Joseph Volpe get pale blue eyes like those?"

And I'd say something like this:

"My dad was born in Genoa and moved here when he was five. But he fell in love with a Norwegian from Minnesota. Opposites attract, I guess. So the recessive gene kicked in, and I wound up with the baby blues."

During one audition I could overhear two of the casting assistants arguing in fierce little whispers.

"Frank Sinatra had blue eyes."

"We're casting gangsters here, not saloon singers."

"Yeah, well, some people think Sinatra *was* a gangster. Besides, the kid is a good actor. He's got an MFA from Yale, for heaven's sake."

"It doesn't look right. David won't like it. I'd rather not bring this guy to him or he'll get angry."

David was David Chase, the creator, director, producer, writer and, show runner on *The Sopranos*. The show was his baby and he made all the important decisions. He made most of the unimportant ones, too.

Finally there was a decision about casting that was so unimportant the casting directors didn't worry about what David Chase would think. A one-line role. So they gave it to me. I think it was their way of thanking me for all those heartbreaking auditions when I came within an eyelash (literally) of landing a big part.

Do I regret being born with blue eyes? Naaah. You've got to take the good with the bad in life. Those eyes helped me score with every decent-looking girl at Bryn Mawr.

You're probably wondering which part I finally landed on *The Sopranos*. That's what everyone wonders! They always get it wrong.

My part was so small that if you were a Talmudic scholar when it comes to *The Sopranos*—and believe me, there are such people—you wouldn't remember it. So I'm not even going to bother trying to explain it. Let it suffice to say that if you blinked, you missed it. Telling the truth about what role I played in *The Sopranos* was embarrassing.

But the funny thing is that after a while I discovered I didn't have to tell anyone which role I played. All I had to do was wait for a while, and they'd come up with the answer themselves. The wrong answer.

"Which part did you play in *The Sopranos*?" they'd say. "I can't quite put my finger on it."

"Well . . ." I'd say. Then I'd wait for them to take a guess.

"No wait, I've got it! You were that guy Christopher killed in the butcher shop and chopped up into little pieces with the meat cleaver. I remember now! He said, 'It's gonna be a long time before I eat at Satriale's again.'"

To which I'd reply, "I'm a method actor, but I draw the line at turning myself into a slice of salami."

No matter which role they guessed, I had a clever answer for them. It made them laugh but would never confirm or deny if they were right.

"Wait, I know!" they'd say. "You were the guy who died on the toilet. You died of a heart attack caused by constipation."

"Nowadays I carry an aspirin *and* an Ex-Lax with me wherever I go," I'd say.

But no, that wasn't me either. That was an excellent actor by the name of John Fiore. I felt sorry for John because he had a nice part and he got written out early. Plus, people will know him as the guy who died on the toilet in *The Sopranos*. Maybe I'm lucky that people can't remember who I was in the show after all.

"I know, I know! You're the guy who hung himself in the basement because Tony wouldn't let you retire to Florida."

"Have you got some Bengay?" I would say. "My neck is *still* killing me,"

Wrong again. That actor's name is Robert Funaro. Really nice guy. He was in the scene with Gandolfini I mentioned earlier. I had time to shoot the shit with him on the set that day. I lost touch with him, though, and I don't know what happened to him after *The Sopranos*.

What about me? What did *I* do after my big scene in *The Sopranos*? Well, they brought me back for two more scenes where my part was even smaller than the first one. I went from having one line to having no lines at all. I didn't even know if I was playing the same character. One time I worked up the courage to ask the director if I was playing the same role I played the previous year. You know what the asshole said to me?

"Does it really matter?"

Does it really matter! I can understand why directors get annoyed with actors for asking, "What's my motivation in this scene?" But don't you think a director should take an actor seriously when he asks, "What's my character in this scene?"

The long and the short of it is I played nobody on *The Sopranos*. Nobody knew my name. Nobody knew who the hell I was. Onscreen or off. Not the director. Not the writer. Not even me. Which is why I was so excited when I got a telephone call from my agent saying that another cable television network had created a spin-off (or a rip-off) of *The Sopranos* called *Button Men*. They wanted me for a recurring role.

The concept behind *Button Men* was that while *The Sopranos* looked at organized crime from the boss's point of view, *Button Men* would focus on the guys who did the dirty work every day. The Mafia called them button men because when the boss says push a button on somebody, they pushed a button. Each week's episode told the story of a different button man. The producers assured me that my starring role would come early in the second year of the series. Meanwhile I appeared as a minor character in several other episodes and got to say a few lines every now and then.

You can't believe how happy Caitlin and I were with this news. After more than ten years in New York, one of us was getting some traction as an actor. We were so excited we decided to celebrate by doing something stupid.

We decided to have a baby.

"If we don't do it now, when?" said Caitlin. "I'm running out of time to get pregnant naturally. Things are starting to happen for you as an actor. I'll stay home with the baby, and we'll focus on your career for a while. Then when the baby is older, I'll go back to acting. It'll work out perfectly."

It worked out like shit.

Not the baby. Her name is Bianca. I love her with all of my heart. The baby turned out just fine. But everything else turned out badly.

When the first ratings book on *Button Men* came out, it was clear there were more people watching cockfights in Spanish Harlem every night than there were viewers around the country watching our show.

The cable network wanted to cancel us right away. The producers came back with the usual argument that a show like ours needs time to find its audience. The network caved in and gave us thirteen episodes (half a season) to show some improvement. But the second ratings book was even worse than the first, and *Button Men* went belly up.

So there you have it. That's my fabulous career in show biz. Do you think the National Academy of Television Arts and Sciences might consider me for a lifetime achievement award?

It's time for me to stop talking about myself and get back to my story.

The morning autograph session came to an end. It was almost time for me to meet Jeremiah Pennington for lunch. First I had to find a phone booth and make a quick phone call.

Who the hell uses a phone booth nowadays?

I do.

I can't afford a cell phone.

5

"So have you gotten laid yet?"

"Please, Caitlin."

"I'm curious."

"Honey, we've been through this a thousand times."

"Who's 'honey'? Is that me or one of your adoring fans?"

"I don't have any adoring fans, Caitlin. If I did, I wouldn't be signing autographs for a living."

"Stop and think about that sentence for a minute, Joey. Tell me if you can find the logic in it, because I can't."

"Look, I made one mistake. Are you going to make me pay for it for the rest of my life?"

The truth is I'd made many such mistakes. Caitlin only knew about one of them, because the crazy girl thought she was in love with me. Somehow she got hold of my home phone number and started calling us day and night. She showed up at our door once in her goddamn Wonder Woman outfit, her face covered with greasepaint and glitter.

Caitlin only knew about the one affair. But I'd jumped into the sack with dozens of fangirls since I'd started going to these conventions. I don't even know why. I was probably soothing my dwindling self-esteem. If I could find some work as an actor and start making some money to support my family, maybe I wouldn't feel the need to sleep with every superhero in a Lycra skirt.

Most of the girls weren't even pretty. They were geeks. Girls can be geeks, too, I've learned. Dressed in Batwoman outfits, wearing vampire dentures, covered from head to toe in purple makeup and glitter, sporting *Star Trek* uniforms. I even did it with a Klingon girl once. I took her up to my room and tried to maintain my erection for forty-five minutes while she removed her makeup. It was an elaborate concoction of latex and modeling wax that makeup artists call build-up. By the time she was ready to hop in bed I was as limp as a piece of overcooked rigatoni.

"I don't want to talk about it now, Joey," said Caitlin. "Why did you call?"

"I wanted to talk to Bianca."

"She's not here. She's on a play date."

I thought Caitlin was lying. When she first picked up the phone, I thought I heard Bianca giggling in the background. If Caitlin was keeping me from talking to my own daughter, I'd shit a brick. That would mark a new low in our relationship.

"Where?"

"Where what?"

"Where's the play date?"

"With the daughter of a friend of mine from work. You don't even know her."

"Well, if I don't even know her, do you think it's a good idea to trust her with our daughter?"

"Who are you, Robert Young in *Father Knows Best*? I trust her. That's all that counts. I trust her more than—"

"What?"

"Never mind."

This was how our conversations went nowadays. Bitter. Nasty, Mean-spirited. Which made me sad because neither one of us was like that. Caitlin used to be the most cheerful, charming, and generous person I'd ever met in my life. I wasn't such a bad guy either. Not really. Now we talked to each other like two heavyweight boxers at a press conference before the weigh-in—hurling jibes, taunts, and threats at each other with reckless abandon. I couldn't stop myself from picking fights with her. So I brought up the other subject I knew would make her mad—money.

"I'm making lots of cash at this convention."

Actually, this was one of the worst attended Fan-Cons I'd ever been to. The Taj Mahal Hotel itself seemed like it was on the verge of bankruptcy—and the demand for my autograph was minimal.

"Must be nice."

"What must be nice?"

"Making money by signing your name on a photograph. Getting your picture taken with some idiot in a zoot suit. It beats waitressing by a long shot."

"I've told you that you can give up that waitressing job whenever you want."

"I thank you for that, Joey, I really do. But I have a weakness for food, clothing, and shelter. So does your five-year-old daughter. That's why I have to keep doing it."

"I can get a regular job to help out."

"Oh, dear Lord," she sighed. "I can't talk about this right now. Not on the telephone. Thanks for calling collect, by the way. Silly me, I thought collect calls had gone out of style. I bet you're in a phone booth," she said with a nasty chuckle. "You've found the last working phone booth in America and used it to call me collect."

Just then I saw Tony Rosetti walk by the bank of phone booths. He didn't see me, thank God. He walked like a lion in the noonday sun. I felt the hair on the back of my neck and on my forearms stand up. What was it about this guy that was so scary? I made a mental note to walk in the opposite direction when I got off the phone.

"Joey, are you still there?"

"Yes, I'm sorry, I got distracted."

"Hot-looking chick in a Wookie suit?"

"Are you sure Bianca isn't there, Caitlin? I'd really like to talk to her."

"Am I *sure*? Gee, let me see. I lose track of her all the time. Maybe she's in Queens betting the exacta on the fifth at Aqueduct. That's where she was the last time I lost her."

"I've got to go. I'm meeting someone for lunch."

"Princess Leia?"

"No, as a matter of fact, it's Jeremiah Pennington."

"Jerry's there?"

I heard a smile in her voice for the first time since the call began. Just like me, just like everybody else in the world, she adored Jerry. We'd had him over to our tiny apartment for dinner several times when he was still living in New York. The two of them got along like a house on fire. They talked about the theater,

Shakespeare, acting, even politics. They agreed on some things, disagreed on others. But they seemed to love talking to each other. He had that effect on people.

"I thought Jerry only went to the big conventions, like the one in San Diego. What's that called again?"

"Comic-Con. I always thought so, too. But he came to this one. Big mistake on his part. The attendance is lousy."

"I thought you said you were making good money."

"Look, Caitlin, I've got to run. I'll call again when Bianca gets back from the racetrack." I hoped for a laugh, but none came. So I said, "Nice talking to you."

"It's been lovely talking to you, too, Joey. Goodbye."

I hung up the phone and poked my head outside the phone booth to look for Rosetti.

Damn! He stood thirty feet away from me and stared in my direction. When our eyes met, he gave me a cold smile and walked toward me.

I bolted in the opposite direction.

"Mr. Volpe, I want to talk to you," he shouted.

I ignored him and picked up my pace. For some reason, I noticed that he'd pronounced my name correctly. Out of a thousand people I meet, most of them call me "Volpee." "It's 'Vol*pay*,'" I correct them. Five minutes later, they're calling me Volpee again. It's a subtle distinction for an American to hear, I guess. In fact, Rosetti's correct pronunciation tempted me to stop and talk to him.

But I wasn't too tempted.

"Mr. Volpe. I'm not going to hurt you. I just want to talk."

I scurried toward the hotel coffee shop where, I hoped, Jerry Pennington would be waiting for me to arrive. I knew Jerry would have some security with him. Not an armed guard or anything. Just some nerdy volunteer assigned to make sure nobody stopped him to ask for an autograph without paying for it.

"Mr. Volpe. Joey. Please. I only need five minutes."

Joey? We were on a first-name basis?

I kept walking.

6

I kept walking as fast as I could.

Not just to put some distance between me and Rosetti. But I was eager to see Jerry. I hadn't seen him in at least three years, except on television. And because of the phone call to Caitlin, I was late.

The only good thing that ever happened to me as a result of doing Equity Showcases in New York was that I met an up-and-coming actor by the name of Jeremiah Pennington in a production of *Cyrano de Bergerac*.

He had the title role, and he was magnificent in it. I played Christian, the handsome young cadet who falls in love with Roxanne but is too tongue-tied, shy, and stupid to succeed with her. So Christian asks Cyrano to write love letters to Roxanne on his behalf and hide in the bushes feeding him romantic lines. I'm sure you know the rest of the story.

Even then I could tell there were bigger and better things destined for Jerry Pennington. It wasn't just his talent onstage, which was considerable. When he did that famous scene in *Cyrano* where his character rips off twenty great one-liners in a row about having a big nose, it triggered some of the loudest laughter I've ever heard in the theater.

Offstage, Jerry had that certain combination of good looks, charm, and *je ne sais quoi* that made everyone he met think they were in the presence of a star. His ruddy complexion and sandy red hair made people think of a young Spencer Tracy. I wish I had a nickel for every time I heard someone say—half-joking, half-serious—"Remember me when you hit it big in Hollywood, Jerry." To which he would reply, "How could I forget *you*?"

Jerry didn't become a *big* star in Hollywood, but he did pretty damn well. His first break was landing a recurring role as a Klingon officer in one of the spin-offs of *Star Trek*. When that series ended, they brought his character back for an even bigger part in another *Star Trek* spin-off. After a few years he left to take a supporting role in a network sitcom, which seemed like a great opportunity at the time. But the network canceled it after two seasons.

Although he doesn't work much as an actor anymore, he still makes a nice living in Hollywood as a TV director. He also makes a nice living signing autographs at Fan-Cons. Which is how we found ourselves at the same Fan-Con in Atlantic City on this day and why we'd made an appointment to have lunch together. Jeremiah Pennington never did forget the little people he met on the way up.

I didn't look back until I got to the long escalator that went from the casino to the shops and restaurants on the mezzanine floor. As soon as my foot hit the first step of the escalator, I swiveled my head around to see if Rosetti was still following me.

He was.

The good news was that I had gained some distance on him. The bad news was that it didn't seem to faze him. He followed me in the patient yet persistent way a predator pursues its prey when he knows it has no way to escape.

The escalator didn't seem to be moving fast enough. So I ran up the steps. Then I took two at a time. When I got to the top of the escalator, the coffee shop was to my right. Unfortunately, it was an open-air sort of restaurant so it wouldn't offer me much cover. As soon as Rosetti got to the top of the escalator, it wouldn't take him more than a minute to see me having lunch with Jerry. I had to hope that Jerry's security escort would be an intimidating-looking guy. A tall, muscular former NFL football player would be perfect.

Alas, he was the exact opposite. Like nearly every other attendee of Fan-a-Palooza Con 2014, he was a skinny, pasty-looking little geek with his belt cinched too high on his waist. The cuffs of his trousers were at flash-flood length, and he wore a short-sleeved white shirt. On the bright side, various lanyards, badges, and ribbons draped over his neck. He must've had at least a dozen buttons and lapel pins on his shirt. He even had a Fan-a-Palooza cravat around his neck and a little sailor's cap that said Fan-a-Palooza 2014 Volunteer Escort Team. In short, he looked *official*.

As I approached the table, he stepped in front of me and said, "Halt!"

Halt? I hadn't heard anyone use that word since Hollywood was still making World War II movies.

"This is Mr. Pennington's private time between appearances. As you can see, he's on the phone right now. If you want Mr. Pennington's autograph, go to Exhibit Hall B at three o'clock for the special guest autograph session. You can also see Mr. Pennington in a panel discussion with other *Star Trek* cast members at two o'clock in the Ivanka Trump Room. Until then, sir, I must ask you to give Mr. Pennington his privacy."

"Look, dude, I'm having lunch with Jerry. That's why he's waiting for me here. We're old friends."

I showed him my own lanyard, which identified me as a "Special Guest" just like Jerry. All pigs are created equal, as George Orwell said, but some pigs are more equal than others.

By this time Jerry saw me standing there and gave me a wink while he continued to talk on his cell phone. He also gave the Nazi Youth Leaguer a hand signal that said something like, "He's okay, let him sit down."

The volunteer saluted me, which I took as an apology. He marched ten feet away from the table and stood at parade rest. I wondered whether his phaser was set on stun or kill. I was hoping for the latter because I figured I only had about thirty seconds before Rosetti tried to crash the luncheon party.

It sounded like Jerry was on the phone with his agent. I could tell they were talking about a voice-over deal, but whether it was for film, television, or just a radio commercial I couldn't say. Jerry asked a few questions about the compensation, but he seemed pretty blasé about the whole thing. I couldn't help but think how excited I would be if I were having a similar conversation with my own agent. Hell, I'd have an orgasm if my own agent called to say hello. I haven't talked to her in years. I wasn't even sure she was my agent anymore.

"Okay, let's do it," said Jerry. "Draw up the papers and send them to my house. I'll sign them as soon as I get back to LA, okay? Good. You're the greatest, kiddo. Bye."

Jerry hung up the phone and stood up to greet me.

"J-Fox, you son of a bitch, you look great! Give me a Beverly Hills man hug, dude!"

I'd forgotten that Jerry always called me J-Fox. Volpe meant fox in Italian. So Jerry had christened me with a superstar nickname like J-Lo or A-Rod.

"Not as great as you," I said. "You haven't aged a bit."

"Yeah, well, don't look too closely," he said as he sat down and waved at the chair across from him to invite me to sit. "Don't look at the crown of my head, You'll find a patch of bare scalp where lovely tresses of rich, red hair once flowed."

"'Uneasy lies the head that wears the crown,'" I said.

I liked to work Shakespearean quotes into my everyday conversation. It was an annoying habit of mine. That particular one came from *Henry IV, Part Two*, Act III, Scene One.

"Nowadays the makeup girls have to spray my head with the paint that Ron Popiel used to sell on those infomercials."

"Speaking of makeup," I said, "I never could understand why the producers of *Star Trek* hired a handsome guy like you and then covered your face with all that Klingon chit. How long did it take to put that stuff on every morning?"

"About three hours. That's how long it took at first, anyway. By the end of the series, the girls had gotten so good at it they cut down to about ninety minutes."

"What did you do the whole time?"

"Learn lines, what else? I had two girls working on my face and one girl sitting next to me running lines. Once I had 'em down pat, I'd ask for a copy of *The Wall Street Journal* and another cup of coffee. It wasn't so bad. The hard part was getting up three hours earlier than everybody else. The good part was that I never had to take any of my own time on weekends or evenings to memorize lines."

Jerry answered these questions in a rote sort of way that led me to believe he'd answered them a million times before. Of course he had, I realized. There were more personal questions I really wanted to ask, but they wouldn't be appropriate. Questions like: How much money do you make in residual checks that show up in your mailbox every week? How much did they pay you to act in the big-screen *Star Trek* movie? How much do you get paid to do a panel discussion at a Fan-Con?

They were paying me a piddling five-hundred dollars for the one I'd be doing after lunch.

"How's Caitlin doing?" he said.

"She's fine."

"And the baby. What's her name again, Becky?"

"Bianca. She's not a baby anymore. She's walking and talking."

"Holy shit! Time flies, man."

I wanted to return the favor and ask him about his wife and kids, but I couldn't remember any of the current details. He was on his third or fourth marriage, and each one had yielded an offspring or two. The only wife I'd ever met was the first one and she was long gone. The fact that he'd had so many divorces caused me to blurt out something I hadn't intended to talk about.

"Caitlin and I are . . . well, we're having some trouble."

"Oh?"

"She caught me dipping my wick where it didn't belong, and she's having a hard time getting over it."

"Uh-oh."

"Plus, money, you know, the usual problems."

He stiffened a bit, and I realized I was talking to someone for whom money was not a problem. I also realized I was talking to someone who got hit up for money by some "old friend" once a week. So I tried to segue out of the subject.

"Hey, speaking of money, I wanted to thank you again for telling me about these Fan-Cons. I never even knew they existed until you told me about them. I didn't even know about Comic-Con. When did you first find out about them?"

"Hell, I was doing these conventions while the first series was still on the air. My agent told me about them. I said, 'Why would I want to do something like that?' He said, 'Well, do you like money or are you some kind of Buddhist monk?' He told me how much money I could make from signing autographs and getting my picture taken with fans. I couldn't believe it until I came home from my first *Star Trek* convention with my pockets filled with cash."

"Wow," I said.

"But at the same time, I've got to admit it's a little demeaning, too. I mean here I was on television in a big role on a hit series, and I'm signing autographs for money. I couldn't exactly picture Clark Gable or Cary Grant doing that. It didn't fit with my self-image, you know what I mean? Plus, there were all sorts of little dings to my dignity."

"Like what?"

"Like one time I was at a Fan-Con in Toronto and I saw a table where they were selling *Star Trek* action figures. They had Shatner. George Takei. Patrick Stewart. Michael Dorn. Jonathan Frakes. Everybody. Then I noticed a little sign in the corner of the table. It said, 'Buy any three action figures and get one Jeremiah Pennington for free.'"

I was sipping some water when he delivered the punch line, and I did a classic spit-take. I mopped up the water with a cocktail napkin.

"True story," he said, "I shit you not."

The waiter came and we ordered lunch. I asked for a cheeseburger and fries. While Jerry glanced at his menu, I looked for Rosetti. There he was. He stationed himself across the hallway a hundred feet away from where we were sitting and stared at me. He had a cup of coffee and a newspaper in his hands. He looked like he would wait as long as necessary.

"I wanted to ask you some questions about how to handle some weird shit that's been happening at these Fan-Cons, Jerry."

"Fire when ready, Gridley. I'm an expert."

"What do you do if a fan asks you to lunch or dinner?"

"Fangirl or fanboy?"

"Fanboy. An older man, actually. I know exactly how to handle the fangirls. That's what got me in trouble with Caitlin."

"Yeah, it sounds like you did too much handling."

"Afraid so. Anyway, this old Italian guy was in the autograph line this morning. He invited me to lunch. He said he needed to talk to me. I told him I was having lunch with you. He said, well, what about a quick drink. I said I don't drink much."

"In other words, you lied?"

"Right. He said let me buy you an Italian Ice on the boardwalk. He called it wooder ice."

"Wooder ice? Ha! Native-born Philadelphian, eh?"

"Exactly. I said I didn't have time for that because I have a panel discussion after lunch, then another autograph session in the afternoon."

"So you blew him off. Good. That's exactly what I'd advise you to do."

"Jerry, I blew and I blew and I blew. But his house did not fall down. He's the most persistent asshole I've ever met in my life. I'm afraid he's going to keep coming back. And there's something else that scares me a little."

"What?"

"He looks like a mobster. Talks like one, too."

"Oh, hell, that doesn't mean anything. Half the people in my autograph line dress in *Star Trek* uniforms. Am I worried that the Romulans might be going to war with the Federation? Not a bit. Don't you get a lot of people in your autograph lines dressed like gangsters? Zoot suits? Spats? Fedoras?"

"Yes, I do. But that's just it. This guy isn't dressed like a movie gangster. He's dressed like a real gangster."

"How the hell would you know what a real gangster dresses like, Joey? You're a Yalie, for heaven's sake."

"We had experts on *Button Men* who were paid to know that stuff. He just looks like the real deal to me. Sounds like it, too.

Plus, I have a little volunteer nerd assigned to me like you do. He said he recognized this guy from some Mafia website."

"You're making a mountain out of a molehill, J-Fox. If he comes back this afternoon, blow him off again. If he comes back a third time, report it to the convention sponsors. They've got some real security guards here. Not like these volunteers who escort us around. I'm talking about guys with guns. They'll talk to your Don Corleone and he'll take a powder. Don't worry about it. You've always been a worrier, Joey. What else are you worried about?"

I didn't want to tell Jerry that Rosetti was standing fifty feet away and staring us down at that moment. I didn't want to alarm him. Nor did I want to drag him into this. Maybe he was right, after all. Maybe all I had to do was tell the convention sponsors that a fan was hassling me and they'd scare Rosetti away.

Meanwhile, our food arrived. I gobbled down my cheeseburger and fries like I hadn't eaten for a day. (Because I hadn't.) Jerry picked at his chef salad. When I came up for air from the plate, I answered his question,

"Well, the other thing I wanted to talk to you about was these panel discussions."

"What about them?"

"I like doing them. I love getting the extra five hundred dollars, but—"

"Five *hundred*?"

"Yes, why?"

"Never mind. Go on."

"I'm a little embarrassed when I do them."

"Why?"

"Because, you know, I just had a tiny part on *The Sopranos* after all."

"But your part on *Button Men* was much bigger. I saw every episode you were on. You did great."

I felt bad. Jerry had made a special effort to watch my show, but for all the hundreds of *Star Trek* episodes he was on I'd seen two or three of them. Every now and then I'd pass one of hi shows when I was channel surfing and I'd stop and watch for a few minutes until he came on. I'm just not a big *Star Trek* fan. I couldn't tell you the difference between a Klingon and a Romulan. I was surprised that Jerry was a hero on the show because I always thought Klingons were the bad guys. Maybe there was an intergalactic peace treaty and I didn't get the memo.

"Thanks, Jerry, but you were only one of three people in America who ever saw *Button Men*. The problem is that when I do these panel discussions I feel like I'm crashing the party. The other actors on the panel are well known. Maybe not their names, but their faces. The audience directs all their questions to them. So I wind up sitting there like an idiot with my thumb up my butt."

"Maybe you could do what I do. I like to go out into the audience and pretend I'm just one of the fans. I raise my hand and start asking the same stupid questions fans ask me all the time, like, "How does it feel when you're beamed down in the transporter room? Does it tingle, or tickle, or what?"

I laughed.

"'How do you talk with the Federation headquarters when the *Enterprise* is traveling at warp speed if the ship is going faster than radio waves?'"

"I've never considered that problem."

"What's the question *you're* asked most often?"

"'What was James Gandolfini really like?'"

"Okay. So you go out into the audience, you raise your hand, and you ask the actors on the panel, 'What was James Gandolfini really like?' What *was* he like, by the way?"

"How the hell should I know? I only met him once and we talked for five seconds. You know, Jerry, I'm not sure that schtick would work for me. Because when you go out into the audience, people know you're one of the stars of the show and they get a big kick out of it. In my case, they'd think I was the emcee or something."

"What's wrong with that? Look, you don't have to go out into the audience if you don't want. All I'm saying is that if you feel like you're the third wheel on the panel, start asking questions of the other actors. You can ask better questions than the fans can, and the actors will appreciate it."

"Okay, I'll try that," I said.

Out of the corner of my eye, I saw someone was approaching our table. Was it Rosetti?

Thank God, no. It was the Nazi Youth Leaguer from the volunteer escort team. He saluted Jerry and held the salute with his body frozen at full attention.

"At ease, Ensign," said Jerry, shooting a wink in my direction.

"Mr. Pennington, sir, it is my duty to inform you that your *Star Trek* panel discussion begins in five minutes. It would be my honor to escort you there myself."

"Okay, okay," said Jerry. "Lunch is over. Let's roll." He tossed a hundred-dollar bill on the table like it was a used cocktail napkin. I did a quick calculation in my head and realized he was leaving a 250 percent tip.

"Thanks for lunch, Jerry," I said.

"Don't mention it, J . It was great to see you again. Please say hello to Caitlin for me. I mean, if she's speaking to you and everything. Bianca, too."

I looked around for Rosetti. He was still standing in the same place. But he could see we were getting ready to leave, so he started getting ready to pounce.

"Jerry, could I ask you for a quick favor?"

He stiffened again. As friendly as Hollywood stars could be with their fans—or even their old friends—the topics of money and favors were sensitive points with them. I could see Jerry's shields go up. (No pun intended.)

"What is it?"

"Could you ask your . . . um, Ensign, if he could escort me to my panel discussion, too? I don't want to run into that fan I was telling you about."

"No problem. Did you hear what Mr. Volpe said, Ensign?"

"Yes, sir."

"Make it so."

"Aye-aye, sir."

So the three of us walked past Rosetti on the way to our panel discussions. The sight of a bona fide television star and a volunteer decorated with official-looking buttons and badges was intimidating enough to keep the gangster at bay.

But not enough to keep him from following us.

7

Rosetti was twenty feet behind us and closing the gap when we reached the meeting room where Jerry and a half dozen other *Star Trek* actors from all different eras were going to hold their panel discussion.

Steven Dubois, who had been in the cast of a *Star Trek* spin-off was standing outside the door. He was shaking hands with fans, and greeting passersby like he was running for office. Dubois was a flamboyant character. I can't remember which role he played—or which series—but I think he was on a space station. He was the chief medical officer. Or the senior science officer. Or the head pastry chef. Like I said, I didn't watch those shows so I can't say for sure.

Over the years, Dubois had become quite well known. In part because he was a militant gay activist who seemed to show up at every political rally in support of gay rights. But mostly because he had just been a bon vivant around Hollywood for years. He was in his late fifties when his show went off the air. He must've been pushing seventy-five by now. He didn't work much as an actor after the network canceled the show. But he attended every cocktail party, supported every liberal cause, and showed up at every showbiz gathering to carry the flag for the *Star Trek* franchise. Plus he attended nearly every one of these Fan-Cons around the country, no matter how small or remote. The joke in Hollywood was that "Wherever two or more people are gathered in the name of *Star Trek*, Steven Dubois is there."

"Jeremiah Pennington, you handsome bastard!" said Dubois when he saw Jerry. "How the heck are you? You keep getting sexier and sexier. I could never understand why they covered your gorgeous face with all that Klingon goop."

"I was just saying the same thing myself," I said.

"Steven, I'd like you to meet an old friend of mine," said Jerry. "Joey Volpe, Steven Dubois. Joey and I worked together off-Broadway many years ago."

"One 'off' or two?" said Dubois, looking into my eyes.

"Two, I'm afraid," I said.

"Hey, don't be ashamed of that. It's a lot better than working *on* Broadway as a stripper in a gay peep show."

"Did you do that?" I said and immediately regretted it. It was widely known that Dubois was gay, but how rude of me to mention it within two seconds of meeting him.

"No, but I knew someone who did! Lovely young man. Tell me, Joey, where did someone named Volpe get such beautiful blue eyes?"

"My mom, I guess."

Jerry glanced at his watch. "Well, Steven," he said, "I think it's time we went in and faced the music. J-Fox, it was great to see you again. Good luck with your stalker. Steven, let's continue our fifty-year mission to boldly go where no man has gone before."

"If there are no men there, Jerry, I'd rather not go at all!"

They laughed and walked into the meeting room side by side, leaving me alone with Jerry's volunteer escort.

Rosetti was standing no more than ten feet away from us now. I'm sure he heard Jerry say "Good luck with your stalker." I glanced at Rosetti. I could tell he was weighing the option of accosting me now or waiting until the volunteer was out of the way. Lucky for me, it looked as if he had decided upon the latter course of action.

"Shall I escort you to your meeting room now, sir?"

"Damn the torpedoes, Ensign, full speed ahead!"

"Aye-aye, sir."

So we marched to the meeting room where the gangster panel discussion would be held. I glanced behind me once and saw that Rosetti was so close that a casual observer would consider us a threesome. The jig was just about up. I would have to confront Rosetti face-to-face—and without protection—within a matter of moments.

Then something surprising happened.

Instead of waltzing into the meeting room the way Pennington and Dubois had done, the volunteer brought me to a nearby door where there was a security guard posted. This guy was big and he had a gun, like the kind of armed security guards Jerry told me about. Plus, he was checking credentials.

"This gentleman is Mr. Joseph Volpe," said the volunteer. "He's one of the special guests for the two o'clock gangster panel."

The security guard took a close look at the credentials on the lanyard hanging around my neck. He checked my name off his clipboard with a ballpoint pen.

"Come in, Mr. Volpe, you're the last to arrive. They're almost ready to begin."

I turned to the volunteer and said, "Thanks for your help."

"Just doing my duty, sir."

I took one last look at Rosetti, who was standing no more than five feet away from me. But he was stymied and not too happy about it. I couldn't resist giving him a little smile that said, *Gotcha, asshole.*

He didn't smile back.

Dear Lord, how many times have I thought how much better my life would've turned out if the situation had been reversed. If only the security guard had let Rosetti go through the door and turned *me* away instead, my life would've been completely different. Rosetti's, too. The actors inside would've loved Tony Rosetti. He would've regaled them with real-life Mafia stories and they would've sat at his feet listening to him. The audience would've loved him, too. Imagine having a real-life mobster on the panel to talk about where the television shows got it right and where they didn't. They would've eaten it up! Best of all, Rosetti would've met *another* actor whom he could enlist in his evil scheme, and he would've forgotten all about me.

I could've returned to New York City that afternoon—it was two and a half hours away from Atlantic City—and tried to rescue my marriage. I could've thrown myself at Caitlin's feet and said, "I'm sorry, darling. I'm sorry for everything. I love you with all of my heart. I'm going to stop cheating on you. I'm going to get a real job and take care of you and Bianca. We'll focus on *your* acting career from now on. You're going to be a big star. We're going to live happily ever after."

But it was not to be. I went through the door, but Tony Rosetti did not.

And I had two long years in federal prison to think about how wonderful my life would've been if the situation were reversed.

8

The security guard led me down a long hall to a little anteroom, or greenroom, so we could make our entrance from the front of the meeting hall.

Walking into that little room was like walking into the room where they kept suspects before they paraded them out in a lineup. The faces of famous criminals filled the room. Of course, they weren't real criminals. They were actors. Sometimes it's hard to tell the difference.

I'd rather not use the real names of these actors for reasons that will become obvious. There was one chubby guy from *The Sopranos* whom I'll call The Fatman. He had a major recurring role in the show. You'd recognize his face in a heartbeat but not his name.

There was another actor from *The Sopranos* whom I'll call The Heckler. He had played the *capo di tutti capi* of one of the rival New York families who were at war with the Soprano family. Plus, he'd played dozens of both large and small roles in other gangster films and TV shows over the years. With his bald head, bushy eyebrows, and hooked nose he was the very picture of an ugly Mafia boss. His most prominent feature was his upper lip. His mouth curled into a permanent snarl, and it made every word that came out seem angry and cruel.

I'm calling him The Heckler because he had a mean-spirited laugh that sounded like a short burst from a machine gun: "Heh-heh-heh." He laughed like that after making a cruel joke at someone else's expense. The laugh was supposed to say, *Hey, I'm just teasing you.* But it usually came after a vicious, ugly, vulgar remark, such as, "Guess what? I just fucked your grandmother and she let me stick it up her ass—heh, heh, heh."

I never figured out who the hell the third actor was, although his face was familiar. He'd been in the movie *Goodfellas*. Do you remember the scene in the Hawaiian restaurant where they introduced all the mobsters in the gang? He was one of them. I couldn't remember if he was Jimmy Two Times, so-named because he always said everything two times ("I'm going to go get the papers, get the papers.") Or Frankie Carbone. Or Freddie No Nose. This guy had a pretty big nose, so I didn't think he was Freddie No Nose, but I couldn't say for sure. Maybe the moniker was supposed to be ironic.

So I'll refer to him as The Goodfella.

"This is Mr. Joseph Volpe," said the security guard, who turned on his heels and left.

"Mr. Volpe has arrived," said a pale, skinny young man who was obviously another convention volunteer. "We're almost ready to begin. Let's wait a few more minutes for the audience to get seated. Then I'll lead you out and introduce you."

It looked like the role of emcee was already taken. Jerry's idea of playing the master of ceremonies during the panel discussion wouldn't work after all.

"Mr. Volpe has arrived," said The Heckler, imitating the volunteer. "The fox is here. The fox is in the henhouse—heh, heh, heh."

He reached to shake my hand. "Which mobster show were you in, kid?"

"*The Sopranos.*"

"Fuck you were."

"Well, it was a very small—"

"The fuck you were on *The Sopranos*. I was on that set for years. I never saw you. And I wouldn't forget. I got a fucking photographical memory." He touched his finger to his temple. "With them blue eyes, you woulda stood out like a wart on a dick—heh, heh, heh."

". . . a very small role." I tried to finish my sentence. "Then later I was on *Button Men.*"

"*Button Men*? What was that, a sewing show? A sewing show on cable television? What channel was it on—nine hundred and ninety-eight? Heh-heh-heh. Look, Mom, I'm sewing a pretty little bow on my panties—heh, heh, heh. I'm making a tea cozy for my balls. Hey, I'm just teasing you, kid. I'm breaking your balls. I'm having some fun with you."

"I know you are," I said and tried to smile.

"But you weren't on no *Sopranos*," he said like he was going to throw me against the wall and choke me until I admitted I was lying.

"Like I said, it was a small—"

"Like *I* said, you weren't on no *Sopranos*. So don't say you was. That insults my intelligence, and it makes me very angry. Do you understand? *Capisci?*"

"It was a small—" I tried to say for the third time without finishing.

"Fuck that. Listen to me, kid. *The Sopranos* was a close-knit cast. We were like a family. Jimmy Gandolfini, *buon anima*, was like a father to me." He crossed himself at the mention of Gandolfini, as if he'd invoked the patron saint of cable-television actors. "So if you're messing with *The Sopranos*, then you're messing with my family. Nobody messes with my family. Got it?"

"It was a small—"

"It's time for us to go out," said the emcee. "Follow me."

9

Rosetti was sitting in the front row staring at me. The Heckler ridiculed and insulted me the entire time. I had a real-life gangster threatening me and a make-believe gangster humiliating me for ninety minutes without a break.

To say that I was the low man on the totem pole in this group would be putting it mildly. The emcee ignored me. The audience didn't even look at me—except for Rosetti who kept his eyes fixed on me the entire time. The other panelists paid no attention to me whatsoever, except for The Heckler who made a point of taunting me now and then.

After being silent for about forty-five minutes, I decided to follow Jerry Pennington's advice and ask a question of my own:

"There's something I always wondered about *The Sopranos*..." I began.

"I thought you said you were *on* the show," said The Heckler.

"Well, I was, but it was a small part," I said to The Heckler for the umpteenth time. "And I'm wondering—"

"I'm wondering what the fuck you're doing up here, kid—heh, heh, heh."

"Well, I—"

"If you want to ask questions about *The Sopranos*, why don't you go down into the audience and wait your turn until the microphone comes around?"

The audience giggled uncomfortably.

"I'm just having a little fun with you, kid," said The Heckler, realizing he'd gone too far. "I'm just breaking your balls. What's your question, young man?" he asked like a kindly grandfather.

"Never mind," I said.

"Let's go back to the audience," said the emcee. "Yes, you in the third row with the blue shirt. What's your question?"

A short guy in chinos and a blue golf shirt stood up and said, "I heard somewhere that Tony Sirico, the guy who played Paulie

Walnuts in *The Sopranos*, was in the Mafia in real life. Is that true?"

"Tony told me he'd had some run-ins with the police when he was younger," said The Fatman, "but I don't think he was actually in the Mafia."

I glanced at Rosetti, who rolled his eyes and shook his head as if to say, "Trust me, there are no actors in the Mafia." What a weird moment. It was as if Rosetti and I were starting to become friends.

Another weird moment. Somebody else in the audience asked a question of The Fatman and Goodfella. "Am I mistaken, or weren't *both* of you in that scene in *Goodfellas* in the Hawaiian restaurant where all the mobsters were introduced?"

The Fatman and Goodfella looked each other over and started laughing.

"I think we were," said The Fatman.

"Yeah, we were both in it," said Goodfella. "I didn't realize it until now. But both of us were in it. That's funny."

"Every Italian actor in New York was in that scene," said The Heckler. "Even my grandmother was in that scene. Well, Mr. Volpe wasn't in it. Even if he says he was."

"No, I wasn't in it," I managed to say.

I should've said, "I wasn't born yet." But the line didn't occur to me until ten seconds too late. Don't you hate when that happens?

I was so humiliated I was giving some serious thought to standing up and walking out of the room. Then something bizarre happened.

Tony Rosetti raised his hand and asked for the microphone.

"My question is for Mr. Joey Volpe," he said.

"The fox is about to speak," said The Heckler. "Everybody be real quiet. This is going to be interesting. Tell us about the time you starred in *Gone with the Wind*, Mr. Volpe."

Rosetti ignored him.

"My question is about your role in *Button Men*," said Rosetti.

"Oh, we have a question about sewing," said The Heckler. "How do you sew a button on your brassiere?"

The audience laughed.

"Is it knit one or purl two? Heh-heh-heh. I don't know whether to sew it by hand or use my Singer sewing machine? Heh-heh-heh."

"SHUT THE FUCK UP, ASSHOLE!"

There was a sharp, collective intake of breath from the audience. Followed by utter and complete silence. *Did that really happen?* Did a member of the audience tell a celebrity on the dais to shut the fuck up?

"If I hear one more word out of you," said Rosetti, "I'm going to come up there and rip your balls off with my bare hands. Then I'm going to stuff them down your fucking throat. Do you understand me? *Capisci?*"

I glanced at The Heckler. He looked like he was melting in his chair. Rosetti waited for a moment to see if he would dare to talk back. He continued in a more measured tone. "Joey, I was a big fan of *Button Men*. I liked it better than *The Sopranos*. It was more—what's the word?—authentic. Every week they'd tell the story of a different soldier, a different button man. I liked your character a lot. So how come they never told your story? I wondered why you never got the big part."

"You and me both!" I said.

There was a nervous titter from the audience.

"No, actually, the producers told me my big episode would come in the second season. But we never got to the second season because our ratings were too low. We got canceled. I'm just sorry there weren't more fans like you out there."

I glanced at The Heckler to see if he had some sarcastic remark to add. There was nothing in his chair but a pool of urine and protoplasm.

"Well, I told everybody I knew to watch the show," said Rosetti. "But the bastards don't always do what I say."

"On that note," said the emcee, "we should wrap this up. Please join me in thanking our gangster panel with a big round of applause."

The Heckler was the first one out the door. He ran into the greenroom like a gazelle that'd caught the scent of a cheetah. The other two actors, bless their hearts, took their time to pat me on the back, shake my hand, and say goodbye. They knew I'd had a rough time of it.

For a moment, I was alone on the dais and wondering what to do next. Although the audience was filing out the door, Rosetti stayed in his seat. He smiled at me.

He had me cornered.

If I tried to go through the main doors of the meeting room, he could block my path. If I tried to go through the greenroom and out the side door, he could intercept me there. The security guard would be long gone.

At that moment, he didn't seem so threatening anymore. He was the only one who came to my defense during the panel discussion, after all. I decided I no longer had a choice. I was postponing the inevitable. Besides, he told me there might be some acting work and some money in it for me. Lord knows, I needed both. So I stepped off the dais and walked up to where he was sitting in the front row.

"Mr. Rosetti," I said. "You wanted to speak with me?"

10

"This is my treat, by the way," said Rosetti, "so feel free to have anything you want. Steak, lobster, whatever."

"Well, it is a steak house," I said. "So you pretty much covered all the choices."

We had decided to meet for dinner at the Taj Mahal's steak house restaurant. Well, *he* decided. I wanted to get the conversation over and done with in the meeting room after the panel discussion. He said he needed more time to talk to me. I had another autograph session in the afternoon, so we agreed to meet in the steak house at eight o'clock. The Taj Mahal decorated their steak house in an African safari theme. I found it appropriate since the lion was sitting down to eat with the antelope. I didn't know if I was eating dinner with him or if I *was* dinner.

"I want to thank you for all the nice things you said about *Button Men* in the panel discussion," I said. "I appreciate it."

"To tell you the truth, I never saw it."

That left me speechless. The waiter chose that moment to come up to our table with a bottle of Dom Perignon in one hand and a wine bucket filled with ice in the other.

"Our executive manager, Mr. Brookstein, would be honored if you gentlemen would accept this bottle of champagne as a personal gift from him," said the waiter.

"That's nice of him," said Rosetti. "Tell him I said thanks. Better yet, tell him to stop by later so I can thank him in person."

After the waiter went through the ritual of opening and pouring the champagne, I had recovered enough to ask about Rosetti's last statement.

"You never saw *Button Men*?"

"No, I'm not a big TV watcher. Except for sports. And that's mostly for business. I like to play cards in the evening. Listen to music. Go to bed early."

"But you seemed to know about the show. You knew that each episode focused on a different button man. You knew I never got my big episode. How could you know all that without seeing the show?"

"An associate briefed me," said Rosetti.

"Oh, I see. Well, it was nice of you to say those things anyway. As you could tell, I was having a hard time up there until you stood up for me."

"That other little prick was treating you with disrespect. If I was you, I would've grabbed the microphone and stuck it in his eyeball."

Rosetti said this like a father handing out practical advice to his son.

"So you never saw *The Sopranos* either?"

"A few times. The guys who work with me loved it. I thought it was like a soap opera. The main character was a pussy. Going to a psychiatrist. Crying and whining all the time like a girl. It gave a bad name to the business."

"And what business is that?" I said with a straight face.

"It's complicated. I have a variety of business interests throughout the Philadelphia and Atlantic City area. That's why I wanted to talk to you."

"How could I possibly help? I'm just an actor."

"Mr. Volpe. Joey. Can I call you Joey?"

"Of course."

"Joey, in my business, we have an interest in cash. We especially like situations where there's a lot of cash and not much security guarding that cash. Brinks Trucks, for example, have a lot of cash. But they also have bulletproof windows, steel-plated doors, and armed guards with automatic weapons. So we tend to steer clear of them."

"Makes sense."

"But every now and then we find situations where there's a lot of cash sitting around, but not too many people guarding that cash. We consider those situations to be good business opportunities. Do you know what I mean, Joey?"

"I think I do."

"Well, a few weeks ago, one of my associates told me about this convention coming to the Taj Mahal in Atlantic City."

He pronounced it, "Lannick See."

"He told me that this was one of hundreds of these, uh, these, what's the word?"

"Fan-Cons."

"Yeah, that's right. He said this was just one of hundreds of these Fan-Cons around the country. Some of them are bigger than others. But all of them are cash businesses. The fans pay cash to get in the door. Some of them use credit cards, but mostly cash. Once they get inside the convention center, they're paying cash for old comic books and, uh, what do you call those little statuette things of Superman or Batman?"

"Action figures."

"Yeah, they pay cash for action figures. They pay cash for other souvenirs. But mostly they pay cash to get autographs from television stars like you."

"Well," I said, "I'm not really a st—"

"I know. But my associates said you were the guy we should talk to."

"Why me?"

"They said most of the other actors are too famous. They're too rich. They think their shit don't stink. They would never work with us. Some of my associates watched *Button Men* on television. They said you were a guy we could reason with. We did a little research and we found out you've been having some money problems. Some marriage problems. Maybe you fucked around a little bit. I'm not judging you, Joey. I'm no saint myself in that department."

"You *researched* me?"

"You've got a young daughter. If your marriage broke up, you'd lose custody of her. Plus, like everybody who lives in New York, you've got to worry about where the kid is going to school when she's ready. You want to put her in public school with a bunch of *animali*? Or do you want to put her in a nice private school with the rich Manhattan kids, give her a good education?"

"We can't afford private school."

"My point exactly."

"What are you driving at, Mr. Rosetti?"

"Call me Tony, please. It's only fair, since I'm calling you Joey."

"All right, Tony, what the heck are you driving at?"

"Joey, let me answer that question with a question. How much cash do you have on you right now?"

"I don't know," I said.

I wasn't lying. I had no idea how much cash I had on me after two autograph sessions. But I knew it was a lot.

"Well, let's find out, why don't we? Empty your right pocket."

I glanced around me.

"Don't worry," he said with a chuckle. "Nobody is going to rob you here."

I pulled a huge wad of bills out of my right pocket and put it on the table.

"Do you mind if I count it?" said Rosetti. "You can trust me."

I nodded and he started counting.

"Three hundred and forty-two dollars," he said. "Is your left pocket about the same?"

"Yes."

"Why don't you put that out on the table, too."

While I was emptying my left pocket and putting the cash on the table, the waiter arrived with two porterhouse steaks with baked potatoes and set the plates down in front of us. I could see the pupils of his eyes widen. He must've thought he was on the verge of getting the biggest tip of his life.

"What about your back pockets, are they full, too?" said Rosetti.

"Yes," I said.

"I can tell you've got some cash in your shirt pocket, too, because I can see it bulging. Either that or you're in the middle of a sex change operation and it's not going well. What about your underpants? Did you stuff some cash down there?"

"Don't make me pull down my pants in the restaurant, Mr. Rosetti."

He laughed. "Don't worry. I don't want to see you do that. What about your shoes?"

"Yeah, I got some in there, too."

"So how much altogether, do you think?"

"Somewhere around a thousand."

"Maybe a little more than that?"

"Maybe."

"And you're not even a big star. You had one line on *The Sopranos*. And *Button Men* got canceled before you had your big show."

"Don't rub it in, Mr. Rosetti."

"Call me Tony, please. What about that little queer who worked on the outer space show?"

"Steven Dubois? What about him?"

"I saw you shake hands with him this afternoon. Do you know him?"

"Yes, I know him, but not well. Jerry Pennington introduced him to me."

Notice how I didn't exactly *deny* knowing Steven Dubois, even though I'd just met him a few hours earlier. That's an actor thing. If you've shaken hands with a Hollywood star you can count him among your inner circle of intimate friends if you ever need to drop his name somewhere. It was a hard habit to break, even when it didn't work in your favor. You'll notice I managed to drop the names of *two* stars in one sentence. It's the actor's equivalent of a double-word score in Scrabble.

"Pennington was the guy you had lunch with? He's a big star, too, right? I didn't recognize his face."

"Well, they covered his face with a ton of makeup when he was in *Star Trek*."

"He was in *Star Trek*, too? I don't remember him at all."

"He was in one of the spin-offs. He was in several of them, as a matter of fact."

"So these bigger stars, like this Pennington guy, how much cash do you think they carry on them?"

"I don't think they carry any cash at all, Mr. Rosetti . . . er, Tony. They have assistants to do that for them."

"You had an assistant, too, but you've got enough cash on you to open up your own bank."

"My assistant is a convention volunteer. I don't trust him with the cash. Most of the big stars bring their own assistants with them. The assistant handles all the money. The stars never get their hands dirty."

"So how much cash do the assistants have on them?"

"After two autograph sessions?"

"There are four autograph sessions over the whole weekend, right?"

"Right."

"So how much cash is a star's assistant carrying after all four autograph sessions?"

"I don't know. Ten thousand. Twenty thousand. In the case of someone like William Shatner or Patrick Stewart or even George Takei, it could be even more."

"So, for the sake of argument, let's say they're each carrying up to twenty grand and there are—what would you say?—fifty actors at these things."

"At a big convention, yes."

"So that's a million bucks in cash. You can see why my associates and I would find this interesting. Can I ask another question?"

I almost said fire away, but thought better of it. "Sure."

"How come you guys don't take credit cards?"

"Well some do. But for most of us, it's just another expense and hassle. As the technology improves, I suppose more actors will start doing it. Five years from now, maybe everyone will take credit cards. But for now it's easier to ask for cash."

"All that cash walking around with no security in sight."

"But there *are* security guards around here, Mr. Rosetti. Don't you remember the one who stopped you from following me into the panel discussion?"

"Oh, yeah, I know. I've checked them out. There are a couple of dozen of them. Most of them look like low-wage *melanzane* who don't know what the fuck they're doing. If they ever had to draw their guns, they'd shoot themselves in the balls."

Melanzane was the Italian word for eggplant. You can figure out what he meant. I won't dignify it with an explanation.

"The biggest problem is the checkpoint outside the exhibit hall," he said. "They've got a big security station there like at an airport. Metal detectors. X-ray machines. Conveyor belts."

"Not only that," I said, "they go over every 'weapon' with a fine-tooth comb. These fans come in with swords, light sabers, sci-fi laser guns, and all sorts of shit. There are a bunch of experts who check out each of them to make sure it can't fire real bullets. Or real lasers. Those rent-a-cop security guards may be nothing to worry about, like you said. But I get the impression the guys who examine the weaponry know their stuff. I bet they're ex-cops or firearms experts of one kind or another."

I couldn't believe I was participating in this conversation!

"That's my take on it exactly," said Rosetti. "That's where you come in, my friend."

He glanced at the waiter and, using nothing more than his eyes, indicated my champagne glass needed filling. The waiter scurried over to our table and started pouring champagne in a heartbeat.

"Wait, Mr. Rosetti, Tony, I'm just an actor. I don't know what the heck you have in mind, but I don't want any part of it. This whole conversation is making me feel uncomfortable. I should be going now."

I tossed my napkin on the table and started to stand up.

"No, no, no, sit down. Finish your steak. Then we'll order some dessert. Gotta polish off this bottle of champagne, too. Probably cost the manager three hundred bucks. It would be an insult if we didn't finish it, and I can't drink it by myself."

I sat down grudgingly. I reached for my champagne and guzzled it in one gulp. No sooner had I put it down on the table than the waiter appeared at my side and refilled it. So I guzzled it again. And the waiter filled it again.

"You can't drink it by yourself either," said Rosetti.

We were silent for a long time. But as the champagne went to my head, I felt myself getting braver.

"Let me ask you a question, Don Rosetti."

"I said call me Tony, please."

"Okay, Don Tony, let me ask you a question."

"Shoot."

"Isn't this kind of crime a little, I don't know, *demeaning* for the Maf . . . er, for a member of your organization? I mean this is basically a rip-and-run you're talking about. I thought you guys were more sophisticated than that."

"Times being what they are," said Rosetti, "we're willing to make money using any illegitimate means available to us."

I'd heard the Philadelphia mob was like the gang that couldn't shoot straight compared to New York, New Jersey, and Chicago— even in the glory days of organized crime. Still, it was hard to imagine they would stoop to stealing from geeky girls dressed like Wonder Woman.

"What exactly does your business consist of nowadays, Tony?"

"Between the government and the internet, there's hardly anything left of our traditional businesses."

"The government?"

"Legalized casinos. Legalized loansharking companies. They're killing us."

"The government legalized loansharking?"

"I'm talking about those so-called payday loan companies Nowadays, the government lets them charge more vigorish on a loan than we ever did. And if you don't pay them back, they take your house. Disgusting."

"And the internet?"

"Completely killed the prostitution business. There are no more whorehouses anymore. The girls don't need them. They put up a web page. They set up a video camera on their computer. Then they sit on their bed all day hawking business from guys who are surfing the web looking for porn. They say, 'Give me your credit card number, honey, and you can jack off while I strip for you. Or, better yet, you can come on over to my house and we'll fuck.' They don't need us anymore. All they need is a good computer guy."

"What about sports betting?" I said. "Casinos aren't allowed to take bets on sports except in Las Vegas."

"For the time being. That may change soon. Meanwhile, the offshore internet casinos can take bets on sports. Fortunately for us, the big punters don't trust their hundred-grand bet with some computer casino in Cameroon. So we hang on to some of the big-money sports betting."

He cut off a piece of steak and chewed on it for a moment, staring off into space—as if he could see the future of his industry and didn't like what he saw. "But it's a risky business," he finally said. "There are easier ways to make a living."

"Like ripping off geeks and nerds in Spiderman outfits?"

"I'm not as interested in the geeks and nerds as I am in the stars. They're the ones who are carrying around all the cash. What did we say it was? A million bucks? That's a lot of money for ten minutes work and three guys to pull it off. Plus, my guys tell me there are Fan-Cons all around the country. All around the world. They say that every weekend someone is holding one of these silly conventions. You do the math."

"I'm not good at math."

"Let's just say it could be a lucrative enterprise. But we need to try it out first. A test case. What do they call it in business school? Put it into the beta phase. That's it."

The dinner was confirming what I suspected from the start. Despite his rough edges and thick Philadelphia accent Tony Rosetti was no one's fool.

"Well, Tony, it all sounds interesting. But you can count me out."

"Why?"

"Because I'm not a crook, that's why. No offense intended. I'm just an actor."

"It's your acting skills I need. Think of it as an acting job. Non-union, of course."

"What do you want me to do? Point a gun at my fellow actors while you empty their pockets?"

"No, no, no. Nothing like that. I just need you to help us with the security problem, that's all."

"No, Mr. Rosetti. I won't do it. I'm not a robber. I'm just an actor. My no is final. That's my final answer."

The waiter filled our champagne flutes and water glasses. Then he tidied up a bit. Meanwhile, Rosetti and I stared at each other in silence.

Although he had struck me as being surprisingly genteel and well-mannered throughout the dinner, he suddenly did something rather crude. He picked up the bone of his porterhouse steak in his hands and began to rip and tear the remaining flesh off it with his teeth like a dog. Or a wolf. After he had picked the bone clean, he dabbed his chin with a napkin and smiled at me. "I'm not sure you understand how we work in our business."

"You just explained it to me."

"I didn't explain it enough, obviously. You're an actor. So you must like movies, right? Have you ever seen *The Godfather*, Joey?"

"Of course. But have you? You said you never watch television or go to the movies."

"Come on, Joey. Do you think someone like me has never seen *The Godfather*?"

"Whatever." Having tried reluctance, righteousness, and anger to no effect, I thought I'd give petulance a whirl.

"Do you remember when Don Corleone said, 'I'll make him an offer he can't refuse?'"

"He never actually said that. Michael said it when he was telling his fiancée a story about his father."

"Whatever," he said.

"Go on."

"Well, my offer is sorta like that," said Rosetti.

"You mean I can't refuse it?"

He made a typical Italian gesture with his hands that meant just so. In fact, it was the kind of gesture Marlon Brando himself would make as Vito Corleone.

"Well, you're wrong about that, Mr. Rosetti. I *can* refuse. And I *do* refuse. I want no part of it."

"Joey, let me be frank with you. When a person in my position makes a business proposition to someone, it's not a yes-or-no deal. It's just a yes deal, if you know what I mean."

"No, I do *not* know what you mean. And I don't want to talk about it any further. Thank you for the steak. Thanks for the champagne. Or maybe I should say please thank the manager for the champagne. But I have to be going now."

"What about my business proposition? Can I count you in?"

"No, you cannot. Look, Mr. Rosetti, congratulations on your new business. I wish you well with it. It doesn't bother me what a man does for a living. Just so long as your interests don't conflict with mine, I've got no problem with it. But I want no part of it." (I didn't realize it until later, but I'd just quoted *The Godfather* myself.)

"I'm just an actor," I continued. "I'm not a common thie . . . I mean, I've never been involved in illegal activities. Thanks again for dinner. And good night."

I stood up and walked away, half expecting to be shot in the back as I did.

But no shots were fired, and the convention ended without me running into Rosetti again. In fact, I didn't hear another word from him.

Until a few days later when he had his goons mug me on the street and kidnap my dog. Then he called to threaten me and my family over the telephone.

11

I opened the door. On the other side was the same son of a bitch who mugged me on the street and stole my dog.

"I found your dog, ma'am," he said to Caitlin as he handed Gizmo over to her.

Caitlin was so overcome with gratitude, she wanted to give the bastard a reward.

"No reward necessary, ma'am, I'm doing what any decent person would do," he said, while shooting me a nasty grin on the sly.

"No, I insist," said Caitlin. "We don't have much cash in this house, I'm afraid, but I want to give you something. Stay there and I'll be right back."

She left the mugger and me standing at the doorway while she went to look for some money, presumably under the sofa cushions.

"Here's your wallet and your watch, man."

"Thanks, I guess."

"Take a look inside the wallet later. Mr. Rosetti put a thousand bucks in there for you. He wants you to come meet him in Philadelphia tomorrow morning. He said to take the Acela train, business class. There's also a card in there with his telephone number and his address. He says buy yourself a decent watch, too."

My wife returned with a fifty-dollar bill in her hands. I have no idea where she found it. Maybe she kept a secret stash somewhere. I wouldn't blame her if she did.

"It's not very much, but it's all we have, and I want you to keep it. We're so grateful to you for finding our dog."

"Thank you, ma'am," he said and he took the bill.

Wouldn't it have been more gracious of him to refuse it, I wondered? Gizmo may have wondered the same thing. He was watching this scene from a safe distance and growling.

We gave the mugger fifty dollars and he gave us a thousand, making it one of the weirdest muggings in history. Caitlin was so happy to have Gizmo back she didn't think to question his quick return. It made it the weirdest dognapping in history, too.

The next morning, with Rosetti's address in my pocket, I took the high-speed Acela train to Philadelphia. An hour and a half later I was in a cab heading through the familiar Philly streets to the Little Italy neighborhood.

That's all I knew. I had no idea if I was going to Rosetti's home. Or his office. Or an old-fashioned Italian restaurant with checkered tablecloths and Chianti bottles covered in candle wax. It turned out to be none of the above. Instead, the cab pulled up to a plain storefront on the ground floor of an ordinary brick building. The sign out front said, "Santa Lucia Hunting & Fishing Club."

I knocked on the door.

Rosetti himself opened it. "Joey, good to see you. I'm glad you came. Come on in."

If you're Catholic, you'll know what I mean when I say the place looked like a Knights of Columbus hall. If you're not Catholic, maybe you can picture it if I told you it looked like an Eagles Club, or an American Legion hall, or a Moose Club. But much smaller. There was one spacious room I'll call a social area with two or three private rooms off to the side, including a tiny kitchen. Faded, dirty linoleum covered the floors. The walls had wood paneling made of knotty pine, probably fake. The furniture looked like the kind of cheap metallic tables and chairs you might see in a small-town diner or tavern. Vinyl cushions padded the backs of the chairs and seats, but they were cracking in several spots. You could see the foam rubber seeping out.

Eight or nine guys sat around doing nothing. Most of them were middle-aged, with a few young guys and a few older men thrown into the mix. Several of them were playing cards around an old poker table. A few of them were having a drink at the counter pass-through between the main room and the kitchen. One was sitting in the corner reading the newspaper. One was clipping his fingernails. Two were having a heated argument, to which the others were paying no attention whatsoever. Rosetti spoke to these two, "You two *cafoni*, shut up. We've got a visitor."

They immediately stopped arguing like someone had flicked off a light switch.

"Everybody, listen up. This is the guy I was telling you about. The actor. Joey Volpe. Joey the Fox, I call him. He's going to be helping us on the convention job."

Joey the Fox? I'd been in the Mafia ten seconds and I already had a moniker.

I didn't have time to think about that because suddenly the whole atmosphere of the room changed. It was if Frank Sinatra had walked through the door. Several of the guys applauded. Some of them made that strange "Whoa" diphthong sound that you would hear on *The Sopranos*. They patted me on the back. They shook my hand. They punched me on the shoulder. And, of course, they began asking questions:

"Hey, you were the one who died on the toilet, right? I had an uncle who died the same way. Heart attack caused by constipation. Can you believe it?"

"Well . . ." I said.

"No, you asshole," said another. "This was the guy who hung himself in his basement because Tony wouldn't let him retire to Florida."

"Fuck both of you idiots," said another guy. "Joey is the one who played the guy that Christopher carved up in the butcher shop. Remember? Christopher said, 'It's going to be a long time before I eat at Satriale's again.'"

"I'm a method actor," I said, "but I draw the line at playing a slice of salami."

Everybody laughed at that. Although I wondered how many of these mobsters knew what a method actor was.

"Hey, Joey, I loved *Button Men*. How come you never got a chance to play the big role on any of the episodes?"

I breathed a sigh of relief. We had gotten through *The Sopranos* interrogation without me having to admit I never had more than a walk-on.

"Well, the producers told me my big show was coming up in the second season. But we never got that far. We got canceled."

"That was a goddamn shame," said one guy. "I loved that show."

"Me too," said several of them at once.

These guys were nicer than I thought they'd be!

"All right, all right," said Rosetti. "You guys sound like a bunch of women at a book-of-the-month club. Before we break out the mah-jongg tiles, we got some business to discuss with Joey. Paulie, Carlo . . . you two come into the back room with Joey and me. Mike, bring us four espressos. Then run down to the pastry shop and buy us a box of *sfogliatelle*. We've got some planning to do."

Rosetti led us into the back room and all four of us sat down at a conference table. It was just another cheap metallic dinette with a dirty Formica top like the ones in the social room.

"Carlo, get the map of the convention center in Boston and lay it out on the table here."

"Wait a second—"

"Hang on, Joey, let's take a look at the lay of the land first. Then we can discuss our strategy."

"But— "

"Hold your horses, Joey."

Carlo laid the map on the table and smoothed out the wrinkles and folds. Mike arrived with five espressos and put one down in front of each of us. Then he left the room and closed the door behind him.

"Okay, here's what we've got."

"Mr. Rosetti . . ."

"What the fuck is it, Joey? It's not time for you to talk yet. I'll let you know when we need your advice."

"I'm not in the Boston convention, sir."

"You're not *in* it? What do you mean?"

"I'm not going to the Boston Fan-Con."

"You sure as hell are. You're going if I have to put a gun to your head and walk your ass all the way up I-95."

"Mr. Rosetti. Tony. Sir. It's not that. I'd *like* to go." (Actually, I wanted to avoid going at all costs.) "But I haven't been invited."

"Not invited?"

"I don't get to go to all these Fan-Cons. I have to apply. I even have to pay a fee. Sometimes my application gets denied. The Boston convention turned me down."

"Turned you down?"

"The big conventions often turn me down."

"Why?"

"Because I'm not William Shatner or Patrick Stewart or George Takei."

"Who the fuck are they?" said the mobster named Carlo, who was obviously not a *Star Trek* fan.

"They are stars. I'm just an actor."

"Oh, shit," said Rosetti. "I hadn't thought of this."

"I'm sorry," I said.

"So what's the next convention you *are* going to?"

"Columbus, Ohio."

"I like Columbus," said the mobster named Paulie.

"You've been there?" asked Rosetti.

"No, I like Columbus the explorer guy. He was Italian."

"Please shut the fuck up," said Rosetti. "Everybody shut the fuck up unless you have something useful to say."

There was a long silence.

"Mr. Rosetti?"

"Is this going to be useful, Joey?"

"I think so."

"Go ahead, then."

"You don't need any maps or blueprints. All these events are set up exactly the same."

"Go on."

"There's a big exhibit hall. The security checkpoint is usually located just outside the exhibit hall at the main doors. The celebrities are sitting at long folding tables lined up along the periphery of the room. Some of the more important celebrities have stanchions set up to control the line. Some of the smaller celebrities . . . like me," I added, "are sitting at tables and the line forms in front of them."

"What's a stanchion?" said Paulie.

"It's like those metal poles and velvet ropes you see when you're waiting in line at the bank," I said.

"I don't wait in the line at the bank," said Carlo. "I go in with my guns blazing."

"Carlo, can we get through this without making any more stupid jokes?" said Rosetti.

"Yeah. Okay. Sorry, boss."

"Let me tell you what we were thinking, Joey," said Rosetti, "and you can tell me if it's a good idea, okay?"

I shrugged my shoulders as if to say I wasn't an expert on these matters. He went on anyway.

"We get Carlo and Paulie here dressed up like movie gangsters. You know, like Edward G. Robinson. Or that other little guy. That Yankee Doodle guy, you know, 'You dirty rat, you killed my brother . . .'"

"James Cagney."

"Yeah, Jimmy Cagney. I always liked him. I liked when he stuck the pineapple in that girl's face."

"Grapefruit."

"What?"

"He stuck a *grapefruit* in his wife's face," I said.

"What the fuck difference does it make? Maybe it was a kumquat. Just shut the fuck up and listen to me."

"Sorry."

"May I continue?"

I nodded.

"So anyway, we dress Carlo and Paulie up in movie gangster outfits. Pinstripe suits. Fedoras. Spats on their shoes. Diamond stickpins in their ties. Pinky rings."

I looked at the guys around the table. All three of them were wearing glittering diamond pinky rings.

"Looks like you've already got that part of the wardrobe covered," I said.

"Yeah, I guess you're right. But listen to this. We give Paulie and Carlo a couple of big machine guns to carry. Real monsters, like they used to use during Prohibition."

"They'll never get past security," I said.

"Shut up and listen. They *will* get past security because they're made of plastic. They're toy guns."

"So you're going to rob people using toy machine guns? That's pretty gutsy. You understand, don't you, that the security guards will have real guns?"

"So will we."

"You just said—"

"I know what I said."

"Then how are you going to get real guns inside?"

"You're going to bring them in for us," said Rosetti with a grin.

His plan stunned me. I almost stood up and walked out. Then I remembered what happened to Gizmo. What could happen, God forbid, to Caitlin or Bianca. So I just sat there without saying a word for what seemed like centuries. It was only a moment before Rosetti asked me a question. "Remember when you did the panel discussion the other day, Joey?"

I nodded.

"The security guard didn't pat you down. He didn't make you walk through a metal detector. He didn't even look through that little girlie purse you carry. He just checked your name off a list, right? Then he let you walk right through. Because you're a big star."

"I'm not a—"

"I *know* you're not a star, Joey. That's why we're going to Columbus Freakin' Ohio instead of Boston. When is the Columbus convention, by the way?"

"Next month."

"Okay, we'll just have to cool our heels for a while. Do you see anything wrong with our plan, Joey? Do you see any holes in it?"

"Even if the security guard doesn't pat me down, I think he'll notice if I'm carrying two machine guns."

"We're going to give you two small pistols, that's all. The newspapers call them Saturday Night Specials. That's all we need to do the job. You can stick them in your underpants. Nobody will notice. Or you can put them in your little purse."

"It's a men's carryall bag," I said.

"Whatever."

I thought about it for a moment.

"What do we do . . . I mean, what do you guys do once you've got the real guns in your hands. What happens then?"

I waited. After a moment or two, it became clear they hadn't thought this far ahead. I remembered the Philadelphia mob didn't have a sterling reputation for competence. "What do you do next?" I said again.

"We rob 'em," said Carlo.

"You rob whom?"

"We rob everyone there. *Whom* do you think?"

"You're going to rob everyone in the main exhibit hall? There may be two or three thousand people there."

"I thought you said Columbus was a small convention," said Rosetti.

"It *is* a small one. At the Comic-Con in San Diego, you might have ten thousand people in the main exhibit hall. In Columbus, there might be two thousand. You're going to rob them all with two guys and two pistols? By the time the security guards are finished with you, you guys will look like Bonnie and Clyde."

Silence.

"You'll look like Sonny Corleone at the tollbooth," I added.

"We get the picture," said Rosetti. "You got a better idea?"

I didn't know whether to help them or hinder them. Part of me wanted them to screw this up, which would get me off the hook for good. I realized Rosetti wasn't even planning to be there himself. If Paulie and Carlo screwed the pooch, I'd still have Rosetti on my ass. Worse yet, he'd be mad. He'd blame me for the mess. So I decided to cooperate.

"Look," I said, "there's no point in robbing all the fans. They don't have any cash on them. Maybe they have some walking-around money, but that's all. You want to rob the *celebrities*. They're the ones with the cash stuck in their underpants and their shoes. It's like what Willie Sutton used to say."

"Who's Willie Sutton?" said Carlo.

I couldn't help but wonder about the sorry state of American education nowadays. I mean, here was a criminal by trade and he had no idea who one of the most notorious criminals in history was.

"He was a famous bank robber."

"So what did he say?" asked Carlo.

"The reporters asked him why he robbed banks, and he said, 'Because that's where the money is.'"

"Well, *duh*," said Paulie. "He doesn't sound so smart to me."

"My point is the celebrities have all the money, so you want to isolate them from the rest of the crowd. Like cutting cattle from the herd. You separate the young bulls who need to be castrated from all the others."

I surprised myself with that analogy. Where does a kid who grew up in the Philadelphia suburbs and went to Haverford and Yale come up with a metaphor from cattle ranching? I guess I saw a lot of Westerns over the years.

"And how do you propose we do that, Tex?" said Rosetti.

I hesitated. Did I want to help them this much? The image of Caitlin and Bianca floating in the East River made me go on.

"It's pretty easy," I said. "You don't want to rob them in the main room. You want to rob them in the greenroom."

"What difference does the color of the room make?" said Paulie.

"No, the greenroom is like a waiting room for actors. Most of the time greenrooms aren't even green. It's just what they're always called in show business. I think it's because the actors are so nervous they turn green. Or maybe the green is supposed to *calm* their nerves. I can never remember which."

"So where's the greenroom?" said Rosetti.

"It's usually behind the flats."

"The flats? What, are you going cowboy on us again? Like the flats in Utah?"

"No, no, no. It's another theatrical term. A flat is a backdrop that's part of the scenery in a play. In this case they're just thin boards covered with black velvet. Or sometimes they use black curtains. They're *behind* the tables where the celebrities are signing autographs."

"Yeah, go on," said Rosetti.

"Well, there are little openings in those flats. When the autograph session is over and it's time for the celebrities to have lunch, they slip through the flats and walk to the greenroom. Usually, there's a buffet for the celebrities and some tables and chairs set up for them to eat lunch at. That's where you want to hit them."

That's where you want to hit them? I couldn't believe I said that.

A slow grin began to form on Rosetti's face.

"That sounds perfect," he said.

I couldn't help smiling myself. I guess I had a natural talent for grand larceny.

"Here's the deal," Rosetti said to his two henchmen. "While Joey is signing autographs, you two guys stand on either side of him with your machine guns like you're his bodyguards. You'll dress like gangsters, so nobody will think anything of it. You'll look like you're part of the show. Half the people at these things dress up in crazy costumes anyway. You'll fit right in."

Carlo and Paulie glanced at each other. They seemed to like this plan.

Rosetti continued, "When Joey breaks for lunch, you two guys go *with* him behind the blackout curtains to the greenroom. Joey, how much security is there in the greenroom? How many guards?"

I tried to remember all the other Fan-Cons I'd been to, and I thought I knew the answer. I considered the possibility of lying to Rosetti to scare him off, but it was too late for that. I was in this too deep now. I decided to tell him the truth.

"Maybe one guard at the door. It's like an airport. The security focuses on the main entrance to the exhibit hall. Once you get past that, you're in the clear. I guess they figure that if you've crossed the main security checkpoint, you're not a threat anymore."

"Perfect," said Rosetti. "At some point while you're signing autographs, you can pass the pistols to Carlo and Paulie. You can do it out in the open if you want. Nobody will give a shit. They'll think it's part of your act."

He turned back to Carlo and Paulie.

"After you get into the greenroom and everybody is eating lunch, you guys grab the security guard. He'll probably be a fat *melanzane*. He won't know what the fuck hit him. Take his gun off him, too. You can put him in his own handcuffs while you're at it. Lock the door behind you. There's only one door in the greenroom, right Joey?"

"I'm pretty sure there's only one, usually, yes."

"So lock the door behind you. Then get the celebrities to cough up their cash. Joey said they could have as much as twenty grand each on them. Don't let them hold out on you. They could have it stuffed in their shoes or in their underpants. Make sure you get it all. Make them take off their clothes if you have to. They're from Hollywood, they probably like taking off their clothes in public."

Paulie and Carlo found that remark amusing.

"Joey, we can work out the minor details from here. I've got to say you've been a big help. I was going to give you ten percent of the haul. I'd like to bump that up to twenty-five because you've shown you're part of the team today."

Paulie and Carlo found this less amusing. They frowned.

"No, sir," I said. "No way."

"I can't go any higher than twenty-five percent, Joey. There are four of us here. That makes you an equal partner, for chrissakes."

"I don't want any money, Mr. Rosetti. I said I'd do this because . . . well, let's be honest, because you *forced* me to do it. But I'm not a criminal. I'm just an actor. I don't want any of the spoils."

"What's spoiled?" said Carlo. "It sounds sweet to me."

"I don't want any of the take. The haul. The action. Whatever you call it. If you're going to make me do this, I'll do it. But I don't want to profit from it."

"Why not?" said Rosetti.

"Well, I don't want to go to prison for one thing."

"Don't worry, Joey, nobody is going to prison. Not you. Not me. Not any of us. We'll make sure of that."

"I hope not," I said. Maybe Rosetti was right, I thought to myself. I needed the money, that's for sure. If I played my cards right, nobody would get hurt and nobody would know I was involved.

"But you're part of this now, Joey," said Rosetti. "If you're in for a dime, you're in for a dollar. So you might as well take the goddamn dollar."

I was in for a dime, that's for sure, because that's what they call a ten-year sentence in federal prison.

12

I got through security carrying two handguns in my pockets with no problem at all. The security guard simply checked my name off a list. Once inside the greenroom, I met my volunteer assistant for the day. She was a mousey-looking girl named Karen Murray. She led me to the main exhibit hall, and we sat down at the table where I'd be signing autographs.

Carlo and Paulie got through the security checkpoint with their two toy machine guns, too. But when they arrived at my table, I forgot which one was which. I looked up at them and said, "Hello, Paulie. Hello, Carlo."

"I'm Paulie. He's Carlo."

"Rosencrantz and Guildenstern," I said. "Or is it Guildenstern and Rosencrantz?"

"Neither one," said Paulie. "It's Bazzoni and Bussetti. We ain't no Jews, for chrissakes."

"Karen," I said. "May I introduce my two . . . er, associates for the day. This is Paulie. And this is Carlo. My agent thought it would be fun if I had a couple of bodyguards in gangster outfits to stand behind me with machine guns."

"Cool idea," said Karen.

"You got something you want to give us?" said Carlo.

"Take it easy, Carlo," I whispered. "Not now. We've got ninety minutes to get that done. Just stand behind me and act like my bodyguards."

Karen paid no attention to us. She was dealing with the first few autograph-seekers that had lined up.

Carlo and Paulie took their places behind me while I started signing autographs. But Carlo and Paulie were not patient actors. They wouldn't have done well on a movie set where 90 percent of the game is learning how to wait for hours on end without going crazy. After a few minutes, Paulie leaned down and whispered in my ear, "What about the guns, Joey?"

"Don't worry about them. Not yet. Just play your part for a while."

"Did you get them through security?"

"Yes, I've got them. No problem. They're in my pants pockets."

"Your pockets? Rosetti told you to put them in your under-wear. You were supposed to excuse yourself and go to the bath-room to get them out."

"It wasn't necessary. They waved me right in. Just be patient, Paulie. That's what being an actor is all about."

"I ain't no actor," he said and resumed his position standing behind me.

His patience lasted another five minutes. He leaned down and whispered into my ear again. I kept shooting furtive glances at Karen to see if she was hearing any of this, but she was busy dealing with the fans.

"Give us the guns now, Joey," said Paulie. "Let's get that part over with. I feel naked here without a gun on me while I'm waiting to do a job."

"All right, for heaven's sake. There's one in my left pocket and one in my right. Reach in and pull them out."

Part of me *wanted* to get caught at this point. No real crime had taken place yet. I could always tell Rosetti that Paulie insisted on taking the guns from me in the exhibit hall. I could tell the cops they weren't my guns anyway. Why would an actor bring guns to an autograph session, after all? I could say the guns belonged to Paulie and Carlo, two known members of the Mafia. If every-thing went well, I'd get off scot-free from both Rosetti and the police.

Karen turned to me and saw Paulie pull the second gun out of my pocket, and a bolt of adrenaline shot through my veins. But I'm an actor, after all. I improvised a line before I had a chance to give it a second thought:

"The more toy guns we have around the better," I said.

"You're right," she said. "If you have any more guns on you, maybe we could put some on the table here. That would look cool."

"No, I'm all out of 'em, I'm afraid. Just two handguns and two machine guns."

"Too bad," she said, and she turned back to selling photos and handling cash.

"All four of them are just harmless plastic toys," I said.

Methinks the actor didst protest too much. But she was no longer listening.

With their guns in hand, Paulie and Carlo calmed down for a while—until the blare of an air horn scared the shit out of all three of us.

Carlo and Paulie raised their machine guns and waved them back and forth until they both remembered they were toys. So they dropped them and drew their pistols instead.

"What the hell was that?" I said to Karen.

"Five-minute warning until the lunch break."

"What do we do now?"

"We sign as many autographs as we can for another five minutes. If there are still people in line, I'll give them a pass for the afternoon session. They can come back after lunch without losing their place."

When the air horn sounded again, announcing the lunch break, Karen said, "Okay, that's it for this morning. Let's go back to the greenroom and get some lunch. We're due back here in ninety minutes."

"Can my bodyguards come to the greenroom with us?" I said, hoping she would say no and this whole nightmare would be over.

"I don't think that'll be a problem," said Karen. "Check in with the security guard and tell him they're with you."

So we did that, and the security guard put up little resistance.

"Who are these guys?" he asked me as we came to the door of the greenroom. "They don't have special guest credentials, just regular fan credentials."

"They're with me," I said. "They're part of my act."

"What are their names?"

Rosencrantz and Guildenstern, I thought. I had forgotten their last names again.

"I'm Carl O'Hara and this is Mr. Paul McPherson," said Carlo, with remarkable poise.

"You're not on the list, fellas," said the security guard, checking his clipboard. "I'm only supposed to let in people who are on the list."

"C'mon," I said. "They're with me. I played a gangster on *The Sopranos*. These are friends of mine pretending to be my body-guards. It's part of our act. See the toy machine guns?"

"Who did you play on *The Sopranos*?" said the security guard. "I loved that show."

This time I didn't mess around with the guessing game. I flat-out lied. "I was the guy who died of a heart attack on the toilet. Remember?"

"Oh, yeah, I remember. That was funny."

"Nowadays I carry an aspirin *and* an Ex-Lax wherever I go."

He laughed.

"Let us in, my friend," I said. "We're hungry and there isn't enough time for us to get lunch anywhere else."

"Well, I don't know . . ." he said.

Then I got some help from an unexpected source.

"They're cool," said Karen, my little volunteer. "I've been working with them all morning. They're very professional gang-sters."

Out of the mouths of babes, I thought.

Karen had so many badges, ribbons, buttons, lanyards, epau-lets, stripes, and medals on her body. It was like getting a direct order from the Chairman of the Joint Chiefs of Staff.

"Okay, I guess it's no big deal," said the guard. "Come on in."

All four of us, including Karen, walked into the greenroom without any more questions.

I turned to Paulie and Carlo and said, "Help yourself to some lunch at the buffet, guys."

Paulie whispered into my ear, "Fuck that. It's time to do the job. Don't chicken out on us now."

"No, it's better if you chill out for a while," I said. "Give it ten or fifteen minutes. Wait until all the celebrities and their assistants are in the room. Otherwise you'll be leaving money on the table. Then make your move." I was trying to put off the inevitable as long as I could. Besides, I was hungry.

After getting some food at the buffet we sat down at a table near the door watching the parade of celebrities come in. And what a parade it was! Sort of like the bar scene from *Star Wars*. Literally.

Among the first in the door were Steven Dubois, of course, with his husband Mitch. Mitch was his full-time assistant, money-handler, and enforcer at these Fan-Cons. Just like in Atlantic City, Dubois walked in the room smiling and glad-handing like he was running for office. I've got to give him credit. He recognized me and remembered my name after meeting me once before.

"Hey, Joey, good to see you again. Say hello to that scoundrel Jerry Pennington for me."

I've never been a big TV watcher, so I didn't recognize a lot of the so-called stars. I kept asking Karen to identify them. Eventually she started announcing them as they walked in. She sounded like the emcee at the Westminster dog show.

"That's Ann Marie Davis from *Buffy the Vampire Slayer* and Jeff Witherspoon from *Flesh Gordon*."

"Flesh or Flash?"

"Flesh." She looked at me like I was an idiot.

"Mary Ellen McEnroe from *Star Trek: The Motion Picture*."

"Which one?"

"When you say '*The Motion Picture*,' you always mean the first one."

"Who's the older woman over there?" I asked.

"Gillian Baker. She was a child actress of some kind."

"Gillian Baker? Are you kidding? She's the most famous person in the room. She played the little girl in that big horror movie from the seventies . . . you know the one I mean. I can't remember the title."

"Before my time," said Karen.

I looked at Gillian Baker. She must've been closing in on sixty. That movie came out before I was born. She was holding up pretty well. She had a nice rack on her for someone her age. Maybe she'd made a deal with the devil.

"That's Kathleen Chase from *Back to the Future*," said Karen.

Back to the Future? Hell, that movie is so old that even the future they were traveling to is now in the past. Michael J. Fox has Parkinson's disease, for heaven's sake.

Karen kept up her running commentary. I kept trying to remember which roles these actors had played in these films and television shows. But it was futile.

"Oh my God!" said Karen.

"What? What?"

"That's Peter Stone from *The Hunger Games*. I forgot he was here. I've got to get his autograph."

"Are you allowed to do that in the greenroom?"

"I don't know. But I'll never forgive myself if I don't. It's now or never. *Carpe Diem*."

Karen got up and left.

"Did she say something in Italian?" said Paulie.

"Latin. Carpe Diem."

"What's that mean?"

"It means seize the day. Take action now or forever regret it."

"She's right. Time to make our move."

"Shouldn't we give it a few more minutes?" said Carlo.

They both looked at me like *I* was the leader of this mob. I had a strong feeling that it was now or never.

"If it were done when 'tis done, then 'twere well it were done quickly," I said. *Macbeth, Act I, Scene Seven.*

"What the fuck do you mean by that, asshole?" said Paulie.

"I *mean* I still don't want any part of this. But if you're going to do it you might as well do it now."

It looked like Carlo and Paulie had rehearsed their next few moves. They drew their pistols and walked over to the security guard who was standing at the door a few feet away from us.

Carlo hit the guard on the back of the head with the butt of his gun and he toppled like a tree in the forest. Paulie closed the door and locked it with the dead bolt. He rejoined Carlo who was relieving the security guard of his gun, nightstick, and handcuffs. Paulie put one handcuff on the guard's left wrist and attached the other to a nearby radiator. The security guard was now neutralized—even if he managed to regain consciousness, which looked unlikely. The locked door would hold off our rescuers for a while. Carlo held his gun in the air and fired two shots into the ceiling.

"This is a stickup. Do exactly what we say and nobody will get hurt."

At that point, the assembled group of has-been actors in the room did something strange:

They did nothing at all.

Most of the actors didn't even look up from their meals. Many of them kept talking. (Presumably about themselves.)

Some of them glanced at Paulie and his smoking gun with a bemused expression on their faces, still chewing their food. They were curious about what was happening but not in the least concerned about it.

I realized these actors had spent so much time on movie sets, so much time rehearsing lines and going to auditions, so many hours practicing stage fighting and shooting guns with blank cartridges that they had a hard time distinguishing fantasy from reality. The fact that some guy stood up and fired a pistol twice into the ceiling struck them as no more unusual than someone clinking their wineglass at a wedding to announce a toast.

So Paulie fired two more shots into the ceiling.

Still no reaction.

He fired one into the window, which shattered into a million pieces. Now—finally!—someone screamed. But it wasn't one of the actors. They were still blasé about the whole thing. It was one of the assistants. It might have been Karen. The gunshots interrupting her in the middle of asking Peter Stone for an autograph may have pissed her off.

"I'm not fucking kidding," Paulie yelled. "This ain't no act. This ain't no show. This is a real stickup."

Paulie had picked up on the same aura of disbelief that I had. He realized his first task would be to convince this group of fantasy addicts this was a bona fide robbery. "I want everyone to get up from your table and line up against that wall over there."

Now a different mood began to prevail in the room. Most actors were accustomed to being herded around like cattle. They were used to being told, "Move over there. No, *there*. Stand there for seven hours. Now move over here. Okay, you're done for the day. We've decided we don't need you for this shot after all."

They did it, and they did it well. But they always did it with a certain attitude, as if they were mumbling to themselves, "Can you believe I once played *Hamlet* off-Broadway and now I'm reduced to getting moved around like a sheep in a pen?"

For all their resistance, reluctance, and disbelief, the group of seventy-five actors and their assistants lined up against the back wall in less than a minute.

I was still sitting at my table watching them.

"You, too, asshole," said Carlo. "What makes you think you're special? Don't think you can get out of this just because you played a gangster on TV."

I realized Carlo was doing me a favor. By lumping me in with everyone else, he was giving me an alibi. Afterward, I could say I had no idea Carlo and Paulie had planned this. I could tell the police I thought they were actors. I might get out of this thing scot-free after all.

I smiled. Then I realized the smile might give me away. So I turned the smile around into a frown. *Acting!* I joined the other actors against the wall and waited for Paulie and Carlo to give their next command. Meanwhile, I tried to act scared.

"I want each of you to put your cash in front of you," said Carlo. "Put your wallet or purse down in front of you. Empty all the cash out of your pockets. Your pants pockets. Your shirt pockets. If you're carrying a cigar box or a pouch for cash, put that down in front of you, too. If I catch any of you trying to hold on to a penny, I'll shoot you in the fucking face. Don't think I won't."

We did what he said.

Paulie took a large plastic trash bag out of his pocket, shook it open, and began to pick up the haul. He turned back to Carlo. "Don't you remember what the boss said?"

"What?"

"He said sometimes they stuff the cash in their underpants and bras. He said we should make 'em strip naked."

I couldn't tell if Paulie's motivation was economic or prurient, but Carlo seemed to like the idea.

"Oh, yeah, that's right," said Carlo. "You heard what my partner said, ladies and gentlemen. Take off your clothes."

There was great reluctance and grumbling. Carlo fired two more shots into the ceiling. Everyone started ripping off their clothes like a bunch of teenagers about to go skinny-dipping at the rock quarry. Me too.

Oh, my dear Lord, what a sorry sight we were. If there's anything more pathetic than an aging actor, it's an aging actor with no clothing. Although Gillian Baker's breasts were nice, and she was—what?—fifty-five years old if she was a day. Some of the younger actors and actresses looked pretty good. Steven Dubois looked like he was seventeen instead of seventy!

I heard someone pounding on the door. The shots had attracted the attention of security. It wouldn't be long before they broke the door down. But Paulie and Carlo remained calm and continued their work methodically.

Once again Paulie started to gather up the booty into his trash bag. Sure enough, Rosetti was right, there was a lot of extra cash stuck in underpants, panties, and bras. A few of the actors had old-fashioned money belts, like American tourists used to carry to Europe. They were jam-packed with bills. Before long Paulie's trash bag was bulging with cash, plus some jewelry and watches, too. I guessed it was about a hundred-thousand-dollars worth altogether. I wondered if it would disappoint Rosetti. He expected more than this. I remembered the figure of a *million* dollars bandied about at our dinner in Atlantic City. We had been talking about one of the big Fan-Cons with stars like William Shatner and Patrick Stewart signing autographs. This was a little bush-league convention in the Midwest. I hoped Rosetti wouldn't blame me for the shortfall.

"Throw their clothes out the window," said Carlo. "That'll slow them down a bit."

Paulie gathered up all the clothing and tossed it out the shattered window.

"How do we get out?" said Paulie.

"We'll use the window, too," said Carlo. "We're on the ground floor."

"Pete is waiting for us in the driveway of the hotel."

"So we'll walk around to the front. Would it kill you to walk a little?"

"No, I guess not."

"Okay, listen up, everybody," said Carlo. "Stand there and be quiet. Sit down if you want. Don't try to follow us or we'll shoot you. I'm not kidding. If you try to crawl through that broken window naked, some of you are going to get your balls sliced off."

I winced.

"Before long, they'll break the door down and save you. You've got nothing to worry about. Stay calm, and everything will turn out fine. Thanks for your cooperation."

"Thanks for your money, too," said Paulie with a laugh.

They both chuckled and started to walk toward the broken window.

13

I didn't know it at the time. Or maybe I'd forgotten. But Steven Dubois had been a real swashbuckler on his television series. He might have been a bit effeminate in real life, but on the show he was constantly getting into (and winning) fist fights with various alien life forms. His character knew all sorts of fancy martial-arts moves and no matter how overwhelming the odds against him—even if two or three monsters from outer space were ganging up on him—he usually came out on top.

Funny thing about being an actor. Once you've played a role, some little part of that character stays with you. If you were a tough guy on a television show twenty years ago, a little voice in your head says you're still a tough guy.

Unfortunately for Steven Dubois, he chose to listen to that voice.

Paulie was halfway through the window, trying to make sure his crotch cleared the jagged edge of broken glass by at least two inches. Carlo was standing right behind him, waiting. Both of them were still holding their guns.

Steven Dubois grabbed a butter knife from one of the tables and started charging toward Carlo. He was swinging the knife around his head and screaming some sort of banshee battle cry.

Carlo swung around and saw this seventy-year-old actor coming at him, stark naked, with a butter knife in his hands and murder in his eyes. So he did the sensible thing.

He shot Dubois in the foot.

Dubois dropped to the floor and grabbed his bleeding foot, howling in pain.

But the gunshot surprised Paulie and he lost his grip on the windowsill. He slipped ever so slightly, but enough for his crotch to land dead center on the same shard of broken glass he'd been trying so hard to avoid. Paulie let out a blood-curdling scream that was louder and more shrill than Steven's. Meanwhile, the pounding on the door was getting louder.

Carlo shoved Paulie the rest of the way through the window to make room for himself to go through. He clambered up and out without harm. I could hear Paulie's screams getting lower and lower in pitch as he moved farther away—the Doppler effect. Meanwhile, Steven Dubois was crying softly near the window and massaging his bleeding foot.

"Is there a doctor in the house?" I said. I kicked myself mentally for saying something so clichéd.

"I'm not a doctor, but I played one on TV," said one of the actors. Talk about clichéd!

"Which show? How many seasons?" said another.

"Two seasons. *ER* with George Clooney."

This was an old actor's trick for padding your résumé. If the part you played in a movie or TV show was so small it was hardly worth mentioning, you mentioned the star in the leading role to make it sound more impressive.

"Did you get residuals?" said the second actor to the one who claimed to be a TV doctor.

"Yes, I'm still getting some. Just a few dollars a month nowadays."

"Still. That's not bad."

I'd heard enough of this nonsense.

"Did George Clooney teach you anything about *medicine*?" I said. "If so, maybe you could go help Mr. Dubois."

The actor's face turned red. Not because he was stark naked, but because I called him out as a fake doctor. He grabbed a couple of napkins and walked over to where Dubois was sitting on the floor. Together they managed to stop the bleeding. Luckily, it turned out to be a flesh wound.

"What do we do now?" said an actress I remembered from an old sitcom.

"We should wait until they find us," said another aging actress.

"Do you want them to find us naked? How's that going to look in the gossip magazines?"

It had been at least thirty years since any gossip magazine had mentioned this woman's name.

"We can't do much of anything until we get our clothes on," said a third actress. "Some brave man has to climb out that window and toss our clothing back inside."

"Not me," said every male actor in the room at the same time.

"What the devil is wrong with you guys?" said Gillian Baker. "Oh, hells bells, I'll do it." And she did. Without any penis or testicles to worry about, she scurried out the window and started tossing clothes back inside.

The mood in the room brightened as we sorted through our clothing and began to put it on piece by piece. It looked like Steven Dubois was going to be fine. Some people made a few jokes to make light of the situation. I can't remember exactly what they said, but I remember we all laughed. Nothing is more exhilarating, Winston Churchill had once said, than being shot at without result. I guess each of us was enjoying some of that sense of exhilaration. (Except for Steven, of course.)

But then Karen—dear, sweet Karen, my loyal assistant—said something that sent a chill down my spine.

"I know it was you, Mr. Volpe," she said. "Those robbers were your friends. You were the inside guy. The three of you planned this whole thing."

Caught.

That was my cue to do the first real acting I'd done in twenty years.

"What are you talking about, Karen?" I said. "I never met them before today. Just like I never met *you* before today."

"You acted like you knew them. You introduced them to me."

"Karen, I didn't even know their names. Remember? I didn't know which was Paulie and which was Carlo. I didn't know their last names at all."

"But you were expecting them."

"I was expecting them because my agent told me she'd hired some guys to act as my bodyguards today. She thought it would help bring more fans to my autograph table and we'd make more money. That's all there was to it. The whole thing was my agent's idea."

Karen wasn't buying it.

"I saw one of those guys reach into your pocket and pull out a gun."

"Karen, those were toy guns."

"What do you mean they were toy guns? Tell that to Mr. Dubois. Look at all the blood on his foot. Look at the bullet holes in the ceiling. Look at the window, for heaven's sake."

"No, I mean I *thought* they were just toy guns. Just like the machine guns those guys were carrying. They were plastic."

"The machine guns were toys, but the pistols were real."

I wondered if Karen was a federal prosecutor when she wasn't volunteering at Fan-Cons.

"I thought they were toys, just like the machine guns."

"You were carrying two pistols in your pockets and you couldn't tell if they were real guns or toys? Isn't a real gun ten times heavier than a plastic one?"

She stumped me with this, and I couldn't reply. Karen continued her final summation to the jury of my peers—a bunch of washed-up actors—who were listening to the whole conversation.

"You did this, Mr. Volpe. Or at least you were in on it. I think you set the whole thing up. You had the two robbers carry plastic machine guns into the exhibit hall. They passed through security because their guns were just toys. But you had two *real* guns in your pockets. You got past security because you came in through the special guest entrance. The security guard at the door checked your name off the list and let you in. He didn't frisk you. He didn't make you walk through a metal detector. You're a big star, after all."

"Well, I'm just an—"

"Then you met up with your accomplices at the autograph table. You passed the real guns to them. When it was time for lunch, you brought them back here to the greenroom. Then they robbed us blind. And they shot Mr. Dubois in the foot. You're responsible for this, Joey. You're the ringleader."

Her case was airtight. I was going to hold out my hands so she could cuff me, but the sheer stupidity, vanity, and greed of my fellow actors saved me.

"Does your agent really help you book these Fan-Cons?" said a guy dressed up like the Green Lantern. "I have to book them myself. I even have to pay an application fee. My agent says they're not worth his time."

"My agent sets them up for me," I lied.

"Do you have to pay him fifteen percent? That's a little steep for something like this. When you subtract the application fee and the other expenses, there's not much left for me. I've got to feed my family."

"Well, it's a cash business," I said. "Your agent doesn't have to know how much you made."

"I don't even tell my agent about this," said an actress I didn't recognize. "Why bother getting him involved? It's just a way to make some money on the side. Would I tell my agent if I opened a lemonade stand at Hollywood and Vine?"

The other actors started discussing this among themselves. They found the topic much more interesting than judging my guilt or innocence in the robbery.

There was a loud bang and we all turned to the door just in time to see it come crashing into the room. With all the confusion and conversation, we had forgotten to unlock the door. Two security guards broke it down by hitting it with their shoulders at the same time. They came flying into the room and wound up splayed on the floor. Five or six other security guards followed them with their guns drawn.

"What the hell happened in here?" said the one in charge. "We've been banging on the door for ten minutes."

"We were robbed," said Karen. "And this guy did it!" She pointed at me. "Joey Volpe of *The Sopranos*."

"Who did you play on *The Sopranos*?" said the security guard.

"Well . . ."

14

You've heard of the good cop/bad cop routine?

Well, something like that happened to me at the downtown police station in Columbus, Ohio. Both cops questioning me knew me from *The Sopranos*. Or thought they did. Each of them had a different take on me. One of them thought I really was a member of the Mafia. The other thought I was just an actor and probably not smart enough to organize a circle jerk in a telephone booth, much less a grand larceny involving three robbers and more than a hundred thousand dollars in cash and jewelry. They argued their cases in front of me.

"He's a known member of an organized-crime family, Jim. According to the RICO statute, we can hold him on that basis alone."

"He's an actor, Bob. Not even an important one. I don't even remember which part he played on *The Sopranos*." He looked at me. "What part did you play again?"

"Well . . ."

"I know which part he played," said the bad cop. "He was the guy who hung himself in the basement because Tony wouldn't let him retire to Florida."

"I thought he was the guy who died on the toilet," said the good cop. He turned to me to settle the dispute.

"Well . . ."

"Oh, never mind," said the good cop. "Does it really matter? Either way his character is dead. It's a television show, Bob. Even James Gandolfini is dead now."

"Hold on a second," I said. "That's still in dispute. I mean, Gandolfini is dead, yes, but is Tony Soprano? The screen just went to black at the end. That could mean they killed Tony. Or it could mean David Chase couldn't come up with a good ending."

"I hated that ending," said the good cop. "I ran to the television set to make sure it wasn't disconnected."

"The ending was a cop-out," said the bad cop. "But that doesn't mean we should cut this guy loose."

So it went back and forth for what seemed like seventy-two hours. Five hours into it, I requested an attorney. They called the public defender's office. Seven hours after that, my attorney showed up. She was a pretty young black woman. She was wearing a visitor's badge that read *Sharon Talley, Public Defender's Office*.

Ms. Talley walked into the interrogation room and pointed at me.

"You, shut up."

Then she pointed at the two cops.

"You two, scram."

They stood up grudgingly and walked out of the room. The bad cop turned over his shoulder and said, "We're not finished with you yet, *paesano*."

"I told you to GET OUT," said the woman. She stared at them until they closed the door. Then she turned to me and held out her hand.

"I'm Sharon Talley. Nice to meet you."

"Joey Volpe. Likewise."

"What did you tell them, Joey?"

"Nothing. We talked a lot about television."

"Television?"

"I'm an actor. They recognized me from TV. They wanted to talk about that."

"Good. So tell me what happened at the hotel. Don't leave anything out."

I gave her my version of the story, the same version I gave Karen. She asked a few questions. She took notes. When I finished, she looked up at the ceiling, tapped her ballpoint pen on her pursed lips, and thought for a few moments.

"Have you ever been in trouble with the law before, Joey?"

"No, never. Not even a parking ticket."

I lived in New York City. I didn't even have a car.

"Have you ever owned a handgun?"

"No, ma'am."

"Don't lie to me. They can check nowadays, you know."

"Sharon, I live in New York City. The only legal way to own a gun in New York is to join the police force."

She laughed.

"Sit tight, Joey. I'll have you out of here in less than an hour."

In the end, the Columbus police couldn't hold me. Oh, they *wanted* to. But they didn't have enough evidence to book me. It was Karen's word against mine. She didn't have enough evidence to support her theory—even though it was perfectly accurate.

"You'll have to come back if they find any new evidence that incriminates you," my lawyer said when she returned to the interrogation room. "But they don't have enough to hold you now."

"Can I go back to New York?"

"They will tell you not to leave town, but they're bullshitting. Once they let you go, you can go anywhere you want. If you were involved, Joey—and I don't believe you were—they can always extradite you. Ohio and New York smokum peace pipe and make treaty."

I laughed. I loved this woman. I wanted to marry her.

Then I remembered I was already married. And my wife would have some questions of her own.

15

"You're almost two days late getting home," said Caitlin.

"I can explain," I said. "And it's not what you think. It's not another woman. But it's a long story. We need to sit down and talk about it. Hey, what happened to the window?"

Our living room window, the one facing the street, was broken. We lived on the second floor of a small brick apartment building on West 112th Street near Broadway. We were almost living in Harlem, but it was all we could afford. Broken windows were not unusual on our block. But this was the first time someone had broken ours. It was the second broken window I'd seen in as many days. Little did I know the same charming group of guys broke both of them.

"I should tell you my story before you tell me yours," said Caitlin.

"Go ahead."

"I was sitting here watching television late last night when I heard something come crashing through the window. It was a brick."

"A brick?"

"Yes, but wait, the story gets weirder. The brick had an envelope taped to it. The envelope was addressed to Joey Volpe. Maybe I shouldn't have opened it, but I couldn't help myself."

"That's okay. What was inside?"

"You're not going to believe this."

"Tell me."

"Five thousand dollars in cash. Fifty hundred-dollar bills. And there was a note, too."

"What did the note say?"

"It was strange. The note said, 'Joey, this is less than we talked about. But you lied to us. You promised us more. We're not amused.'"

I was silent.

"Can you explain that?" said Caitlin.

"Was the note signed?" I said.

"No."

"Where is it now?"

"I don't have it."

"You don't *have* it?"

"No."

"Why not?"

"Well, it was a threatening note. You had disappeared. I thought maybe someone had kidnapped you. So I called the police."

"You called the police?"

"Of course."

"Caitlin, when someone is kidnapped, you're supposed to give the kidnappers money. They don't give *you* money."

"What do I know about kidnapping?"

"Jesus Christ. Just give me the note and the money."

"I said I don't have it."

"What did you do with it?"

"The police took it. They said it was evidence of a crime."

"Oh my God."

"I'm sorry. Did I do the wrong thing?"

"Please tell me you at least took some of the money out of the envelope."

"No, the cops took all the money. And the note. The brick, too."

Too bad, I thought. We could've used that money. I could've hired a decent lawyer.

16

Speaking of throwing bricks, Caitlin hit me with a ton of bricks a couple of weeks later. Not literally. But when you consider the damage it did to my mental and emotional health, it was almost as bad.

The public defender assigned to my case in New York got me released on my own recognizance. I was sitting in our living room, watching television, and drinking a beer. Ever since my release, I was drinking and watching television constantly. It was a desperate attempt to deaden my senses and forget about the trial and possibly prison. I was on my fifth beer and third rerun of *Law & Order* when Caitlin walked in and nailed me.

She took one look at me sitting on the couch with a can of beer in my hands, staring at the television with bloodshot eyes, and she said: "I want a trial separation."

At first I thought she was kidding. So I answered back with some gallows humor of my own: "Well, honey, it looks like that's exactly what you're going to get. There's going to be a trial, and afterwards you and I are going to separate for seven to ten years."

"I'm not kidding." I looked up from the television to see if she was smiling. From the moment our eyes met, I could tell she was serious.

I dropped the beer on the floor. There was only a sip or two left in the can so it didn't make a mess. I tried to turn off the television set so we could talk. But the remote had vanished. Remotes have a way of doing that. I looked under the seat cushion. Under the couch. Under Gizmo, who was fast asleep next to me. I got up from the couch and turned off the television the old-fashioned way. When I turned to face her, Caitlin was still standing in the same spot with the same serious look.

"You're joking, right?"

"Do I look like I'm joking?"

"Why?"

"Why what?"

"Why do you want a separation?"

"Now *you're* the one who's got to be joking."

"No, I'm serious. Why do you want a separation? Why *now* of all times? I told you I'd stop messing around and I did. I haven't even left the apartment for weeks. Do you think I'm having an affair with Mrs. Morgenstern?"

Mrs. Morgenstern was our ninety-six-year-old neighbor. The only attractive thing about her was that she was living in one of the last fully rent-controlled apartments in New York. She was paying two hundred and fifty dollars a month for a three-bedroom apartment in Manhattan with a market value of five thousand. Which made her as rare as a bird-of-paradise with a nest in Central Park.

"It's not just the other women," she said.

"There was one other woman, Caitlin. How many times do I have to tell you that?"

"Don't play me for a fool, Joey. If there's one woman I know about, there's got to be others. Women who sleep with married men are like cockroaches. For every one you see, there must be a million hiding in the cupboard."

"There was only one, I swear."

"To tell you the truth, it doesn't even matter at this point."

"Well, if it isn't about the other women . . . I mean woman, what is it?"

"Joey, I don't even feel like I know you anymore."

"You don't know me? We've known each other since we were in college. We were Romeo and Juliet, for heaven's sake. We were twenty-one years old when we met. We've grown up together. We've had a child together." I lowered my voice. "Where is she, by the way? I don't want her to hear this conversation."

"She went to a friend's house. I didn't want her to hear it either. You were so busy with your beer and your television show, you didn't even notice her leave. So don't try to tell me what a loving father you are because I'm not in the mood to hear it."

"Caitlin, you can't leave me now. Not when I'm about to go on trial. Not when I'm at the lowest point of life. You can't leave me here alone."

"I'm not going to leave you here alone."

"Good."

"I want you to pack your things and get out."

"Where am I supposed to go?"

"I don't know and I don't care. Go live with your parents in Gladwyne."

"I'm not allowed to leave New York."

I was telling the truth. It was okay for me to leave Ohio after the robbery because the cops in Columbus never booked me. Now that I'd been arraigned in New York, staying in town was a condition of my release. If I went to Gladwyne, I'd go straight to jail. My father was so mad at me, he'd be the one to drop the dime.

Caitlin stood firm and silent. She said nothing. But the expression on her face still said, "Get out." So I came up with a strategy that had often worked in our marital arguments before: I started to cry.

Maybe it was because I was an actor and, as the saying goes, I wore my heart on my sleeve. I couldn't argue with Caitlin for five minutes before I started to cry. Not just arguments with Caitlin. I've cried in arguments with my mother, my father, my sister, even my male friends. I used to cry in school, where it was mortifying for a kid to cry—even a girl. I'm not just talking about grade school. I'm talking about grad school! I cried in an argument with the butcher at a grocery store because he overcharged me for a leg of lamb. I'm not faking it. The tears are real. I'm just lachrymose. What can I say?

Crying always made me feel like a pathetic weakling. But it usually got me what I wanted. (The butcher wound up giving me a discount on the lamb.) This ability, if you want to call it that, came in mighty handy as an actor. Even in rehearsal, I could manufacture tears at the drop of a hat. When I did it in performance, I often overheard audience members turn to each other and say, "What an actor!" One time I glanced down at the audience through my tears and saw that everyone in the front row was crying, too.

Caitlin and I had been married twenty years at this point, and it'd been a long time since my tears had moved her. "Crying isn't going to help you this time, Joey."

"I don't understand why you're doing this to me *now*," I wailed. "When I need you the most."

"I already told you. I don't even know who you are anymore. I can't go on living with a stranger in my house. I can't let Bianca live with a stranger."

"I'm not a stranger."

"Yes, you are. I'm not talking about your girlfriend now, Joey. Or your girlfriends, whatever the case may be. I've forgotten about that. Well, I haven't forgotten, but that's not what this is about. Joey, you were arrested for *armed robbery*? That's not the man I married."

I had no response for this. So I just kept sniveling and wiping my nose with the back of my hand.

"The guy I married was such a beautiful boy. With curly hair and blue eyes. You were so romantic. So funny and charming. You wouldn't hurt a flea. And you were so *sensitive*. You know, Joey, sometimes I can't even blame these women for jumping into bed with you. I've been there myself. I know what you're like."

I had to file that away as the most unusual thing a husband ever heard from his wife.

"Until I met you," she went on, "nobody had ever really *listened* to me. Even onstage, I could tell you were hearing every word I was saying. I could see it in those eyes of yours. I don't know if the audience could see it, but I sure could. We connected in a way I've never connected with another human being before. It didn't matter if we were onstage or off, I always knew you could hear me. And I could always tell what was in your heart."

In the middle of my mewling and blubbering, I smiled for a moment when Caitlin complimented my acting. Actors love compliments more than life itself. If an actor was about to be guillotined and the executioner paused for a moment to say, "By the way, I loved you in *Tartuffe*," he would die happy.

"But now look at you," she said in a different tone. "You don't listen. You don't talk. You won't tell me what happened in Columbus. My God, Joey, how could you do this? How could someone even accuse you of such a thing? How could you come up with the idea of stealing from people at gunpoint? I didn't even know you owned a gun. And stealing from other actors, no less? Stealing from our own people. How could you *do* that?"

She was starting to cry now, and this only made my own crying worse.

"It wasn't my idea," I protested.

"Then whose idea was it?"

"I can't tell you. I just can't."

I couldn't take the risk of telling anyone, not even Caitlin. If I told her about Rosetti, she'd want me to tell my lawyer. My lawyer would want me to tell the cops. And if the cops found out, Rosetti would put Caitlin, Bianca, and me in the East River.

"That's exactly what I'm talking about, Joey. Every time I try to find out what happened in Columbus, you clam up. Maybe if you'd tell me what happened, I could help with your defense. We could work on this problem together, the way a married couple is supposed to work on things together. Maybe I could help you."

My tears weren't working so I decided to change strategy and go on the offensive. Her last line gave me an opening to land a punch of my own.

"Yeah, right. You've been a big help. If it weren't for you, we wouldn't be in this mess."

"What the hell do you mean by that, Joey? How in the world is this *my* fault?"

"When a brick comes through the window with five thousand dollars taped to it, you don't call the police and let them take the money."

"What was I supposed to do?"

"Keep the money and shut up, that's what. If you'd done that, we would've had five thousand bucks, and I would've gotten away with this thing. We needed money, Caitlin. That's why I got involved in the first place."

"We needed money so you decided to become an armed robber? Is that what you're telling me? I can understand how some of our neighbors in Harlem might come up with a bright idea like that, Joey. They've never had any other options in life. But it's not a good excuse for someone with degrees from Haverford and Yale. With that kind of education, you could at least get a job at Starbucks. Hell, you could even be a taxi driver with an education like that. Did you really have to shoot a member of the cast of *Star Trek* to make a buck?"

"I didn't shoot him. Somebody else did."

"Who?"

"I can't tell you."

"Here we go again."

"I don't know, Caitlin, I don't know."

"You don't know what?"

"You've got a degree from Yale, too," I said. "Granted, it's a worthless degree in fine arts. But still. You should be smart enough to know that when someone *gives* you money, it's not a kidnapping. I don't know if you were being stupid, or—"

"Or what?"

"Or maybe you *wanted* to get me in trouble. You were mad at me for screwing around with other women, and you figured that would be a good way to get back at me. To call the cops on me and turn me in."

"I don't know how you could even think such a thing." She stormed out of the room in tears.

It was a ridiculous thing to accuse her of, I know. But I was desperate. I couldn't let her kick me out of the house. Not right then. I needed a place to stay in New York. And with seven dollars in my pocket, it wasn't going to be the Sherry Netherland. After the trial, if I was found not guilty, Caitlin and I could work something out. Until then, I'd have to stay put. I walked to the kitchen to grab another beer. Then I plopped myself back down on the couch and turned on the TV. Gizmo rolled over and snuggled up to me.

"After the trial, things will get better between me and Mommy," I said to Gizmo. "You'll see. After the trial, everything will work out fine."

That's how low I'd sunk. I was lying to my own dog.

17

A few days later, as I was heading out the door for my first strategy meeting with my public defender, I received a disturbing telephone call.

"Is that you, Joey?" said the familiar voice on the other end of the line.

"Yes, Mr. Rosetti, it's me."

"I know you're meeting with your attorney today, so I wanted to give you some legal advice. After all, I've got lots of experience with this kind of thing."

"What advice?"

"My advice is that trying to blame this on Paulie or Carlo, or even me, would be a shortsighted strategy."

"Shortsighted?"

"Yes. It might get you off the hook in the short term. But in the long term, it wouldn't be good for Gizmo."

I was silent for a while, so he went on.

"Let me make myself clear, Joey. I won't kidnap your family and bring them right back like I did before. There won't be any happy ending this time. I'll make them suffer. Maybe not your little girl. I'm not an animal, after all. I'll put a bullet through her brain to make it quick. Because I'm a nice guy. But I'll make your wife watch me do it. Then I'll have some fun with her before I kill her. And I'll take my sweet time doing it, too. *Capisci?*"

"*Si, capisco bene.*" I understand very well.

I could tell he was about to hang up, but I stopped him. "I have one question for you, Mr. Rosetti."

"Fire away."

"Why me? With all the other actors you could've forced to do this, how did I get so lucky?"

"I told you at our dinner in Atlantic City, Joey. We did some research on you. We knew you had some money problems. We knew you had some problems in your marriage. Remember *Wild Kingdom* with Marlin Perkins, Joey?"

He was talking about a television show that went off the air when I was still a kid, but I remembered it.

"Mutual of Omaha?"

"Yeah, that's the one. Well, when the lion attacks the antelope, he doesn't go after the fastest and the strongest one in the herd. He goes after the young ones. The sick ones. The old ones that are half-dead already. It's easier that way."

I was going to mention that it's the females, not the males, who do all the hunting in a lion pride. But I got his point.

"Well, that's pretty much the way we work in our business. If we need help from a civilian, we tend to look for ones who won't give us a lot of trouble."

"I see."

"Let's face it, Joey, you're weak."

"I guess I am."

"So let me give you some more advice. Don't look weak in prison. Use all your acting ability not to seem weak. Because if you look weak in prison, five years is going to seem like five hundred."

"Good advice, I guess."

"Now I gotta go, Joey. Good luck with your trial. Don't forget what we talked about, okay?"

"Okay."

He hung up.

And I clicked off my tape recorder.

I rewound the tape a bit to make sure it had recorded. I heard Rosetti's voice say, *"Let's face it, Joey, you're weak."*

"Maybe I'm not so weak after all, asshole," I said to the tape recorder.

I knew this call was coming eventually, so I was ready for it. I already had the tape recorder hooked up to the phone. All I had to do was press the button marked "Record" as soon as the call came in.

But let's get real, okay? I wasn't going to use this tape recording in court. Heck, I wasn't even going to let my lawyer listen to it. The thing about fighting the Mafia is that it's like fighting a zombie. When you think you've killed it, it springs back to life and keeps coming after you. Suppose I did succeed in getting off the hook by ratting out Rosetti, Paulie, or Carlo. What good would it do me? Some other Mafia boss would come and kill me. They'd kill my family, too. No, I had to take my chances in court and hope to get off on a technicality. Ratting out Rosetti would be trading a prison cell for a gravestone.

I made this tape for one reason and one reason only. And there was only one person in the world I wanted to hear it. So I popped the cassette out of the tape recorder and put it into an envelope. I grabbed a Sharpie from the kitchen counter and wrote on the outside of the envelope:

FOR CAITLIN'S EYES ONLY
Do not open until one week before I get out of prison.

There was a notepad nearby that we kept in the kitchen for writing grocery lists. It wasn't big, so I had to keep it short. I wrote the first words that came to my mind:

Dear Juliet. I love you. I've loved you from the first moment I heard you speak. And I love our daughter. You know I would do anything for both of you. Even go to prison.

I know I fucked up. I'm so sorry. I don't have any excuses for my behavior over the last few years. But if you listen to this tape, you'll understand what happened in Columbus and why. And why I couldn't confide in you.

Caitlin, listen to me. PLEASE, PLEASE, PLEASE don't give this tape to the police or let anyone listen to it. Not even my lawyer. I'll be out of prison soon. And if you still want me in your life, we can play it by ear from there.

I'll love you forever and a day,

Romeo

I put the note in with the cassette, licked the envelope flap, and sealed it. If things started to look like they were going badly in the trial, my plan was to give it to my lawyer and tell him to hold it until I was almost out of prison.

Little did I know that things would start to go badly from the moment I met him.

18

I knew I was in trouble the moment I showed up in my public defender's office to discuss our legal strategy. My previous experience with a public defender, Sharon Talley, had been pretty good so I was optimistic. But the lawyer assigned to my case made Sharon Talley look like Clarence Darrow.

It turned out they didn't have to extradite me to Ohio, after all. The prosecution charged me under the RICO Act, which stands for Racketeering-Influenced and Corrupt Organizations. They created the criminal statute to put Mafia bosses in jail. RICO is a federal law, so I got to be tried in my hometown of New York City. Lucky me!

Unlike Sharon Talley, my new attorney didn't work for the Public Defender's Office itself. Instead, he was one of the hundreds of young, inexperienced attorneys in New York hired by the courts to defend poor clients like me. This kind of freelance work didn't attract the city's best attorneys. But he had done a decent job of getting me out on bail and released on my own recognizance. So I had no reason to believe Michael Willis would turn out to be the worst lawyer in the history of jurisprudence.

Do you know how you sit in a doctor's office and try to figure out what disease the other people in the waiting room have? Well, I realized the same thing is true in a lawyer's office.

There was one teenage black kid with dreadlocks, a dirty T-shirt, holes in his jeans, and a pair of four-hundred-dollar sneakers. I had him pegged for someone who grabbed iPhones from people on the subway. In fact, he was texting on an iPhone at that moment. I assumed he had stolen it because of the feminine-looking pink-and-gold-glitter case.

A middle-aged working class guy sat across from me. He had rheumy eyes and a bulbous nose laced with broken capillaries. I had him figured for a DWI, maybe his third. One more and he might lose his driver's license for good, which would cost him his job. He looked as depressed as I felt.

A Latino couple sat together on the couch next to me arguing in Spanish. I guessed that one was an American citizen and the other wasn't. It looked like they were here for some help with immigration. My Italian could help me understand the gist of what was being said in Spanish. But these two were talking fast and with some kind of South American accent that made it hard for me to follow. I heard the words for *green card*, *marriage*, and *daughter* several times.

I realized Michael Willis's office was the legal equivalent of what my mother scornfully referred to as a Doc-in-the-Box. In the New York City judicial system, freelance public defenders like these were called 18B Lawyers. Eighteen, I presume, because that was their average age. And the B, of course, stood for bad.

Speaking of my mother, I wondered if I should break down and ask my parents to lend me some money for a real attorney. But I was already hundreds of thousands of dollars in debt to them. Starting with graduate school, which wasn't so bad. After all, it was Dad's idea for me to go to grad school in the first place. Then there were thousands of dollars that Caitlin and I borrowed from them when I was out of work. My parents helped pay for the rent. They helped pay for the baby. They helped pay for everything. Two years ago, my father said, *"Basta!"* Enough! He cut me off. No more money for any reason. Now I was afraid to ask. And too proud. I'd have to take my chances with this Shyster-in-a-Box. I glanced at the wall where Michael Willis, Esq., displayed his college diplomas. One was from the University of Kalispell, the other was from the Lake Tahoe Law School.

The University of Kalispell?

I confess to being something of an academic snob. I went to one of the top liberal arts colleges in the country for my BA and followed that up with an MFA from Yale. My father was a full professor at another Ivy League university. My mom did her undergraduate work at Carleton College in Minnesota and got her MD at Johns Hopkins.

The University of Kalispell, as I understood it, was an online correspondence school. They passed out bachelor's degrees like jellybeans. And the Lake Tahoe Law School? Well, I decided to walk over and take a closer look at that diploma. There was a little gold seal on the diploma saying *The Remote Electronic Education Association* had granted the school's accreditation. *Remote electronic education?* I assumed that meant the Lake Tahoe Law School was online, too. Could you practice law in the City of New York with that kind of academic pedigree?

I guess you could if you passed the bar exam. Someone once told me you could practice law with a kindergarten diploma in some states as long as you passed the bar exam. I'm not sure whether that was true of New York or not. Let's just say these two diplomas did not fill me with confidence.

"You're next, Mr. Volpe," said the Lake Tahoe Law School's answer to F. Lee Bailey, beckoning me into his tiny office.

"I have some news for you," he said, as he took his seat behind a large desk and indicated that I should sit in the small folding chair opposite him.

"Good news or bad?"

"Well, that depends on your point of view. The assistant US attorney has offered us a plea bargain."

"Take it."

"Wait until you hear it first. It's five years. But you'll only serve one. They'll make sure you go to the cushiest prison in the system, or the one nearest your family, whichever you prefer. Then maybe you'll do another year or two of probation and community service."

"Take it."

"There's a catch."

"What?"

"You have to allocute."

My perfect score of 800 on the verbal part of the SATs suddenly failed me.

"I'm sorry. I forget what that means."

"Don't worry, I had to look it up myself."

This *did* make me worry. He had to look up a legal term?

"It means you have to stand up in court and admit you did it," he said. "You'll have to explain exactly how you planned the crime and how it took place. You'll also have to reveal the names of your two accomplices."

"I can't do that. We discussed this before. They'll kill me."

"Are you sure about that, Joey? I mean, we're talking about two small-time crooks here. All three of you will spend some time in prison to cool off. They can't hurt you if you go to different prisons, and the judge will make sure you do. It's not like you're dealing with the Gambino crime family where they could kill you anywhere. You're not really in the Mafia, are you?"

"Of course not."

"So why not give them up and save your own skin?"

"I can't do it. That's all I can say about it."

"Okay. If that's the way you want it, fine. It's my duty to present you with all plea bargains and let you make the decision for yourself. But you know what?"

"What?"

"I'm glad you turned it down."

"You are? Why?"

"Because I've been thinking a lot about your case, Joey, and I've come up with an idea. I have a little trick up my sleeve. It's something that can win us an acquittal and let you walk out of that courtroom a free man."

"What is it?"

"I'm not going to tell you. I want it to be a surprise. To the jury. To the judge. Even to you. The element of surprise is critical. But it might work. You're going to have to trust me."

"Are you sure?" I said.

"It's a bit of a long shot, I admit. But if you're not going to take the plea bargain, it may be our *best* shot."

"Well, I've been thinking a lot about the case, too," I said. "And I've come up with an idea of my own."

"Yes?" he said with an indulgent smile.

"I think they've charged me with the wrong crime. I looked up the RICO Act on the internet and I don't think it applies to me."

"Joey . . ."

"Hear me out for a second. It turns out that there are about twenty-five different crimes that are RICO predicates."

"Like the predicate of a sentence?"

That made two legal terms that our Lake Tahoe Law School graduate failed to recognize. It made me wonder if I'd be better off defending myself. They say the man who acts as his own lawyer has a fool for a client. It was hard to imagine any bigger fool than the one representing me.

"No, not like the predicate of a sentence. These are more like conditions that must be met for the statute to take effect. These crimes include bribery, kidnapping, extortion, gambling, murder . . . here, I wrote down the whole list for you."

I pulled a sheet of paper from my men's carryall bag and put it on his desk. He ignored it, so I continued.

"Of all the crimes on that list, I only committed *one* of them—robbery."

"So?"

"Here's the thing. To convict someone under RICO, you've got to prove he committed at least *two* of those crimes. Or he ordered someone else to commit at least two of those crimes."

"Are you sure about that?"

"I found it on Wikipedia. They gave the history of RICO. You see, they designed the whole thing to catch Mafia bosses, not two-bit thieves. They wrote the law to prevent bosses from getting off the hook just because they didn't commit any crimes themselves. RICO says that if you run an organization where you tell people to rob, steal, kidnap, kill, and so on, you're as guilty as the guy who actually does it. That's how they finally put John Gotti in jail. Plus all the other heads of the five families in New York. But it has nothing to do with someone like me."

"I have a cousin who lived near John Gotti in Queens."

Was this guy even listening to me?

"Look, Michael, they charged me with the wrong crime. They should've charged me with plain old armed robbery and let the City of Columbus, Ohio, take the case. They made a stupid mistake by charging me with RICO."

"It's a technicality, Joey."

"Technicalities are what let guys like me go free, Michael!"

"No, no, no, I don't like it. Trust me. I've got a little trick up my sleeve that's going to work like a charm. You're going to walk out of there a free man."

Over the course of the next three months, he must've said, "I've got a trick up my sleeve," more often than I said, "I'm just an actor." We would've made a nice pair of parrots in a cage.

"Well, I'm just an actor," I said. "I guess you know best. I suppose I shouldn't try to defend myself with legal precedents from Wikipedia."

"Now you're talking sense, Joey. Trust me. Everything's going to be fine. I've got a little trick up my sleeve."

19

"If the defendant's face looks familiar to you," said the assistant US attorney, Richard Fineman, "there's a simple reason for it: he's a known member of an organized-crime family."

I grabbed my attorney by the arm, pulled him over to me, and whispered into his ear. "Object to that, for Christ's sake. I'm not a member of any organized crime family. I'm just an actor."

"I can't object during an opening statement," said my attorney.

"Who made up that rule? He's telling a flat-out lie."

"That's what they told us in law school. You shouldn't object during the opponent's opening or closing statement. It's a matter of professional courtesy."

"I'm sure you can object. I've seen it on TV a hundred times. And I don't even watch that much television."

"You can't get your law degree from watching TV, Joey."

"But I suppose you can get it from surfing the internet," I said.

I sat back and listened to the prosecutor tell lie after lie for the next half hour. My dumbass defense attorney, Michael Willis, did nothing but sit there and make stick-figure doodles on his yellow pad.

"We will show you in painstaking detail how the defendant, Joey Volpe—which means The Fox in Italian—conspired with two other Mafia members to steal more than one hundred thousand dollars in cash and jewelry from celebrities who attended the fan convention in Columbus, Ohio.

"We will show how the defendant smuggled two semi-automatic pistols past security by using the entrance reserved for special guests of the convention. In a classic diversionary tactic, his two accomplices brought toy machine guns in through the main entrance. While the firearms experts posted at the main entrance were going over those plastic machine guns to verify that they were toys, Mr. Volpe, aka The Fox, was sneaking two deadly handguns into the side door.

"We will present an eyewitness who was sitting less than two feet away from The Fox when she saw him pass two handguns to his fellow Mafia soldiers. We have pictures taken on the cell phones of convention attendees showing The Fox and his accomplices discussing their strategy for the robbery and deciding when to make their move. When a horn blew to indicate the lunch break was at hand, The Fox's two accomplices dropped their toy machine guns and began threatening the crowd with genuine handguns loaded with deadly thirty-eight caliber bullets.

"The robbery itself took place in an area called the greenroom. It involved many actors and actresses whose faces you will recognize from stage and screen. We will put several of these celebrities on the witness stand so they can tell you what they saw with their own eyes. They will describe their humiliation when The Fox and his henchmen forced them to strip naked. You will hear one celebrity in particular, Mr. Steven Dubois of *Star Trek*, recall how he was shot in the foot by one of The Fox's henchmen as he tried to stop the thugs from getting away. Ladies and gentlemen, you can trust the testimony of these actors and actresses. They have been guests in your homes on television."

I turned to my attorney. "Object to that! They're all professional liars, for heaven's sake."

"I told you I can't object to an opening statement."

"Can't you at least get him to stop calling me The Fox? It's prejudicial."

"I've met Mr. Fineman before. I don't think he's prejudiced at all."

The prosecutor continued. "If the defendant has the guts to take the stand in his own defense—and I'm not sure he does—you're going to hear him say the words 'I'm just an actor' often. Let me remind you, ladies and gentlemen, you can be an actor and a member of the Mafia at the same time. David Chase, the producer of *The Sopranos*, was famous for casting ex-Mafia members. There were rumors that Tony Sirico, the actor who played Paulie Walnuts, was an ex-mobster. One of the other stars of the show, the so-called Bevilaqua Kid, was convicted of burglary. Being an actor and a criminal are not mutually exclusive."

The Bevilaqua Kid was in prison? That was news to me. But I wasn't surprised. I heard that kid was a bad seed. When he was seventeen years old, he was in *A Bronx Tale* with Robert DeNiro. He'd been playing mobsters for so long he was having trouble telling fantasy from reality.

"Finally, ladies and gentlemen," said Fineman, "you have to ask yourself why The Fox's two accomplices are not in the courtroom sitting at the defendant's table today. The answer to that question is simple. It is the Mafia's code of silence, or *omertà* in Italian, that prevents The Fox from identifying his accomplices. If he snitched on them, they would kill him. That's why he refused several plea bargains . . ."

"Is he allowed to mention plea bargains?" I said to Michael. "I thought those negotiations were confidential."

"I can't remember if that's allowed or not," said my brilliant attorney.

The prosecutor concluded. "So instead of serving just one or two years in jail, he decided to keep his mouth shut and serve ten years in federal prison. Ladies and gentleman, I would submit to you that if ten years in federal prison is what The Fox wants, then ten years in federal prison is what The Fox should get. Thank you very much."

"Mr. Willis," said the judge. "Your opening statement?"

"Yes, Your Honor. The defense is ready to proceed with our opening statement."

"Well, all righty then. Please proceed."

"Oh, okay, yes, of course."

Michael charged up to the jury box, leaving his yellow pad filled with notes behind on the defendant's table. He got five words into his delivery—"Good morning, ladies and gentlemen"—when he forgot his lines.

Michael stared at the jury for a few moments, and they stared back at him. He decided to repeat his greeting in the hope it would jump-start the opening statement. "Good morning, ladies and gentlemen."

Again he forgot his lines. The jury took Michael's repetition to mean he was expecting a response, so they said "Good morning" in ragged unison.

To which Michael replied, "Good morning," yet again.

"Now that the salutations are out of the way, Mr. Willis," said the judge, "I suggest you go ahead with the substance of your case."

At this point Michael realized he was not going to be able to remember his lines, so he scurried back to the defendant's table to pick his yellow pad. Unfortunately, the yellow pad did not contain a written script for the opening statement. It was several pages of handwritten notes and sentence fragments to jog his memory if he got stuck. By now, Michael's memory was un-joggable. So he read his notes word for word:

"Good morning . . . er, good morning *again* . . . defendant . . . Joseph Volpe . . . innocent . . . not Mafia . . . Yale graduate . . . father professor . . . mother doctor . . . good education . . . happily married fifteen years . . . five-year-old child . . . no criminal record . . . no Mafia involvement . . . played mobster on TV . . . not real life . . . Italian heritage . . . victim of racial stereotyping . . . not involved in robbery . . . never saw robbers before in his life . . . robbers planted handguns in Joey's purse . . ."

"It's a men's carryall bag, goddammit," I muttered to myself. "Is that so hard to say?"

"Robbers stole Joey's purse . . . put guns inside . . . followed Joey into greenroom . . . slipped past security guard . . . robbed celebrities . . . shot Dubois . . . Joey forced to strip naked . . . like the other actors . . . Joey's money stolen, too . . . robbers left scene of crime . . . Joey left behind naked with other actors . . . Joey innocent . . . thank you."

Michael returned to the defendant's table and plopped down next to me drenched in flop sweat.

"Please don't tell me this is your first time in a courtroom, Michael."

By choosing not to reply, he gave me the answer loud and clear.

"The government calls its first witness, Your Honor," said Mr. Fineman. "We call Ms. Karen Murray to the stand."

In walked my loyal assistant Karen dressed in her full Columbus Fan-Con official volunteer regalia, with hat, scarf, epaulets, lanyards, badges, the works.

"Object to the way she's dressed," I said to Michael. "That's outrageous. And it's prejudicial. I'm surprised the judge would even allow it."

"No, no, no," said Michael with a smile. "That's perfect. It fits with what I have planned later."

"Your up-the-sleeve trick?"

"Yes. Wait and see. This is perfect."

"Ms. Murray, could you tell the jury why you're dressed in this unusual way," said Fineman.

"Because you told me to."

"No, I mean, well, let me rephrase the question. Is the manner in which you are dressed today similar to how you were dressed on October 13, 2014?"

"Yes, exactly."

"And what were you doing on that day?"

"I was serving as an official volunteer at the Columbus Fan-Con."

"What are the duties of an official volunteer?"

"They vary. But on that day, I served as the assistant to Mr. Joey Volpe, who was a special guest at the convention."

"A special guest is usually a movie or television star, am I correct?"

"Well, you could say they're stars."

The jury giggled a bit. I grimaced.

"But they're not always actors, are they? Sometimes they can be real people, right?"

"Right. Sometimes they're comic book artists. Or writers. Or people who are famous for one reason or another. I went to a Fan-Con once where Joe the Plumber was signing autographs."

"So it wouldn't be unusual for, let's say, a famous Mafia boss or hit man to be at one of these conventions."

"Not unusual at all."

"What are the duties of a special guest's assistant?"

"I was helping him manage his autograph line. Selling eight-by-ten photos, handling the cash, taking pictures of Mr. Volpe with his fans, and so on."

"Your Honor, I have in my hand People's Exhibit A. May I approach the witness and show it to her."

"You may."

"Ms. Murray, can you identify this photograph?"

"Yes, that's a photograph of Mr. Volpe with one of his fans that I took using the fan's smartphone. I remember that guy because he was dressed as one of the characters in the *The Hunger Games*. I'm a big fan of *The Hunger Games*."

"Ms. Murray, let me direct your attention to the two men standing behind Mr. Volpe. Do you recognize those two men?"

"I do. Those were Joey's personal friends and bodyguards."

"Object, for chrissakes!" I said to Michael, loud enough for everyone in the courtroom to hear.

"Objection, your honor!" said Michael, rising to his feet.

"On what grounds, Mr. Willis?"

Michael turned to me and whispered, "On what grounds exactly?"

"On the grounds that they were not my friends or my bodyguards."

I could see the gears in Michael's brain grinding. He reviewed his entire Lake Tahoe Law School curriculum in search of the right way to translate this into acceptable legal verbiage.

"Relevance?"

"Overruled."

"Wait, no. Not relevance. Scratch that. My mistake. I'm objecting because it assumes facts not in evidence."

The judge pondered this a moment. "You've got a point, Mr. Willis. Sustained."

Michael sat down and slapped my thigh under the table like he'd just caught a game-winning pass in the Super Bowl.

"I'll rephrase my question," said Fineman. "Ms. Murray, with regard to these two men standing behind Mr. Volpe, when did you first meet them?"

"Objection!" said Michael. "Assumes facts not in evidence. Who said she ever met them?"

"Overruled. Don't press your luck, Mr. Willis. Proceed, Mr. Fineman."

"When did you first *notice* these two men, Ms. Murray?"

"When they walked into the convention hall carrying two gigantic machine guns. They said hello to Mr. Volpe, and he introduced them to me."

"Were you under the impression he was acquainted with these men prior to that morning?"

"I got the impression they knew each other, yes."

"What did The Fox . . . er, what did Mr. Volpe say to you about the role of these two men at the convention?"

"He said they were there to act as his bodyguards. He said their presence would enable him to make more money at the convention. He told them to stand behind him, hold their machine guns, and look tough. I got the impression that Mr. Volpe was in charge. He was the ringleader."

"At any point, did you notice Mr. Volpe giving anything to his bodyguards?"

"Yes, I did."

"Could you elaborate?"

"About half an hour after they showed up, I could hear them whispering to each other. I couldn't tell what they were saying because I was dealing with the fans in line. When I turned to look at Mr. Volpe, one of his bodyguards had his hand in Mr. Volpe's right pocket. He was pulling a pistol out of it."

"Anything else?"

"Yes, he pulled another pistol out of Mr. Volpe's left pocket."

"What did you think about that?"

"I thought it was strange. I asked him what the pistols were for."

"What did he say?"

"He said they were toys like the machine guns. He said they were part of his 'act.'" She made air quotes around the word *act* with her fingers.

"And you believed him?"

"Why wouldn't I? I've volunteered at dozens of these Fan-Cons over the years. Everybody is carrying weapons of one kind or another. Light sabers. Samurai swords. *Star Trek* phasers. They're all made of plastic. They're all toys."

"But you were about to find out that those pistols were not plastic toys at all, weren't you?"

"Yes, sir," said Karen. She dabbed at the tears in the corner of her eyes with the official volunteer kerchief.

Oh, *puh-leeze*, I thought. I also thought I was 99 percent convicted at this point. Mr. Fineman had made his ice-cream sundae. It would just be a matter of putting nuts, sprinkles, marshmallows, chocolate chips, whipped cream, and a cherry on top. I glanced at Michael. He was doodling on his yellow pad again. I think he was playing a solitaire version of Hangman. How appropriate.

"At a certain point, you broke for lunch. Is that correct?"

"Yes."

"Tell the jury in your own words what happened next."

Karen turned to the jury and directed her well-rehearsed speech to them.

"Mr. Volpe asked me if his two bodyguards could come with us into the greenroom for lunch. I said it was okay with me, but the security guard might stop them because they didn't have the right credentials. I was right. The security guard tried to keep them from going into the greenroom. But Mr. Volpe made a big fuss. He threw a temper tantrum. He threatened to call the guard's supervisor. He threw his weight around like a big Hollywood star. Finally, the guard gave up and let them all in. Once they got inside, all three of them headed for the buffet line. I sat at their table for a while. But they were whispering to each other and not including me in the conversation. So at a certain point I decided to get up and sit at a different table."

What a pack of lies, I thought. I glanced at the jury and I could tell they were eating it up with a spoon. Their attention got more rapt as Fineman walked Karen through the robbery and its aftermath. The warning shots fired into the ceiling. The single shot that shattered the window. How the robbers lined everyone up against the wall and forced us to strip naked. How they put all the loot into plastic trash bags and tossed our clothing out the window. Steven Dubois's ill-fated attempt to stop the robbery. The moment Paulie slipped and almost castrated himself on the shard of glass. Putting our clothing back on. Trying to stop Steven Dubois from bleeding to death. How we all stood talking about what just happened.

"You confronted Mr. Volpe at that point, did you not?"

"Yes, I did."

"What did you say?"

"I said he was responsible for the whole thing. I said he planned it. He was the inside guy. He was the ringleader. He smuggled the handguns into the exhibit hall. He was going to meet up with his bodyguards later and split the money. He was the mastermind. And everybody around me said they agreed with me a hundred percent."

"For God's sake, Michael, make an objection," I said.

"Object to what, exactly?"

"She's acting as judge and jury. She's assuming facts not in evidence. She's speculating. She's quoting hearsay. She's . . ."

"Naaah, that'll never work," said Michael, and he turned back to his yellow pad.

It was at that moment I realized you can get a *better* legal education from watching television than you can from attending an online law school.

"No further questions for this witness, Your Honor," said Fineman. He returned to his seat with a smug look on his face.

"Your cross-examination, Mr. Willis?"

"I have one question, Ms. Murray. Did you see someone dressed as Darth Vader waiting in the autograph line?"

"Yes, I did. He bought Mr. Volpe's photograph, asked Mr. Volpe to sign it, and left without saying anything."

"I have no further questions for this witness," said Michael and sat down.

"You don't have any more questions for her?" I said.

"Nope."

"You could make mincemeat out of her."

"Don't worry, Joey, I have— "

"I know. You have a goddamn trick up your sleeve. Well, your trick better make Harry Houdini's heart skip a beat, Michael, because we're in serious trouble here."

Over the next few days, Fineman called a series of witnesses to the stand who linked me to Paulie and Carlo. Many of them had taken photographs of all three of us on their smartphones. In some of those pictures, Carlo and Paulie were whispering into my ear. Someone snapped a photo at the critical moment when the lunch horn went off and the two gangsters dropped their toy machine guns and drew real handguns.

I had to give Fineman his due. He was damn good at his job. He had charts, diagrams, and hotel surveillance photos that showed exactly where we were standing in the exhibit hall. He used a map of the hotel meeting rooms to show how we ducked behind the flats and walked to the greenroom in the back. Fineman questioned the security guard who stopped us at the door to the greenroom. His testimony was damaging. He made it sound like the three of us were in cahoots and that I'd used my influence as a celebrity to wheedle our way past him. He overstated his testimony almost to the point of perjury, but I couldn't blame him. Other than Steven Dubois, the guard was the only one to get hurt in the heist. In fact, he was hurt *worse* than Dubois. He was still suffering headaches and double vision as a result of the blow to the head from the butt of Carlo's gun.

As witness after witness took the stand, Fineman built his case, and the honorable Michael Willis, Esquire said next to nothing. "I have no questions for this witness, Your Honor," was his mantra. Fineman dug my grave one shovelful after another, and Michael didn't even bother to kick a few clods of dirt back into the hole. I sat there helpless and depressed.

Finally, Fineman called his star witness. Literally.

20

"The people call Mr. Steven Dubois to the witness stand," said Fineman.

Steven Dubois limped down the aisle on two crutches, with his left foot wrapped in white bandages. I knew he was overplaying it. The TV doctor had stopped the bleeding with a couple of napkins, for heaven's sake. But it worked. The jury stood up and applauded.

"I've never seen that before," said Michael.

"This is your first time in a courtroom," I reminded him.

"I haven't even seen it on television, though."

"Ladies and gentlemen of the jury, please!" said the judge. "This is highly irregular. Take your seats. You don't applaud a witness as he takes the stand. This is a trial, not a stage show. In thirty years on the bench, I've never seen that before."

Michael gave me a told-you-so look.

"I'm sorry, Your Honor," said Dubois. "Because of my foot, I'm still walking slowly. The jury was just trying to give me some encouragement. They were sharing the love. Bless your hearts, jury people."

"Very well, Mr. Dubois. Mr. Fineman, please proceed. Let's keep the histrionics to a minimum."

"Mr. Dubois, you are an actor, correct?" said Fineman.

"I plead guilty to that charge."

The jury laughed like it was the opening gag in a stand-up comedy routine. The judge put the kibosh on that right away.

"Mr. Dubois, try to make your answers as brief and to the point as possible. Our goal here is to find the truth, not to make the jury laugh."

"Aye-aye, sir."

Another laugh from the jury.

"I mean, yes, Your Honor."

"Mr. Dubois," said Fineman, "can you identify the defendant in the courtroom?"

"He's that handsome young man with the curly black hair and pale blue eyes seated at the table over there."

Dubois pointed at me and smiled. I smiled back. Weird moment.

"Where have you seen the defendant before?"

"He was in the greenroom at the Columbus Fan-Con where the robbery took place."

"Had you ever seen the defendant before that day? Other than on television, of course."

"Yes, Jeremiah Pennington introduced him to me at another Fan-Con in Atlantic City."

"Jeremiah Pennington is also an actor, isn't that true?"

"You could say so."

A big laugh from the jury.

"I'm sorry. Yes, Jerry is an actor and a friend of mine."

"In fact, like you, he was an actor on the *Star Trek* television show, was he not?"

We were on different versions of *Star Trek*. But we did a few episodes and two feature films together."

"So when you walked into the greenroom for lunch, did you recognize Mr. Volpe?"

"I did. I said hello to him. And I told him to give my regards to Jerry."

"Tell us in your own words what happened after you entered the greenroom that day."

Dubois told his version of events in great detail, and his story matched Karen's exactly. There were no gaps or discrepancies for my attorney to exploit—even if he was the type of attorney who asked questions.

When Dubois finished telling his story, Fineman rewound his testimony to take a closer look at one critical moment. "Let me take you back to the time when the two men with guns were forcing everyone up against the wall. What was The Fox . . . er, Mr. Volpe doing at that time?"

"Well, it was strange. Joey sat in his chair while everyone else lined up against the wall. Finally, one of the gunmen noticed him sitting there. He said something like, 'You, too, ass—' Your Honor, can I say asshole in court?"

"You just did."

Laughter.

"Ooops, I guess you're right. He said something like, 'You, too, asshole. Don't think you can get out of this just because you played a mobster on TV.'"

"What did Mr. Volpe do then?"

"He smiled."

"He smiled like a fox?"

"Yes."

I glanced at Michael in the desperate hope he might object. But he hadn't made an objection since the judge overruled his last one. He had a .500 batting average when it came to objections, and he was willing to rest on that record.

"What did he do then?"

"Well, his smile turned into a frown. It looked like he was acting."

"And you're an expert on acting, correct?"

"I guess I am. Then Joey walked over to the wall with the rest of us. From that point forward, he acted like he was being robbed like everybody else."

"He *acted* like he was being robbed?"

"Yes."

"He took his clothes off and everything?"

"Yes. He's in good shape for a man his age."

"He put his money down on the floor and let the gunmen take it?"

"He did. But he seemed less angry about it than the rest of us."

"One last question. What made you, armed with a butter knife, think you could overcome two robbers with guns?"

"Well, I've studied stage fighting since I was a child actor. I've taken many martial arts classes. I'm in pretty good shape for a man my age, too, if I do say so myself. Plus, I had the advantage of surprise on my side. I could tell the problem of climbing through a broken window occupied the robbers. I just thought I'd take a shot. Come to think of it, that's what I did. I took a shot in the foot!"

The jury laughed. Even the judge cracked a smile at that one.

"Well, it was very brave of you," said Fineman. "There's a lesson in there for all of us. Your behavior shows that actors on television often play a version of themselves in real life. If they play a hero on TV, they are brave in real life. And if they play a lowlife criminal on television, they're often a crook in real life, too."

I almost stood up and objected to that myself. It wasn't even a question, it was a closing argument. I looked at Michael, but he wasn't listening. The judge himself must've been asleep to let that one go by, I thought.

"That's all I have for you, Mr. Dubois," said Fineman. "On behalf of the jury and the court, thank you for taking the time out of your busy schedule to talk to us—especially given your grievous gunshot wound. Now, if you can spare us a few more minutes, I'm sure Mr. Willis will have some questions for you."

No reaction from Michael. I jabbed him with my elbow and he stood up.

"I have no questions for this witness, Your Honor."

He sat down and I pulled him over to me by the collar of his shirt. That didn't look good to the jury, but I was past the point of caring how it looked.

"Ask a goddamn question, Michael. I don't care what it us. You can't keep saying, 'I have no questions.' You'll make the jury think you've given up. They'll think you know I'm guilty and you're just going through the motions. So ask one damn question."

"What do I ask?"

"Any goddamn thing at all. Just let them know you're not a potted plant."

Michael stood up.

"Your Honor, on second thought, I do have a question for this witness. Two questions, actually."

"It's nice to see you've rejoined the land of the living, Mr. Willis," said the judge. "Fire away."

"Mr. Dubois, there's something I've always wondered about . . ."

"Yes?"

"When you're beamed up to the transporter room, does it tingle or tickle or what?"

The jury laughed. The judge was too dumbfounded to say a word.

"I get asked this a lot. To tell you the truth, you just stand there. They add the sound and the visual effects in post."

"In post?"

"In post-production."

"And one last question, if I may?"

"Yes?"

"When the *Enterprise* is flying at warp speed, how do you communicate with Starfleet Command if the ship is traveling faster than radio waves?"

"I find that question offensive."

Michael looked shocked. "Offensive? Why?"

"My series took place on a space station, not a starship. When you ask a question like that, it tells me you never even saw the show."

That was my lawyer for you. He couldn't even ask a question about *Star Trek* without screwing it up.

Michael stood still for a few moments until the judge snapped him out of it.

"Any more questions for this witness, Mr. Willis?"

"I have no more questions, Your Honor."

"Thank God," said the judge. "Mr. Dubois, you may step down. The court thanks you for your testimony. Call your next witness, Mr. Fineman."

"Your Honor, the government rests," said Fineman.

"Very well," said the judge. He glanced at the clock on the back wall of the courtroom. "We still have an hour before lunch. Is the defense prepared to call its first witness, Mr. Willis?"

"We are indeed, Your Honor."

"Please proceed."

"Here goes nothing," Michael whispered to me.

Here goes ten years of my life, I thought.

"The defense calls Mr. David Kandinsky."

And in walked Darth Vader.

21

Of course, it wasn't really Darth Vader. It was some nerd named David Kandinsky dressed up as Darth Vader. But it was a convincing costume.

As he walked down the center aisle of the courtroom, he made that distinctive iron-lung sound Darth Vader made in *Star Wars*. When he sat down in the jury box and said good morning to the judge and jury—as witnesses are advised to do—he sounded like James Earl Jones. He must've been speaking through a voice modification system built into his helmet.

To say that the unflappable Richard Fineman went ballistic would be putting it mildly.

"Sidebar, Your Honor!" he said.

"Approach!" said the judge who was just as upset.

It was indicative of the laziness and stupidity of Michael Willis, Esquire, that this was the first judicial sidebar conference of the entire trial. I had a pair of headphones on the defendant's table I could use to listen in to the discussion while the jury heard nothing but white noise. I donned the headsets and got ready for the fireworks. What I heard would've been hilarious, had it not been that a decade of my life was at stake.

"Your Honor, this is beyond outrageous. Counsel is turning this trial into a three-ring circus. I object in the strongest possible terms."

"What in the name of God do you think you're doing, Mr. Willis?"

"Your Honor, this witness is critical to my case."

"Then why didn't you tell him to show up in street clothes?" asked the judge. "What could you hope to gain by letting him take the stand in a *Star Wars* costume?"

"That will become clear during my questioning, Your Honor."

"Your Honor," said Fineman, "it's inflammatory. It's not in the least bit probative. It makes a mockery of the judicial system to the point where it should be considered contempt of court."

Fineman shouldn't have said the words contempt of court. That decision was solely under the discretion of the judge and he seemed protective of it.

"I'll decide what's contempt of court and what isn't, Mr. Fineman."

I could see Fineman bow his head and step back like the Queen of England herself had rebuked him. The judge turned back to Michael in a conciliatory, almost fatherly tone. "Mr. Willis, you've been quiet during this whole trial. There have been times when I was afraid you were asleep. And you seem to be working on some kind of elaborate drawing on your yellow pad. I'd love to take a look at that, by the way, after the trial is over. But now, out of the blue, you come up with this bizarre display of showmanship and histrionics. What possible reason could you have for asking your witness to testify in costume?"

"Your Honor, as I said, if you'll give me just a few questions my reasoning will become clear."

"Your Honor, I cannot allow—" said Fineman.

A petulant Michael Willis suddenly cut him off. "Your Honor, it's only fair! Mr. Fineman brought that volunteer girl in here dressed in her convention get-up. She had that kerchief around her neck and all those badges, medals, and buttons on her chest. *What was the reason for that?* I listened to her entire testimony. Well, most of it. And I still don't know why she was all dressed up like that."

"He has a point, Mr. Fineman. I wondered about that myself at the time. I kept waiting for Mr. Willis to object, but he was busy with his artwork."

"Your Honor," said Fineman, "I simply thought her attire would lend some credibility to her testimony and help the jury understand she was in a position of authority at the convention."

"I rest my case, Your Honor," said Michael.

"You rest your case? *Now?*"

"I mean Mr. Fineman made my point for me."

"Mr. Willis, when you say 'I rest my case,' it has a specific meaning in the courtroom. You don't say those words colloquially. You say them when you're really ready to rest your case."

"I'm sorry. But you know what I mean."

All three of them were silent for a minute while the judge stared at the ceiling and pondered his decision.

"Okay, look, here's the deal," he said. "I'm going to allow it—"

"Your Honor—"

"Shut up, Mr. Fineman. Consider yourself lucky this trial has gone like a wet dream for you so far. You've been taking batting practice against a pitching machine set on 'slow.' For whatever reason, Mr. Willis has chosen to let you get away with murder. He says this witness is critical to his case, so I'm going to allow it."

"Thank you, Your Honor," said Michael.

"Listen to me, Mr. Willis, and listen good. I'm going to give you five minutes of questioning to prove this demonstration is probative. If I don't understand your reasoning within five minutes, I'm going to put an end to it. Understood?"

"Yes, sir."

The attorneys walked back to their tables.

When Michael reached the defendant's table, he picked up his yellow pad and leaned over to whisper something to me, "Hey, Joey, you're good with words. What does *probative* mean again?"

"It's an adjective that means useful for uncovering evidence or proof. Like you're trying to ferret out the truth."

"Okay, cool. That's what I thought it meant. Just checking. Wish me luck."

Instead of wishing him luck, I closed my eyes and said a quick Hail Mary.

Michael stepped up to the attorney's podium, checked his notepad, and asked his first question.

"Sir, would you please state your whole name and occupation for the record."

"Darth Vader, supreme commander of the Galactic Empire."

"Objection!" said Fineman.

"Sustained. Mr. Willis, please remember what we talked about up here."

"Yes, Your Honor. Let's try that again. Could you please state your *real* name and occupation for the record."

"David Kandinsky. I work in a shoe store."

"And where do you reside, Mr. Kandinsky?"

"Middletown, Ohio."

"Is that near Columbus, Ohio?"

"About ninety minutes."

"So is it fair to say that when you heard a Fan-Con was coming to Columbus, Ohio, you were excited about going to the convention and wearing your Darth Vader costume?"

"Objection, Your Honor! Counsel is putting words in the witness's mouth."

"Sustained."

"Let me rephrase that. Did you wear your Darth Vader costume to the Columbus Fan-Con last October?"

"I did."

"And were you the only one there dressed as Darth Vader?"

"No, I counted five Darth Vaders, including me."

"Objection, Your Honor. The witness is not in a position to say with certainty how many Darth Vaders were at the convention."

I could tell Fineman's strategy was to make an objection every minute or two to throw Michael off his game—to the extent Michael had a game.

"Overruled," said the judge. "He's only testifying to how many Darth Vaders he saw."

Michael did a little fist pump, like Tiger Woods after sinking a twenty-foot putt.

"Would you say there were a lot of people in costume at the convention?" said Michael.

"Yes, there were thousands of people in costume."

"Three more minutes, Mr. Willis." The judge tapped his watch. "Three more minutes."

"Yes, Your Honor. We're really close now. Mr. Kandinsky, would you say that many of those costumes were as elaborate as yours?"

"Most of them were."

"Is it fair to say that many of them included helmets, masks, and other kinds of headgear that completely covered the person's face and eyes?"

"Yes, definitely."

"Mr. Kandinsky, can you tell me how many fingers I am holding up right now?"

"Objection, Your Honor," said Fineman. "Relevance."

"I'll allow it," said the judge.

"How many fingers, Mr. Kandinsky?"

"I can't tell. I can't see that far in this helmet."

"Can you even see me?"

"Just barely."

"Your Honor, may I approach the witness?"

"You may."

Michael walked to within ten feet of the witness stand.

"Can you see me now?"

"A little better."

"How many fingers?"

"I still can't make out your hands at all."

Michael walked right up to the witness stand and put his hand six inches away from Darth Vader's face.

"What about now, how many fingers?"

"Two?"

"Let the record show that I'm holding up three fingers," said Michael to the court reporter. He gave a meaningful glance to the jury, too.

I looked over at Fineman to see how he was reacting to this. He had his hands over his eyes, and his shoulders were heaving up and down. I couldn't tell if he was crying or laughing. I'm pretty sure it was the latter.

"Just a few more questions, Mr. Kandinsky."

"Okay, cool."

"Did you wait in line to get Mr. Volpe's autograph?"

"Mr. who?"

"Mr. Volpe. The man sitting at the defendant's table."

"I told you I can't see that far."

"Mr. Joseph Volpe, the man who robbed all those—er, I mean the defendant in this case."

"Oh, yes, the Mafia hit man. Yes, I got his autograph."

"Did you see two bodyguards standing behind him holding machine guns?"

"No, I couldn't see them. Like I said, I can't really see more than about five feet in this thing."

"It's your testimony, is it not, that the kind of helmet you're wearing is typical of those worn by most people at the convention."

"Yes, very typical."

"So you're saying that most of the people at the convention could not see very well and could not make a positive identification of my client or his accomplices?"

"Objection, Your Honor," said Fineman. "Counsel is asking the witness to speculate and draw a conclusion based on facts he could not possess."

"Sustained," said the judge with a heavy sigh.

"Your Honor, I rest my case," said Michael.

"You're resting your case *again*?"

"No, I mean I have no further questions for this witness."

Michael walked back to the defendant's table with a triumphant smile on his face and sat down like a prince taking his throne.

"That's it?" I said. "That's all you've got? That was the trick up your sleeve? That was the trick I've been waiting to see for three months?"

"Yep! We nailed him, baby."

"The only thing you put a nail in, Michael, was my coffin."

"Mr. Fineman, I presume you have some questions to ask on cross?" said the judge. I thought I heard a chuckle in his voice.

"Just a few, Your Honor." Fineman walked to the attorney's podium and smiled. "Mr. Kandinsky, were you ever in the greenroom at the convention?"

"I couldn't tell the color of the room, sir. Like I said, I can barely see anything in this helmet. Everything is kind of dark and blurry in here. I can't see colors at all."

"No, the greenroom is an anteroom behind the curtains in the exhibition hall. Were you ever in there?"

"No."

"Did you know that the greenroom was where the robbery took place?"

"No, I didn't."

"When you say that a lot of people were wearing helmets like yours, what percentage of the total number of attendees were dressed like you?"

"I can't say for sure."

"Give me a guess."

"About half of them, I'd say."

"So if there were two thousand people on the floor of the convention hall, about one thousand of them were wearing helmets like yours?"

"Well, maybe a thousand were in costume and maybe two hundred and fifty or so were wearing helmets or masks."

"And the rest of them were dressed normally, correct?"

"Objection, Your Honor," said Michael. "What is normal?"

"I was wondering the same thing, Mr. Willis," said the judge. "I have no idea what normal is anymore. Your objection, however, is overruled."

"The rest of them were in street clothes?" said Fineman.

"Yes."

"The rest of them had unimpeded vision, in other words?"

"Yes."

"No further questions, Your Honor."

"Redirect, Mr. Willis?"

"No, Your Honor, I rest my case."

"Mr. Willis, what did I tell you about saying that?"

"No, I really mean it this time. I'm done. I'm through. I'm finished."

So was I.

The jury found me guilty. It took an hour of deliberation. Well, it probably took them three minutes of deliberation. They spent the other fifty-seven minutes playing cards and reading the newspaper to make it look like they talked about the trial.

The jury sent a note to the judge asking if they could meet me before they went home. While they waited in the jury room, the judge discussed their request with the attorneys in the courtroom.

"I've heard this request after a not-guilty verdict," said the judge, "but it's unusual with a guilty verdict. After a guilty verdict, everybody is too depressed to talk about the case any further—except the prosecutor, of course. I'm going to leave it up to Mr. Volpe. If he wants to meet with the jury, he can. I want the US Marshall to put him in handcuffs though. The man has a history of passing guns back and forth."

I indicated my assent by flicking my wrist in resignation. I was too depressed and worried about prison to speak.

Why did the jury want to meet me?

They wanted my autograph.

22

Federal minimum-security prison is a) not as bad, and b) not as good as it's cracked up to be.

I say not as good because some people call it Club Fed. They think it's a place with swimming pools, tennis courts, golf courses, and surf-and-turf dinners on Saturday night. Trust me, it's not like that at all. It's a downright miserable and wretched way to spend two years of your life.

When I say it's not as bad as some people think, I mean there is no violence. No homosexual rape. No solitary confinement. It's nothing like the horror stories you've heard when it comes to maximum- or even medium-security prisons.

We federal inmates referred to those prisons as big-boy jail, as in "Don't let the guards catch you outside the perimeter or they'll put you in big-boy jail."

The perimeter? That's right. There were no fences or walls either. In fact, there was no surveillance at all. If you wanted to break out of prison, all you had to do was pack up your kit bag and walk away. There was no barbed wire. No electronic monitors. The only thing keeping you inside was the certain knowledge that if they caught you, they'd take you to big-boy jail. As far as I was concerned that worked as well as a high tower manned by sharpshooters with sniper rifles. I never got within a hundred feet of the perimeter.

Frankly, I considered myself lucky to be there. After all, they convicted me of a RICO crime involving guns in which two men were wounded. The judge could've sent me to Leavenworth if he wanted. But he sensed something was wrong during the sentencing hearing.

The judge said to the district attorney, "Mr. Fineman, I've read the presentencing investigation report and I'm deeply troubled by it."

"How so, Your Honor?"

"I don't see any evidence here that the convict was involved with organized crime in any way, shape, or form."

I noticed they called me the convict rather than the defendant. I was moving down in the world.

The judge continued. "He's never been seen in the presence of known criminals. He's never been convicted of or even charged with a crime. Or arrested. Or even picked up and questioned about a crime. There is no record of him in the criminal justice system at all. Not even a traffic violation."

"Your Honor," said Fineman, "the jury convicted him in less than an hour."

"I'm well aware of that, Mr. Fineman. I had just taken one bite of my steak at Morton's when my cell phone rang. I'm not questioning his guilt. He clearly took part in the robbery. I'm questioning whether this was a RICO trial in the first place."

"Well, Your Honor, of course, we discussed—"

The judge cut him off. "Please review your RICO predicates for me again."

"Well, there was robbery, of course . . ."

"Yes. *And?* You're a federal prosecutor, Mr. Fineman. You must know you need at least two predicates to make a RICO case."

Fineman started rifling through papers like a maniac. Documents, briefs, notebooks, pens, and pencils were flying off the side of the desk while he kept saying, "Robbery and . . . robbery and . . . robbery and . . ."

"And *what*, Mr. Fineman?"

"I'll find it, sir. Prostitution? Gambling? Kidnapping? No. Wait."

"Mr. Fineman, you can stop looking. I don't think you're going to find it. If this were *your* mistake, I wouldn't be so concerned. I don't give a damn about your career. Unfortunately, this is my mistake, too, and I don't like getting overturned on appeal. In fact, I hate it. Of course, maybe I wouldn't have made this mistake if there had been a defense attorney working the case."

The judge stared at Michael Willis, who shrunk into his chair. Up until this point, Michael had been smart enough to sit there without saying anything.

"Mr. Volpe," said the judge, "I'm going to address you directly. Your attorney can listen in if he's not too busy with his fantasy football league. I believe you're guilty of taking part in an armed robbery. I don't believe you're guilty of violating the RICO statute. I don't think you're a member of the Mafia. I think you're just an actor."

The expression on my face said, *What have I been trying to tell you people for the last six months?*

"You're an actor who got mixed up in some bad business. I don't know how and I don't why. What I do know is you didn't belong in my courtroom," said the judge. "You should've been tried in Ohio under the local statutes against armed robbery."

I looked up at him with a glimmer of hope in my eyes.

He continued. "Having said that, armed robbery is a serious crime—especially when the gun goes off and hurts somebody. I couldn't let you walk out of here, even if I wanted to. Which I don't."

"Your Honor—" said Fineman.

"Shut up, Mr. Fineman, you've done enough damage already. What I *can* do for you, Mr. Volpe, is reduce your sentence to five years. I'll suspend half of it so you'll serve two and a half years. If you keep your nose clean, you'll get good time, which means you'll only serve twenty-four months. I'm also allowing you to self-surrender. You have thirty days of freedom to put your affairs in order. I can also put you in a minimum-security prison and let you choose which one."

"Thank you, sir," I managed to say.

"It's been my experience, Mr. Volpe, that convicts either choose a prison close to home or one known for being gentle. Which would you prefer?"

"Gentle, please."

"You don't care if it's someplace like Arizona or New Mexico? Your family won't be able to visit you often."

"Things aren't going great at home, Your Honor. I doubt my wife would come visit me even if I were in Queens."

"I see. Well, I'll try to make that happen for you. Meanwhile, if I were you, Mr. Volpe, I'd think about hiring an attorney for your appeal who has an IQ above room temperature. There's a good chance he could get you off the hook entirely."

The judge turned to Fineman and Willis and continued, "I must say, you gentlemen are two of the worst lawyers with whom I've ever had the displeasure of working. Court is adjourned."

So the judge walked out of the courtroom and thirty days later, I was part of the federal prison system. My last official act as a free man was to give the envelope with the tape recording in it to Michael Willis and tell him to give it to Caitlin one week before my release. I knew I'd have a lot of time to worry about him screwing that up, but what choice did I have? He was my so-called attorney and my only connection to the outside world.

They assigned me to the Hoover Federal Correctional Complex. It was in the desert not far from Tucson, Arizona. I don't know if it was technically a desert, but it sure looked like the desert to a New Yorker. The minimum-security prison was attached to a medium-security prison *and* a maximum-security prison. It was like one of those senior citizen homes that have three levels of care: people who live independently, people who need some supervision, and people who require attention twenty-four hours a day.

The intake for all three prisons was in the same building. So the guards handled me rather roughly at first and it scared the shit out of me. Literally. I had to ask to use the toilet three times during my brief orientation, at which they gave me my prison uniform and a manual of rules and regulations.

The guard who escorted me over to the minimum-security area noticed how pale and sweaty I was and took pity on me. "Don't worry, kid. You're going to spend two years in summer camp, and then you're going to walk out of here and get on with the rest of your life." He nodded in the direction of the maximum-security area. "Some of the guys over there are never going to see the light of day again. You're one of the lucky ones. So cheer up."

I did cheer up when I got my first look at the place where I'd be spending the next couple of years. It looked like my college dormitory at Haverford! The only way I could tell it *wasn't* Haverford at first glance was that college students didn't wear orange jumpsuits and white slip-on tennis shoes. We were younger back then, too. But the large common area looked much like the main lobby of the dorm. There were overstuffed chairs and couches scattered about, where inmates sat reading or talking among themselves. A big television set dominated one corner of the room, and several inmates were watching a basketball game. Both a billiard table on one side of the room and a Ping-Pong table on the other were in use. Strange as it may sound, it struck me as a rather welcoming environment.

"You're in cubicle one hundred and eighty-eight," said the guard. "I'll walk you there and then you're on your own."

There was something comforting about the word *cubicle*. It sounded less threatening than *cell*. As we walked down a long corridor, I peeked into the other cubicles. Each had two bunk beds, a set of lockers, and two small desks. Most of the cubicles were empty, but here and there I saw an inmate lying on his bed reading a magazine. There were no bars on the doors or windows. The floors were carpeted and clean. Unlike every other jail cell I'd ever seen in the movies or on television, there were no toilets or sinks in the rooms. Presumably, I'd find a central restroom and shower area. I breathed a little easier with every step we took toward my new home.

When we finally arrived at my cubicle, the guard said, "Okay, here you go, Mr. Capone. Put your stuff in the empty locker. You'll have to find out from your cellmates which bed you're in. The new guy usually gets the top bunk. Good luck to you, young man."

There was one inmate in the room. He'd been sitting at the little desk and writing something in longhand in a spiral notebook. Now he turned to greet me.

"Ah, our new cubie has arrived." He stuck out his hand. "I'm Charlie Scott. Mail fraud. But I didn't do it. Well, I sort of did it, but I shouldn't be in jail for it. Of course, that's what everybody says."

This struck me as surprising, because I'd done some research on the internet about prison life to prepare myself. One piece of advice I saw was that you should never ask another inmate what he was in for. I was under the impression it was a taboo subject. Maybe it was, but not in cubicle 188. So I responded in kind.

"Joey Volpe, armed robbery."

"*Armed robbery?* Whoa! What the hell are you doing in *here?* You should be in big-boy jail. That's where they put the armed robbers."

"Well, it wasn't really armed robbery. Technically, it was a violation of the Racketeer-Influenced and Corrupt Organizations Act."

"RICO? You're a mobster? Holy shit!"

"Well . . ."

"Can you cook spaghetti? Can you slice a clove of garlic with a razor like Paul Sorvino in *Goodfellas?*"

"I can't cook at all, I'm afraid. I'm an actor. I did work with Sorvino once, though."

There I go again! Remember when I told you that one of the ways an actor pads his résumé is by mentioning the name of the star in a show where he only had a small part? Well, Paul Sorvino was the guest star in an episode of *Button Men* one week. I had one line in that episode, and it wasn't in the same scene with Sorvino. I never even got a chance to see him from a distance. But I had no reservations about dropping his name whenever I thought it could help.

"That's pretty cool, dude," said Charlie. "You're a major improvement over the guy you're replacing. He was just a garden-variety embezzler. Dull as dishwater, that one. Trust me, an actor who moonlights as a Mafia soldier is going to make things much more interesting around here."

"Where are the other two guys?" I asked.

"Oh, they're around somewhere. Nigel is a big card player. Steve likes to exercise. If I had to guess, I would say Nigel is in the rec room right now and Steve is in the gym."

Nigel? Now, there's a name I didn't expect. Not after all the jokes you hear about, "Hi, my name is Bubba. I'm your new cellmate and I'm looking forward to getting to know you better." So I was expecting Bubba. The names Killer, Tex, or Spike wouldn't have surprised me either. *But Nigel?*

"They'll be back soon. The morning count is coming up."

"The count?"

"Yeah, we all have to muster in our rooms twice a day so the guards can count us and make sure we haven't gone to Las Vegas for the weekend."

At that moment, a distinguished-looking older gentleman with a pencil-thin mustache walked into the cubicle. Well, he was as distinguished as one can be when wearing an orange jumpsuit with white tennis shoes. Even in the prison garb, he reminded me of David Niven or Fred Astaire.

"Speak of the devil and he doth appear," said Charlie. "Nigel, this is our new cubie, Joey Volpe. He's an armed robber *and* a made-man in the Mafia."

"I'm duly impressed," said Nigel.

I thought I detected a slight British accent. Or maybe it was an upper-class American accent.

"What are you in for, Nigel?" I said.

"Dear boy, it's considered bad form to ask a fellow inmate for the cause of his incarceration. He will share that information when and if he chooses to do so."

Dammit, I *thought* so. Charlie's instant confession had thrown me off. It was going to take me a while to master the etiquette around here.

"Oh, don't get a stick up your ass, Nigel. He was born with a stick up his ass, Joey. Nigel is what's politely known as a flimflam man. So am I. The only difference between the two of us is that I do it in the mail and he does it in person."

"In other words," said Nigel, "the only difference between the two of us is that you're a pusillanimous milksop and I'm not."

It was a rather nasty insult. I backed off thinking that someone might pull a knife or—what do you call it?—a shiv out of his shoe and stab the other in the chest. Charlie just laughed.

"Good one, Nigel! I hope you brought your thesaurus with you, Joey, because Nigel talks like he swallowed a dictionary. I'm the writer around here, but he comes up with words I've never heard before."

"Well, I did score eight hundred on the verbal part of my SAT," I said before I realized what an inappropriate thing that was to say. In prison, no less. To people I'd just met. Under any circumstances, really, unless you were applying for college.

"Okay, let me get this straight," said Charlie. "You're a Rhodes Scholar. You're a Mafia hit man. You're an armed robber. And you're a Hollywood actor. Nigel, I think we've just added the third con man to our little band of brothers here."

"For he today that sheds his blood with me shall be my brother . . ." said Nigel.

"Be he ne'er so vile, this day shall gentle his condition," I added.

"And gentlemen in England now abed," said Nigel, as he swept his arm and pointed to the bunk beds, "shall think themselves accursed they were not here . . ."

"And hold their manhoods cheap," I continued, "whiles any speaks who fought with us . . ."

We finished the famous speech from *Henry V* shouting in unison:

"ON SAINT CRISPIN'S DAY!"

Nigel and I shook hands and he patted me on the back.

"I am honored and delighted, sir, to share a cubicle with a fellow scholar of the Bard of Avon."

"Shakespeare?" said Charlie. "I thought you guys were doing Mel Gibson from *Braveheart*."

"Philistine," said Nigel with a wink in my direction.

At that moment, another man walked into the room and said, "Have they done the count yet? I hope not."

"You're just in time," said Charlie. "Steve, this is our new cubie, Joey Volpe, Shakespearean scholar and Mafia button man."

"Pleased to meet you," said Steve. He was an ordinary-looking middle-aged guy. Rimless glasses. Mostly bald. Overweight, especially in the belly. Charlie had said he was an avid exerciser, but it didn't look like it was doing him much good.

"Steve is a con man, too," said Charlie.

"I object to that. I was in the investment banking business on Wall Street."

"He ran a pyramid scheme," said Charlie.

"The Carlo Ponzi of our time," said Nigel.

"Nonsense," said Steve. "Don't believe a word these guys tell you, Mr. Volpe. They sound like the prosecutors in my case. I ran a legitimate brokerage firm and investment bank on Wall Street. Then 2008 hit and we got caught short of cash. Some of our clients wanted their money back and we weren't able to pay them. Next thing you know, I've got the SEC up my ass saying I'm running a Ponzi scheme. Outrageous."

"The defense rests, Your Honor," said Charlie. And we all laughed.

At that moment, a guard poked his head into the cubicle.

"I see the Barrow gang is all here," he said, and made a check mark on his clipboard. "Plus, you have a brand-new member." He looked at the clipboard again and said, "May I give you a word of advice, Mr. Joseph Volpe?"

"Yes, sir?"

"If you've just shaken hands with your new cubies, I suggest you look carefully to see how many fingers you have left."

"Oh, get the fuck out of here, Swanson," said Charlie.

"I'm going, I'm going," said the guard.

Prison was an entirely different experience from what I'd expected.

23

The worst part of prison?

The food, of course. But that was second worst. First worst was the sheer, unrelenting, oppressive boredom of it.

The best part? The best part was all the interesting, intelligent, and complex people I met there. No, not everyone you meet in minimum-security federal prison is a nice person. Not by a long shot. Some of them are downright evil. But surprisingly few.

The food was the institutional slop provided by the same private contractor who ran the cafeterias at Haverford. As bad as the food was at Haverford, it was much worse at Hoover. I assume the food-service company had a range of plans they offered their clients from the Caviar Plan to the Dogshit Plan. Hoover was on the latter. The best thing you could say about the food in prison was that it was capable of sustaining human life. Barely.

The biggest difference between the food at Haverford and the food at Hoover, however, was not the food itself, but the role food played in your life. At Haverford, there were lots of interesting things to do each day from attending classes to going on panty raids at Bryn Mawr. Food played a relatively small role in campus life. It was bad, but so what?

In prison, you *lived* for breakfast, lunch, and dinner. Those three occasions were the highlights of your day. When the highlight of your day is terrible, then your life really sucks. We did have a commissary where you could buy snacks, candy, and an occasional piece of fruit. When you purchased something from the commissary, they deducted the cost from the money in your prison bank account.

How did you get money into your account?

Either by working a prison job or having your family send it in from the outside. There was a limit to how much money you could keep in your account, and the Bureau of Prisons deducted a certain amount each month to pay restitution to your victims.

That's right, a few pennies of the measly paycheck I earned from scrubbing prison toilets went into the mailbox of Steven Dubois—where I'm sure it was lost among the thousands of dollars he earned from *Star Trek* residuals.

As I said before, the worst part of prison was the crushing boredom. Every day you faced hours with nothing to do but tedious manual labor, three god-awful meals, and the constant blare of a communal television set that was tuned to the lowest of lowest-common-denominator programming.

Different inmates dealt with the boredom of prison in different ways. My cubie Charlie, for example, who wrote letters for a living (he was a freelance junk-mail copywriter by trade) was writing a series of long letters to his two young sons. He wrote in a spiral notebook and when he finished ten pages or so, he'd rip them out and send them home. He let me read each installment before he put it in the mail.

"Are you sure it's not too personal?" I asked. "It's a letter to your family, after all."

"You're part of my family now, Joey. Besides, I'm going to publish them someday. I'll charge ninety-nine nighty-five and discount it to forty-nine bucks. I've got a mailing list in the millions. At a two percent response rate, I'll net several hundred thousand dollars from this project. When I get out of the slammer, I'm going to need that money."

"No offense, Charlie, but why would anyone want to buy your letters to your kids from prison?"

"There's a lot of advice in there on copywriting and marketing. That's what I'm known for. Don't worry, people will buy it."

So I read the letters. They were beautiful. They contained a lot of advice about advertising. I wasn't in any position to tell whether the advice was brilliant or bullshit. But the affection he felt for his two boys was palpable on every page. On one page he'd tell them how to write a headline on an envelope, then on the next page he'd talk about how to use a razor without nicking your chin. He was such a good writer, he could make anything interesting. I got more pleasure out of reading Charlie's letters

than any of the hundreds of books I read in the prison library—
except, of course, for Shakespeare.

As I mentioned earlier, my cubie Steve, the Wall Street broker,
tried to fight the boredom with exercise. He'd hit the gym at dawn
and wouldn't stop until lunchtime. After lunch, he'd go back and
exercise some more. Four hours, five hours, six hours a day he'd
be jogging on the track, lifting weights, climbing the Stairmaster,
or cycling on the stationary bike. But he never lost much weight.
He was still doughy, bloated, and unhealthy looking. Probably
because our food was loaded with simple carbs and other empty
calories. I wondered if the exercise was doing him more harm
than good and I told him so a few times.

"Steve, why don't you back off on the exercise for a day or two?
Give your body a chance to repair itself. That's how you build
muscle. Or so I've heard."

"Naaah, I'm not doing it to build muscle. Just to pass the time."

"That much exercise isn't good for you. Not unless you're an
Olympic athlete. If you don't mind me saying so, I don't think
you're an Olympic athlete."

"It gives me something to do with my day, Joey."

"Why don't you take a job?"

"I hate those prison jobs. Look at *your* job, for chrissakes. Do
you think I want to clean toilets all day? I used to have lunch
every afternoon at Le Bernardin. I had a house on the beach in
the Hamptons, for heaven's sake. *I still do!* I've got plenty of money
in my prison account. My wife sends a check to the prison every
month. After all, she's got a hundred million in the bank. That
money will be waiting for me when I get out in ten years. But I've
got to make sure I live that long. That's why I exercise."

Nigel was a different story. He liked to read. He liked to talk
to people. I think he knew every single inmate in the joint. And
he loved to play cards, especially poker. Of course, we weren't
allowed to play poker. But Nigel came up with a system whereby
four guys could play poker and make it look like they were
playing bridge. They didn't use poker chips. Instead, they'd make
their bets using code words. When somebody said, "I bid four

no-trump," for example, it meant "I bet four stamps." (Stamps became the main currency in federal prison after cigarettes were banned.) One of the guys kept track of the bets in a notebook. The guards didn't know bridge was played with thirteen cards to a hand and poker with five. Or maybe they did, but didn't care.

Nigel almost always won at poker. I think the only times he didn't win were the times when he thought it would be a good idea to let someone else win for a change.

"They shouldn't let me play cards in this place, Joey," he said to me one day in our cubicle.

"Why not?"

"I'll show you why not." He pulled out a deck of cards and fanned them in front of me on the bunk bed. "Pick a card. Any card you want. Look at it and memorize it, but don't show it to me."

I pulled the nine of spades.

"Put it back in, but be careful not to let me see it."

I did so.

"Shuffle the deck thoroughly."

I played a lot of bridge at Haverford, so I was a pretty good card handler. I shuffled the hell of that deck and slid it over to him on the bunk.

"No, I don't need to touch the deck," he said. "Just leave it in the center of the bed. Now take off your left shoe."

"Take off my left shoe?"

"Do as I say."

I slipped off my left tennis shoe.

"Hold the shoe upside down over the bunk and shake it."

When I did that, a single card fluttered out of the shoe and landed face down on the bed.

"Turn over the card."

Do I need to tell you which card it was?

"And that, my dear boy, is why they should not allow a scoundrel like me to play cards in prison," he said with a devilish glitter in his eye.

What about me? How did I pass the time in the joint? Reading. Mostly drama, because that's what I loved best. I read all of Shakespeare. *Again.* I memorized a lot of the soliloquies and other famous passages, so that I could quote them even more than I used to—which drove my friends crazy, but tickled me to no end. I read the Holy Bible front to back, just for the hell of it. The prison library would order any book or play you wanted, so I continued to study the work of my favorite modern playwright, David Mamet. I tried to keep up with what was happening on Broadway and off-Broadway, ordering the plays when they were available and reading reviews in the newspaper when they were not. I nurtured a dream of working as an actor when I got out of prison.

Oh, and I also worked on my appeal, of course. I asked the government for a new public defender. He assured me I had been wrongly tried under the RICO Act and I would be out of jail in no time.

"What exactly is 'no time?'" I asked him during one of our first meetings. "From start to finish, how long will the appeal process take?"

He said, "About two years, give or take."

"That's the length of my sentence."

"Oh."

"What happens if we win?"

"You walk out of here a free man with no criminal record." He hesitated. "Unless . . ."

"Unless what?"

"Well, there's a chance that if the RICO charge is vacated, the State of Ohio might want to try you for armed robbery."

"Isn't that double jeopardy?"

"We would make that argument, of course, but I can't guarantee we'd prevail."

"What is the penalty for armed robbery in Ohio?"

"I've never taken the bar exam in Ohio, but I guess it's around twenty years."

"So I could walk out of here a free man with no criminal record in two years and then go into some Ohio state prison for the next twenty years?"

"The good news is you'd only serve half of that," he said.

I decided to fire my lawyer, serve my two stinking years at Hoover, and be done with this nightmare once and for all.

But I spent most of my time in prison thinking, thinking, thinking.

I thought about my wife, even though I didn't get many letters from her and no visits. I came to realize the reason I kept cheating on Caitlin was because I felt guilty for not being able to support her and Bianca. I didn't feel like a real man, so I tried to make up for that by screwing any woman who walked into my life. Richard Burton once said, "An actor is something less than a man, but an actress is something more than a woman." *How true!* I was something less than a man, that's for sure. I was starting to realize Caitlin was something more than an ordinary woman.

I spent most of my time thinking about how I got into this mess. Thinking about Rosetti. Thinking about revenge. Could I really get revenge on a Mafia boss? Don't be ridiculous, I told myself. You've heard the expression cutting off your nose to spite your face? Getting revenge on a Mafia boss would be like slitting your throat to get revenge on your head. I'd be a dead man.

Speaking of dead men, one afternoon after lunch something awful happened.

Steve had a heart attack.

Let me give you some advice. If you're planning to spend any time in federal prison, please don't get sick in there. See your doctor and dentist before you go. Your podiatrist and chiropractor, too. The quality of the medical care you get in prison is abysmal. Prison is where young doctors go when they've graduated from medical school in a small Caribbean island. At the bottom of their class. After cheating on the final exam.

Even worse than the quality of prison medical care is the speed at which it's delivered. If you're suffering from a minor illness like the flu, for example, the doctor will see you a month or two after the disease has run its course. If you're suffering from an urgent illness like a stroke or a heart attack, medical care will arrive much faster. Six or seven hours, or so.

I happened to be in the gym when Steve's heart attack hit. I wasn't exercising. I was looking for a quiet place to read. I chose a different place to read every day, just to add a little variety to my life. I was reading *Troilus and Cressida* near the running track, and every three minutes Steve would jog by me. Once in a while, he said something snarky like, "Keep at it, Lord Olivier."

"You, too, Jesse Owens," I replied.

Troilus and Cressida is not exactly gripping reading, but I was getting into it and I didn't notice that Steve hadn't passed me in a while. When I looked up I saw him lying facedown on the track opposite from where I was sitting. At first, I thought he was stretching or cooling off. But he wasn't moving. I got up and walked over to him. I wasn't worried until I saw his face.

"You okay, Steve?"

"No."

"What's the matter?"

"Chest hurts."

Then he vomited.

I rolled him over on his side. His face was as pale and pasty as a fan at a *Star Trek* convention. I knew he was having a heart attack.

"Guard!" I yelled. "Emergency!"

No guard was in sight. They were never around when you needed them. There was one other inmate in the gym lifting weights. I said, "Go find a guard. My cubie is having a heart attack." The guy dropped a two-hundred-pound barbell on the ground and ran out the door.

Everything after that seemed to happen in super-slow motion. It must've taken fifteen minutes for a guard to show up. He took one look at Steve and got on his walkie-talkie to call some more guards. Ten minutes after that, two more guards arrived. They talked among themselves for five minutes or so and concluded that Steve was indeed having a heart attack. They talked about calling the medical unit at the big-boy jail, but decided it would take too long for them to send a doctor to us. We were fifteen minutes into Steve's cardiac arrest when one guard had the bright idea of calling 911.

I held Steve's hand and said, "It won't be long now, buddy. They've called the ambulance. It's on its way. You're going to be fine."

His eyes were starting to glaze over.

Unfortunately, an ambulance cannot pull up at a prison and let the EMTs run inside and do their job like they would anywhere else. It's not that easy. First of all, this was Nowheresville, Arizona, and the nearest hospital was forty-five minutes away. Secondly, the ambulance has to stop at the gate and pass a security check. Third, the EMTs cannot rush inside without being frisked, questioned, and cleared. Ironically, at a federal minimum-security prison, it was much easier to break out than break in.

All told, it took ninety minutes for the EMTs to reach us. Steve was just barely alive when they got to him. They did CPR on him again and again, but it wouldn't take. They couldn't get his heart in rhythm. Finally, it stopped.

Steve was dead.

That night, after lights-out, the three of us stayed up late talking in the dark. The emptiness of Steve's bunk bed was a heavy presence in the room. We replayed the events of the day over and over again.

"Ironically," said Charlie, "I think Steve was the only one of the three of us who was truly innocent. He told me the whole story once. They railroaded him. Somebody had to pay for the stock market crash and they chose Steve. Even if he didn't dot every I and cross every T, I don't think he was any more guilty than ten thousand other assholes on Wall Street. In fact, I think he was completely legit."

"What about you, Charlie? Were you innocent?" I said.

We'd never talked in detail about our crimes before. Something about lying there in the dark after Steve's untimely death made it seem like a good time for confession.

"I was innocent," he said, "but not very smart. I wrote an ad for a guy who was selling nutritional supplements for high cholesterol. The capsules were supposed to be filled with an exotic herb from the rainforest in the Amazon. The Federal Trade Commission didn't seem to think baking soda was an exotic herb."

"That's your client's fault, not yours," I said.

"Yes, but I made some stupid mistakes. I should've checked out the client more carefully. It turned out he had a long history of pulling the same kind of scam. He'd done some time in prison himself. Plus, I didn't take a fee for services. He talked me into sharing the profits with him. So from the government's point of view, I wasn't just a copywriter for hire. I was a full partner. They made a deal with the bastard to testify against me, and they let him off with a slap on the wrist. I wound up with two years."

"For what it's worth, you sound innocent to me," I said.

"Thanks," said Charlie. "What about you, Joey? How did you find yourself pursuing a career in armed robbery and organized crime?"

So I told them the whole pathetic story. It took thirty minutes from beginning to end. I left out the part about Rosetti kidnapping my dog and threatening my family.

"One thing I don't understand," said Charlie. "Why did you do it? When your acting gig dried up, was robbery really the only way you could earn a living?"

There was a long silence. Finally, Nigel spoke up. "He was forced to do it."

"Who forced you?" said Charlie.

Another long silence.

"He'd rather not talk about it," said Nigel. "And frankly, I don't blame him."

"What about you, Nigel?" I said, eager to change the subject.

"I'm guilty, my dear boys. I'm not only guilty, but I'm also unrepentant. I'm a career criminal and proud of it."

"What kind of criminal exactly?" I asked.

"I told you on the first day we met. I'm a confidence man. A grifter. A flimflam artist. A swindler. Scoundrels of my ilk go by many names."

"But what crime did you commit to land here?"

"It was pretty much the same crime I've been committing for the last thirty years, but this time I got caught. I can't give away all of my trade secrets. There's a code of honor among con men. The basic scenario goes something like this: I have a team of people around the country who are good at spotting individuals who have a unique combination of great wealth and lack of sophistication. We call them marks. We call the people who find them ropers, because they rope the marks and bring them to me."

"Like a cowboy roping a calf," said Charlie.

"Precisely, my dear boy. I am the manager and grand poobah of something we call the big store, which in my case is a stock brokerage firm. Much like the one our dearly departed friend Steven once ran—only his was legitimate, and mine is entirely phony. Once we get the mark inside the store, we convince him we've come up with a clever way to beat the stock market. Our store, or office, looks just like any other brokerage firm. Desktop computers and printers are cranking out important-looking documents. Secretaries and clerks are running around looking busy. But they are all actors. Just like you, Joey. In fact, I might have some lucrative employment for you when we both get out of here."

"It'll be the first time I've worked as an actor in years."

"You don't need to be Lionel Barrymore for this kind of acting. You don't need to say a word. I do most of the talking myself. I show the mark some fancy computers and some wires. All very hush-hush, you know. I explain how my brokerage firm has figured out a way to get the stock prices from Wall Street a hundredth of a second before everyone else gets them."

"One hundredth of a second?"

"Yes. That's all you need nowadays. Computers can execute a trade in a *thousandth* of a second, ten times faster. In that blink of an eye, you can make money by knowing which way the stock is moving before anyone else does. I show them a closet full of wires and cables and mainframe computers that make all this happen."

"Wow," I said.

"Actually, we bought the wires and cables at a hardware store for a hundred bucks. They're not hooked up to anything at all."

"And the computers?"

"Big empty boxes with lots of dials and flashing lights. I hired a theatrical set designer to build and paint them. He did a lovely job and charged me a pittance. They look quite realistic."

"The marks believe this is real?"

"The play's the thing, my dear boy, the play's the thing."

"*Hamlet*, Act II, Scene Two," I said.

Then Charlie asked, "What happens next?"

"Well, now it's time for The Convincer. We show the mark how our secret system works. Then we ask him to test the system for himself by investing a small amount of money. Let's say a thousand dollars. He writes us a check. We show him a computer with the ticker prices from Wall Street. The computer goes through all sorts of gyrations. Bells and whistles go off. The next thing you know, we've turned his thousand dollars into five thousand. So we write him a check for five grand."

"Is it a good check?" I said.

"It's as good as gold. Do you think I'm a common paper hanger?"

"Paper hanger?"

"Someone who writes bad checks," Charlie said.

"Sometimes we give the mark five thousand in cash. Cash works even better. Something about all that green triggers the hormones in his greed glands."

"Then what happens?"

"Then we put him 'on the send.' In other words, we send him home to get some real money. A hundred thousand at least. Preferably a million or two. The biggest score I had was five million. Ah, what a lovely day that was."

"You mean he withdraws a million bucks from his bank and gives it to you?"

"You catch on fast, Joey. Are you sure you're an actor? You seem too sharp to be a thespian."

"What happens next?"

"Well, we have to wait for his check to clear. Meanwhile, the mark stays in the finest hotel in town at our expense. He's drinking champagne and eating caviar on our tab. Having a lovely time. When he shows up at our office three days later to execute the stock trade, a curious thing has happened."

"What?"

"Our office has quite thoroughly vanished, dear boy. 'Melted into air, into *thin* air.'"

"Prospero from *The Tempest*."

"Actors may be a bit slow," said Nigel, "but you cannot deny they have prodigious memories. Rather like elephants, I should say."

We were silent for a while. A scary thought crossed my mind. So scary I almost didn't say anything. But I couldn't help myself.

"These con jobs of yours, Nigel, do you always do them for money? Or do you sometimes do them for revenge?"

"Money, mostly. That's the beauty of con games. They work well for both money *and* revenge. Why do you ask? Is there someone you want vengeance on?"

"Maybe."

"Who?"

"I'd rather not say. Besides, it probably wouldn't work. He's rich, but he's not stupid. In fact, he's very intelligent. Just a little unsophisticated."

"We're not looking for stupid people, Joey. We're looking for greedy people. Stupid people don't work. They can't grasp the opportunity and act on it quickly. But smart people who are too greedy for their own good work like a charm. They see the chance and grab it before they take the time to think it through."

"Well, the guy I have in mind is perfect for the part. But he's too dangerous to mess with. Besides, I'm taking the straight and narrow when I get out of here. If I can't make it as an actor, I'll wash dishes to support my family."

"Not sure whether you want to take revenge or not, Prince Hamlet? I understand. If you ever want to talk more about it, you know where to find me. I'm not going anywhere for the next seven months and twenty-three days."

"Okay, but I'm too tired to talk any more tonight."

"Me too," said Charlie.

"Sweet dreams," said Nigel.

"We are such stuff as dreams are made on." I continued Prospero's famous speech from *The Tempest*. "And our little lives are rounded with a sleep."

Soon the three of us were rounded with a sleep as well.

24

A week after Steve died, I was walking into our cubicle with my nose stuck in a copy of *Richard II*, when I saw somebody lying in Steve's bunk.

"Hello there," I said.

He stood up and held out his hand, "I'm Mario Spagnuola. People call me Spags. I'm your new cellie."

"Cubie."

"What?"

"We call our roommates cubie's here. Cellie is a word reserved for the big-boy jail."

"Oh, okay. This is my fourth time in the slammer. But I've got to say, I've never seen one cushier than this."

"Fourth time?"

"Occupational hazard."

"Dare I ask what occupation?"

"Waste management and related activities."

"That's illegal?"

"The waste management is not illegal. Some of the related activities are."

"I see."

"What's your name? You look familiar," he said.

"Joey Volpe. I was on television once. Sometimes people recognize me."

"What show?"

"Small role on *The Sopranos*. Then a slightly bigger one on *Button Men*."

"My two favorite shows! No wonder you look familiar. I remember you from *Button Men*."

I loved this guy at first sight. He recognized me from *Button Men* and he didn't want to question me about *The Sopranos*. He was my favorite kind of fan.

"Do I detect a Philly accent?" I said.

"Born and raised a block from Geno's. Cut open my veins and I bleed Cheese Whiz."

"Do you know a guy by the name of Tony Rosetti?"

"Of course. *Do you?*"

For a moment, he looked like he might strangle me.

"No, no, no. Just what I've read in the newspapers."

"Trust me, you don't *want* to know him. When I say he's a bad actor, I don't mean he couldn't remember his lines—if you know what I mean."

"You've worked with him?"

"More like I've worked against him. I worked for one of his competitors, so to speak. Rosetti and I have worked together on a few projects, too. It's complicated in my business. Listen, Joey, we just met. Maybe it's best if we don't talk about my work."

"I agree. I'm sorry to pry. Welcome to our cubicle."

"Thanks. I think I'm going to like it here. I could do twenty-five years here standing on my head."

"Twenty-five years, really?"

"Naaah, just a few months. Even less if my lawyer gets off his lazy ass and does his job."

"I hear you."

Then I answered some of his questions about how to get along and get by at the Hoover Federal Correctional Complex.

Getting along and getting by is exactly what I did for the next year and a half. Then one beautiful day in May, the most wonderful thing happened to me.

I was released.

And you'll never guess who was standing outside the prison doors waiting to meet me.

25

It was Caitlin.

This was the first time I'd seen her in over two years. We had agreed that she would not visit me in prison. For two reasons. Plus a third reason that was unspoken but understood.

The first reason was that it was too expensive. She would have to fly from New York to Tucson, rent a car, and stay in a motel for at least one or two nights. We couldn't afford it on her waitress's salary. We knew that seeing each other in this setting would be depressing for both of us, so why spend a ton of money to feel sad?

Secondly, we agreed it wouldn't be good for Bianca to see her daddy in prison. We came up with a cover story that I was on the road with a national touring production of *The Music Man*, which was kind of an inside joke between Caitlin and me. As I mentioned before, I can't dance worth shit. On the day I land a role in *The Music Man*, you'll know the world has come to an end. But Bianca bought the story hook, line, and sinker. Caitlin went so far as to buy little postcards and write notes from me to Bianca so she could get them in the mail. She was too young to notice they all had New York postmarks on them.

The third unspoken reason Caitlin never came to visit me in prison was because our marriage was still in tatters. She was still mad at me for cheating on her when suddenly I was arrested, tried, and convicted for armed robbery. Who could blame her?

So every month she sent me an unemotional letter from home, filled with pictures of Bianca growing up—and Gizmo getting older—without a single word about us. Or whether there still was such a thing as "us." I had to assume there wasn't. I figured I'd take the prison bus back to Tucson, then hitchhike to New York—where I expected to find her dating a hedge-fund manager and ready to move on with her life.

But when I saw her standing outside the prison gates in front of a little red rental car, I knew my plan had worked.

"You listened to the tape?"

"I did."

"Where's Bianca?"

"With my friend Patty from work."

"Is she doing okay?"

"She's doing fine."

"Where'd you tell her you were going?"

"I told her I was going to Arizona to bring her daddy home."

"*The Music Man* tour is over?"

"Yes," she said. "Professor Hill has turned his life around. No more con games. No more girlfriends in every town. He's going to settle down with Marian the Librarian in River City. And they're going to live happily ever after."

I walked slowly toward her. I reached for her hand, and she gave it to me. I put my other hand on her shoulder to see if she'd let me hug her. She did. And the next thing I knew we were hugging like we hadn't hugged since the balcony scene in *Romeo and Juliet*. We hugged so long I thought we'd stand there in the desert until we turned to dust.

I got into the car, put on the seat belt, and immediately started to cry.

Not just "cry." I'm talking huge, heaving sobs. I was drawing deep breaths into my lungs and letting them out in whining, plaintive wails. My shoulders were rising and falling. My eyes were gushing with tears. My nose was overflowing with snot. I couldn't catch my breath and was afraid I might pass out. Caitlin remained silent. I kept crying like this for five, ten, twenty miles down the road until she said something:

"You remind me of Gizmo."

I started to laugh. But I couldn't stop crying. So I was still making these pathetic sobs and laughing at the same time.

What was so funny?

Whenever we picked up Gizmo at the kennel after coming home from a trip, he'd cry exactly like that. We'd hop into a taxi and he'd whine and wail all the way the home, as if to say, "You people have no idea what you just put me through. You cannot even begin to comprehend the pain and misery I've been suffering. I hope you're proud of yourselves for treating a helpless little dog with such cruelty." He'd keep crying like that until we got home and then about five minutes later he'd be his happy old self.

I was crying *and* laughing as we drove down the lonely Arizona two-lane highway. Gradually my laughter subsided and I continued to cry softly, tears streaming down my face. I saw a sign to Tucson, but Caitlin drove past it without turning off.

"Where are we going?" I said, my voice still choked with tears.

"Phoenix airport."

"Why?"

"It was cheaper to fly into Phoenix than Tucson. One flight instead of two. Saves money."

"Even with the rental car?"

"You have to rent a car no matter which airport you come into. Plus, the mileage is free. It just means we have to drive a little farther, that's all."

It meant we had to drive a lot farther, but that was fine with me. It felt so good to be out of prison, I could drive all the way back to New York with my head out of the window and my tongue flapping in the wind. But we fell into a deep and lengthy silence. Ten miles passed. Then twenty. Then fifty miles without either one of us saying a word. Finally, I said something quietly.

"I still love you, you know."

"And I never stopped loving you."

We fell silent again for another twenty miles or so. I spoke up in a tiny voice, almost a whisper:

"The quality of mercy is not strained. It droppeth as the gentle rain from heaven upon the place beneath."

"It is twice blessed," she said in that melodic voice she used whenever she quoted Shakespeare. "It blesseth him that gives and him that takes."

"It blesses *her* that gives and him that takes," I said.

She was silent.

"I feel blessed," I said.

"Me too," she said.

Before I knew it we were back in New York City. Where my reunion with Bianca didn't go quite as well as I'd hoped. For two years I'd pictured her jumping into my arms and smothering me with kisses, like a returning veteran from Iraq. Instead she was quiet and shy. At first she let me give her a long hug. Then she retreated behind her mother's legs and observed me cautiously from there. "Give her time," Caitlin whispered to me. I caught her watching me from a distance several times that first night. But when I waved her over to come talk to me, she turned away. After three hours of careful observation, she finally approached me and said something.

"May I make you a mustard sandwich?"

"Why yes," I said, "I'd like that very much. But only if you're having one yourself."

So the two of us sat on the living room floor eating mustard sandwiches, and I knew from that moment forward everything would be fine with me and Bianca.

It also took me some time to adjust to my old bed. Caitlin and I didn't have any problem making love there, that's for sure. We did that several times the first night and every night afterward for a week or two. But I couldn't fall asleep on the damn thing. It was too soft. My bunk bed at the Hoover Federal Correctional Complex had a mattress that was two inches thick with no box spring. I couldn't sleep on our cushy queen-size bed at home. So I started sleeping on the floor.

But that drove Gizmo crazy, because he wanted all three of us on the bed. So Gizmo would join me on the floor for a while, then jump up and nestle under the covers with Caitlin, then get back down with me. None of us were getting any sleep. Finally Caitlin got out of bed and all three of us slept on the floor. Bianca, who slept in a little nook off the living room, would join us in the morning. We slept like that for a month until I got used to living softly again.

But New York City is not a soft place to live. For two years at Hoover I'd harbored this ridiculous notion that I would get back to New York and immediately start working as an actor. What a pipe dream that turned out to be! New York City was as good as ever at taking someone's dream and grinding it like a cigarette on the sidewalk.

While Caitlin kept supporting our family as a waitress, I mailed out thousands of eight-by-ten photos, résumés, and postcards to agents and casting directors. The response was minimal as usual. For every hundred I sent out, I might get one agent to call me in for an interview. He'd make me wait in his reception room for an hour or two. Then call me back into his office long enough to say, "We're not really looking for your type right now."

Plus, I was facing a new obstacle. I'd sprouted some gray hair in prison and I was looking older than my years. Theatrical agents and casting directors weren't known for their tact. They took a certain pleasure in being rude. I started hearing something along these lines: "This résumé is mighty thin for someone your age. What are you, fifty? Sixty?"

"Forty-two."

"Yeah, right. Well, even if you were still in your forties, this résumé tells me you've spent most of your career on the moon. You got your MFA in acting from Yale twenty years ago and since that time you've had a few walk-ons in *The Sopranos* and another bit part on a cable television show that got canceled after a year. No movies. No Broadway. No off-Broadway. Just a bunch of equity showcases from fifteen years ago. What's your problem? Have you been in prison?"

"Well . . ."

"Look, I'm sorry, Mr. Volpe. I'm just not seeing enough evidence of acting ability to send you out on any auditions, much less sign you as a client of this agency. Even if I got a casting call for elderly Italians with blue eyes, I'd hesitate to send you out. Thanks for coming in. Good luck to you."

I spent hundreds of hours and thousands of dollars in postage to land one interview with an agent and that was how it went.

Discouraging? My first day in prison was more encouraging than trying to get traction as an actor in New York.

I turned to the way I used to make money before I went into prison—signing autographs at Fan-Cons. This was even more discouraging. Convention after convention turned me down. Had I gone from being a D-minus celebrity to an F-minus celebrity? After getting rejected two dozen times—including a convention in Gary, Indiana, for heaven's sake—I called the woman responsible for hiring talent at the convention and asked her point-blank why they rejected me.

"Are you kidding me, Mr. Volpe?"

"No, I'm serious. I'd like an answer. I want to know why my application was denied. Am I not famous enough anymore?"

"Oh, you're famous all right, Mr. Volpe, but not in a good way."

"What do you mean?"

"You're the guy who ripped off the Columbus Fan-Con and shot that *Star Trek* star in the foot."

"Well, I didn't exactly shoot . . ."

"Do you think word doesn't get around in this business, Mr. Volpe? Do you think I'd invite someone to our convention so he could rob the other celebrities and take a potshot at them?"

I had to admit she had a point. What a fool I'd been to think I could ever sign autographs at a Fan-Con again. I also had to admit to myself I wasn't an actor anymore. I wasn't even an ex-actor. I didn't know what the hell I was. I'd spent so many years of my life dreaming about becoming a rich and famous actor, I never gave much thought to becoming a man. One thing was for sure, though. Unless I wanted my family to starve, I had to find some way to make money.

Getting a regular job like a dishwasher or office clerk wasn't easy either. Do you know what the first question on nearly every job application is? "Have you ever been convicted of a felony?" Do you know what happens when you answer that question with a yes?

After six months of banging my head against the wall trying to find work in New York, I took the step I didn't want to take. The business card was exactly where I'd left it three years earlier—sitting on the kitchen counter. Caitlin, bless her heart, wasn't the world's best housekeeper. Neither was I. I dialed the phone number and held my breath.

Two rings. Three rings. Four rings. Finally, he answered:

"Who the fuck is this and what do you want?"

ACT TWO
THE CONVINCER

26

"It's Joey Volpe. I want to talk to you."

"Joey Volpe?"

"That's right. I want to talk to you. When can I see you?"

"If you want to talk, then talk."

"Is it safe to talk on the telephone?"

"My phone is swept every day. As far as your phone goes, well, you've already been tried and convicted. I doubt if anybody wants to bug your phone anymore."

"Tried, convicted, and served two years in prison."

"Take it easy, Joey. It's not like you're the first guy in the world to go to the joint for something you didn't do. Hell, I did two stretches in jail for shit I didn't do. But I kept my mouth shut and did my time. That's what you should do, too."

"I already did."

"So why make a fuss about ancient history? There's nothing more to talk about."

"I want to come visit you."

"To kill me? Joey, do you have any idea how stupid that would be?"

"I need money, Mr. Rosetti."

"Oh, don't get me started on that, Joey. You promised us a million bucks. Do you know how much we made?"

"No, I don't. I never saw a penny of it."

"What do you mean you never saw a penny? We sent you five grand by airmail."

"Yeah, well, the cops took that. They said it was evidence."

"Tough luck, kid. That's the way the cannoli crumbles sometimes. You need to suck it up and get over it. Get on with your life."

"I think you just sent me that money to set me up."

"That's what you think, huh?"

"Yes, I do. If you sent me five thousand dollars to take the fall, that means you got away with a hell of a lot more than that."

"I'll tell you how much we got, Joey, and it wasn't much. After we fenced the jewelry, it came to a grand total of a hundred and seventeen large. I've never seen so many fake Rolexes in my life, by the way. Half the diamond rings and earrings were fake, too."

"It's called costume jewelry. These are actors. What did you expect?"

Ironically, knowing actors as well as I do, I'd be willing to bet some of them paid twenty-five thousand for those fake Rolexes. They got a "deal" from some con man that was too good to turn down. They probably bought the watch after signing their first big movie or television contract. But who was I to judge? I made a bigger financial mistake after signing my first big contract. I decided to have a baby.

"What did I expect?" said Rosetti. "I expected a million bucks like you promised."

"Hold on a second, Mr. Rosetti. I didn't *promise* you anything. I told you that if we hit a big national convention like Comic-Con in San Diego, we could make as much as a million. This was just a little spin-off convention in Columbus, Ohio. It doesn't attract big stars who draw the big money."

"Tell me about it."

"I did tell you about it. I warned you about it when we talked in Philadelphia. I told you we should wait for a bigger convention. But you were raring to go."

"I don't remember it that way."

"Still, a hundred thousand dollars is nothing to sneeze at, Mr. Rosetti."

"That's the gross. We had expenses, too. Plus, in our business, it's customary to kick some up to your bosses. Carlo, Paulie, and me split the rest evenly. So I wound up with about twenty-five grand. Chump change. It wasn't worth the effort."

"But a million would be worth the effort, wouldn't it?"

"What the fuck are you getting at, kid?"

Long pause.

"I want to do it again."

"You want to do it again?"

"Yes."

"You're fuckin' nuts."

"Maybe. Maybe not."

"You spent two years in prison, Joey. You've got a criminal record now. You didn't make any money the first time. You're out of jail for—what?—two or three months. Now you call me and say you want to try it again. You're a glutton for punishment, kid."

"I think we can do it right this time. I think we can make some real money."

"What are you planning to do different?"

"Well, we'll hit a bigger convention for starters. Maybe even the biggest one, the Comic-Con in San Diego. We'll take advantage of some of the things that worked last time. After all, Mr. Rosetti, some of our tactics were perfect. We'll fix the things that didn't work. Plus, I learned a few tricks in prison that might be helpful."

"Now that makes me sad," said Rosetti. "It's just like the newspapers always say. Our prison system doesn't rehabilitate criminals. It just teaches them how to be better criminals when they get out."

"What do you think, Mr. Rosetti?"

"I think you're nuts. But I'm glad there are no hard feelings about what happened. We can take a meeting about it, if that's what you want. I guess I owe you that much."

"Thank you, Mr. Rosetti."

"Come to Philadelphia next Monday morning. You know the place."

27

I hung up the phone. Then I picked up the receiver and dialed another number. A familiar voice answered.

"Royal Bank of Luxembourg. Wealth Management Department. Beason speaking."

"Is that you, Nigel? It's me, Joey."

"Don't use that name," he said.

"What should I call you?"

"Beason. Jonathan Beason."

He said it like Sean Connery as James Bond.

"Okay, Jonathan. I'm just calling to say I want to put Plan B into effect."

"The plan we discussed in Arizona?"

"Exactly. I was wondering if maybe we could get together and talk about it a bit. I have a meeting with Rosetti set up for next Monday."

"Why don't you come to my office this afternoon at two o'clock? I've got a little acting job you could do for me if you're interested. There might be some money in it for you."

"I'd be very interested in that. Where are you located?"

"Our offices are at Fifty-five Wall Street, near the Stock Exchange."

"Fancy address."

"Don't be too impressed, Joey. By tomorrow morning, this place will look like a barn. That's why I need you to be on time. No later than two o'clock. The mark arrives at half past two and he'll be gone in an hour. Then we can talk about your Plan B. But we've got to tear down the offices by no later than five o'clock. After that I have to go on the lam for a few days, as you mobsters say."

"Well, I'm really just an—" I stopped myself. I wasn't an actor anymore. I didn't know what I was at this point.

I left the apartment before one o'clock and took the express subway on the West Side Line down to Wall Street. It took me twenty minutes to get down there. After all my years of living in New York City, I could count the number of times I'd been to the financial district on the fingers of one hand. When I climbed the stairs and got to the surface, I was a little lost. I had to ask for directions to Fifty-five Wall Street like a tourist. Some guy in a three-piece suit pointed me in the right direction. It turned out to be a few blocks from the subway stop. When I got to the building, I walked into the lobby and stopped at a security desk where visitors had to check in and get a badge.

"What's your name and who are you here to see?" said the security guard.

"My name is Joseph Volpe and I'm here to see Jonathan Beason."

"Which company?"

Oh, shit. What did Jonathan say? The Royal Bank of Somewhere. Someplace in Europe. Some small country. Monaco? *Did Grace Kelly own a bank?* Was she even still alive? No, it started with an L. Liechtenstein? Latvia? Finally, it came to me. "The Royal Bank of Luxembourg."

The guard punched some numbers on his telephone and said, "Mr. Joseph Volpe is here to see Jonathan Beason." Pause. "Okay, he'll be right up."

The guard prepared a visitor's badge for me and said, "Wear this at all times. The office is on the thirty-seventh floor, suite number thirty-seven forty-one. Bring the badge back to me before you leave."

It was harder to get into this place than it was to break out of the Hoover Federal Correctional Complex.

When I walked into the door of the Royal Bank of Luxembourg, something strange happened. In the first millisecond after I entered the offices, I could see a bunch of people lounging around, reading magazines, and chatting with each other. But as soon as they saw me, they sprang into action. They started answering phones, typing on keyboards, running fax machines, and in general, looking busy. It was as if the boss made a surprise visit after a long vacation.

Then I saw Nigel.

"Take it easy everyone," he said. "False alarm. We're still thirty minutes away from showtime. This is just a friend I made during my vacation at Club Fed. Joey's going to help us out by playing a small role in our drama today. Joey Volpe, this is my little band of Merry Men. Merry women, too, of course."

"Hi, everybody," I said.

They said "Hi, Joey" in ragged unison, then resumed the relaxed and casual postures they were in before I walked through the door.

"I'll introduce each of them to you later, Joey. But first, let's you and I duck into my office and rehearse your line."

"My line?"

"Yes, my dear boy. Did you think I'd give an actor of your stature a nonspeaking role? I'm afraid it's just a cameo. You didn't give me much notice."

Nigel led me into a gorgeous corner office with a 180-degree view of the Lower Manhattan skyline and the New York Harbor, including the Statue of Liberty and the Verrazano Bridge glittering in the sunlight.

"Wow."

"I know. Breathtaking, isn't it? It's a pity I only have a few more hours to enjoy it."

"As great as the view is, Nigel, it's just as good to see you again."

"And you, too, my dear boy. I've missed you. But you really must call me Mr. Beason from now on. Or Jonathan. We can't afford to make a mistake. At this point in the con, the smallest gaff can ruin everything. The mark will be skittish and looking for any reason to call it off."

"Yes, Mr. Beason."

"That's better. I've written your line on this piece of paper. Can you memorize it within the next half hour?" He handed me the paper. "Try reading it aloud for me once."

I read the line as Nigel had written it: "The strike price on the put option just fell to one hundred and twenty-three and three-eighths before the triple witching hour. We've got to move fast now."

"Excellent."

"What does it mean?"

"I haven't the foggiest idea, my dear boy, but it sounds lovely, doesn't it?"

"The triple witching hour sounds like something from the Scottish Play."

"Macbeth was a clever guy, Joey, but he wouldn't understand this. The triple witching hour is when three different types of security options expire on the same day. Let me hear you read it again."

"Let me try it off-book this time."

"Without the script? Already?"

"I've always been a fast study. 'The strike price on the put option just fell to one hundred and twenty-three and . . .'"

"Three-eighths."

"Right. '. . . just fell to one hundred and twenty-three and three-eighths before the triple witching hour. We've got to act fast now.'"

"Bravo, dear boy, bravo!"

"I'm still a little shaky," I said, "but give me ten minutes with the script and I'll have it down cold."

"Excellent. Now here's what's going to happen." Beason glanced at his watch. "About twenty-five minutes from now, we'll get word from downstairs that the mark is on his way up to the suite. My Merry Men are going to leap into action as you saw them do before. Three minutes later, the mark will walk through the front door of our suite and the receptionist will ask him to take a seat while she lets me know he's here. I'll make him cool his heels in the reception area for a few minutes—just to make sure he sees what a prosperous little firm we are. Then I'll go out and greet him."

"Where will I be?"

"You'll be stationed behind the glass windows next to the receptionist staring at a computer screen. After I've made some small talk with the poor bastard, I want you to act like you've seen something surprising on your computer screen. I want you to leap out of your seat and dash into the waiting room. Interrupt my conversation and say your line as urgently as you can. Can you handle that, Mr. Barrymore?"

"Of course, I can. It's a classic 'Hark, I hear the cannons roar!' line."

"A what?"

"Oh, it's an old theater joke. An actor gets his first speaking role in a Broadway play. He's only got one line. All he has to say is 'Hark, I hear the cannons roar.' He practices the line several hours every day: 'Hark, I hear the cannons roar.' For six weeks of rehearsal, he says the line perfectly: 'Hark, I hear the cannons roar.' Then finally it's opening night. It's the last act before the big battle scene and it's time for him to say his line. The sound man cues the cannons, which make a loud roar. And the actor runs out on stage and says, *'What the hell was that racket?'*"

"Yes," said Beason, chuckling. "That's exactly the kind of line it is. Just remember. We can't afford to make any mistakes."

"You can count on me, Mr. Beason."

"Okay, take your place out front. You've got twenty minutes to study your line. After you've said it, I'm going to bring the mark back to my office. He's going to leave here with a briefcase filled with cash. Then we're going to strike the set, as you actors say. You and I will have a few minutes to discuss how we're going to handle your Italian friend in Philadelphia before I leave. Okay?"

"One last question," I said.

"Yes?"

"Who would've said this line if I hadn't called you this morning?"

"One of the other guys, I guess."

"In other words, I'm indispensable?"

"Utterly indispensable, my dear boy, and you'll be compensated accordingly."

I left Beason's office and took my seat in front of a computer screen behind a glass window near the reception area.

The con went down exactly as Beason said it would. At twenty-eight minutes past two o'clock, the pretty girl playing the role of receptionist received a phone call from downstairs saying the mark was on his way upstairs. Everyone started shouting into telephones, printing documents, typing on computer keyboards. I was staring intently at my computer screen when the mark walked in the door.

"We've been expecting you, Mr. Wilson," said the receptionist. "I'll let Mr. Beason know you're here. Meanwhile, please have a seat. Can I get you a cup of coffee while you wait?"

The mark declined the coffee and sat down in a plush chair in the waiting room. He picked up a *Forbes* magazine from the coffee table, but immediately put it down again. He seemed nervous.

After a few minutes, Nigel . . . er, I mean Mr. Beason came out and greeted the mark warmly. They started making some small talk. I could hear Beason ask him about his flight from Nebraska and the cab ride from LaGuardia. That was my cue.

I pretended to see something on the computer screen that surprised me. I jumped out of my seat, ran into the waiting room, and grabbed Beason by the sleeve.

"Mr. Beason, sir. The strike price on the put option fell to one hundred twenty three and three eighths before the triple witching hour. We've got to act fast."

"You're right, Volpe, there's no time to waste. Mr. Wilson, if you'll just follow me into my office, I'll show you how our system works. If we place our order in time, you're going to walk out of here with a significant profit today."

Beason took the mark into his office and shut the door. Immediately, everyone in the office relaxed and stopped pretending to be so busy. I resumed my seat behind the glass windows. I turned to the cute receptionist and said, "How do we know when the client is ready to come out of Beason's office so we can start acting busy again?"

"Mr. Beason has a button on his desk that triggers a red light on mine. When that light starts flashing, we leap into action." She flashed me a big smile and said, "I'm Jennifer, by the way. Who are you?"

We shook hands and she held my hand perhaps a little too long.

"Joey. Joey Volpe."

"Italian?"

"If you prick me, do I not bleed olive oil?"

"Ha, that's funny!" She fingered a glittery bauble on a gold necklace that dangled just above her neckline. "So tell me, Mr. Joey Volpe, how does an Italian with curly black hair like yours get such beautiful blue eyes?"

Oh boy, here we go again. Three years ago, I would've killed the time by letting Jennifer give me a quick blowjob in the nearest broom closet. But I'd learned my lesson. I was in it with Caitlin through thick and thin now. Better or worse. Sickness or health. Richer or poorer. (Mostly poorer, so far.)

"It's funny," I said. "My wife has blue eyes, too. But our little daughter has brown eyes. I never took biology in college, so I have no idea how that genetic stuff works. All I know is that I love my wife's blue eyes, and she loves mine."

"Aw, that's so sweet," she said. "Well, Mr. Beason said I should use this time to call the furniture-rental company to make sure they're ready with the moving van. So I guess I better do that."

"Good idea."

After a few minutes, I felt that familiar tingle in my pants begin to subside. Marital fidelity was going to be a full-time job for a guy like me. But I learned the hard way that it's worth it.

An hour later, the red light on Jennifer's desk flashed. She said, "They're coming out." The office sprang to life again. Beason and the mark walked out of his office together. The mark was carrying a fat briefcase and wearing a dopey grin on his face. Beason, on the other hand, was betraying no emotion whatsoever. He had the kind of beatific smile on his face that one saw on funeral directors at a wake. They exchanged a few pleasantries at the door. I couldn't quite make out everything they were saying, but I thought I heard the mark say something like, "It will take a few days for me to sell some assets." And I thought I heard Beason reply by saying, "Take your time. Enjoy the St. Regis."

Beason walked the mark into the hallway and waited with him until the elevator arrived. When the elevator doors opened, they shook hands one more time, the mark stepped inside, and Beason watched as the doors closed. He watched the dial above the elevator door to make sure it went all the way down to the first floor and stayed there. Finally, he walked back into the office and said simply:

"I have done the deed." *Macbeth*, Act II, Scene Two.

Everyone in the office cheered, hugged each other, and exchanged high fives.

"Jennifer," said Beason, "call the furniture-rental company and tell them they can start moving stuff out immediately. Joey, come back into my office with me. We've got about thirty minutes to talk about our next project. Then I've got to make like Banquo's ghost and vanish."

"What just happened?" I said when I took my seat in Beason's office.

"Mr. Wilson turned a five-hundred dollar investment into five thousand by using our system. We gave it to him in cash, small bills, and he carried it out in a briefcase. Now he wants to turn two million into twenty million. But he's got to liquidate some stock and sell some assets to pull the money together."

"You put him 'on the send?'"

"Your memory always amazes me," said Beason.

"And your ingenuity amazes me."

"Meanwhile," Beason said, "our gullible friend will stay at the St. Regis Hotel on us. He'll be eating caviar and macadamia nuts until he gets sick to his stomach. A few days from now, his two million dollars will reach our offshore bank, and we'll call him to come in and make the trade. Unfortunately for Mr. Wilson, when he gets to Fifty-five Wall Street he'll find that this office is quite empty. Broom clean, as they say."

"You're a scoundrel," I said.

"Have I ever claimed to be anything else? Speaking of scoundrels, where do things stand with your Italian friend?"

"I told him I want to pull another heist at a Fan-Con. He wasn't very enthusiastic, but he agreed to talk with me about it. We set a time for next Monday morning at his office. Which I must say is somewhat less luxurious than this one."

"That's the difference between running numbers and running collateralized debt obligations, I suppose. How do you plan to handle that conversation?"

"I'm going to come right out and say I lied to him on the phone."

"He may not like that."

"It's a chance I have to take."

There was a knock at the door.

"Come in," said Beason.

It was Jennifer, the pretty receptionist.

"The movers from the rental company are here, Mr. Beason. They want to know if they can start taking furniture from your office."

"Just leave us these two chairs," said Beason. He turned back to me and said, "Go on."

"I'll tell Rosetti I really don't want to rob any more Fan-Cons, but I have a better idea. I have an idea that can make us some real money. Then I'll give him the spiel you and I came up with in prison."

Two burly guys entered the room and carried out the desk that was between Beason and me. Beason didn't seem to notice. He said, "When do you want me to make my entrance?"

"I was thinking I'd tell him that you happened to be in Philadelphia on business that very day. I'll suggest that the three of us meet the next morning for breakfast at the Four Seasons."

Two different guys walked into the office and carried out the bookcase, the credenza, and the coffee table. Beason didn't even glance at them.

"We're talking about next Tuesday morning?"

"Yes."

"That works fine for me. One last thing, Joey, I know I prom-ised to pay you for your acting work today."

"Oh, don't mention it, Nigel . . . I mean, Jonathan. It was fun. I haven't done any acting for years. You don't have to pay me a penny."

"I insist. Unfortunately, I can't do it today. Until Mr. Wilson's money comes in, we're tapped. We had to pay for all of this, after all." He swept his hand to take in the magnificent view of New York harbor outside the windows. "But I'll have the money by the time I get to Philadelphia. I'll write you a check for five thousand dollars."

"Five thousand? For saying one line? Even George Clooney doesn't get paid that much for one line."

"You're a better actor than George Clooney, Joey. Besides, you're going to have to use some of that money to buy some airline tickets for you and your Mafia friend. But the rest is yours to keep. And now, my dear boy, I'm afraid I must take my leave of you."

"You cannot take from me, sir, anything which I would more willingly part withal."

He laughed.

"*Hamlet*, Act II, Scene Two," I said. "Hamlet is talking to that old gasbag Pollonius. I think it's one of the funniest lines in Shakespeare."

"*Hamlet* is a tragedy, but there are some amusing lines in there. You do realize you just insulted me, don't you?" said Beason. "I've always wondered if Shakespearean actors actually under-stand the things they're saying."

"Who's insulting whom now? To tell you the truth, Mr. Beason, there's only one line I've ever uttered onstage that I didn't under-stand."

"What was that?"

"'The strike price on the put options just fell to one hundred twenty-three and three-eighths before the triple witching hour.'"

"That makes two of us," said Beason.

Then we shook hands, which somehow turned into a long and heartfelt hug. Even if your cellmate is not named Bubba, the bond between the two of you is strong and can last forever.

28

I didn't take the Acela train to Philadelphia this time. I couldn't afford it. I took the ultra-cheap BoltBus instead. Which made a two-hour trip seem like twenty. The guy sitting next to me was playing music in his earphones so loud I might as well have been sitting next to the subwoofer at a rock concert. The person behind me vomited outside of Trenton, some of which splattered into my hair. And the inevitable screaming baby was a few rows ahead of me. All of which made it very hard for me to focus on my pitch to Rosetti.

No, I wasn't crazy enough to suggest we rob another Fan-Con. As I told Nigel, I was lying to Rosetti on the telephone. Nor was I stupid enough to be planning a hit on Rosetti. What Nigel and I had in mind was something a bit more complicated and I needed a face-to-face meeting with Rosetti to explain it. I knew Rosetti would reject the idea if I tried to pitch it over the telephone. That's why I had to ask for the "sit-down," as we say in the Mafia.

When I got off the bus in Philly, I realized I didn't have enough money for a cab. I had to take a city bus to the Santa Lucia Hunting & Fishing Club in Little Italy. I knocked on the door, and just as before, Tony Rosetti himself opened it.

"Come in, Joey. It's good to see you again."

I walked inside and as my eyes adjusted to the gloom I could see that nothing had changed in the past three years. The same guys were sitting around talking, drinking, or playing cards. The place was furnished with the same ratty furniture. Perhaps another hole or two had sprouted up in the vinyl seat cushions with foam rubber spilling out.

My reception this time was much cooler than before. Nobody rushed up to shake my hand, pat me on the back, or ask me questions about *The Sopranos*. Most of the guys looked up, glared at me for a moment, and went back to what they were doing. Except for Carlo and Paulie who came up to say hello for old time's sake.

"It's Joey the Fox!" said Paulie. "Remember me? Good to see you again. How are you doing?"

"Good to see you, too, Paulie," I said. "How are your, uh, well . . ." I glanced down at his crotch. I was trying to think of a delicate way to inquire after the health of his testicles.

"*Stugotz*? They're doin' fine. Thanks for asking. Just a couple of stitches. Good as new. Spraying like a fire hose."

"Glad to hear it," I said, trying to shake that image out of my head.

"Hey, Joey," said Carlo. "How'd you do in the slammer?"

"Kept my nose clean and did my time."

"Good thinking. Where'd they put you?"

"Hoover Federal Correctional Complex in Arizona."

"Minimum or medium? They couldn't put you in max. You're a first offender."

"Minimum."

"Minimum? *At Hoover?* Oh, shit, man, that's fucking Disneyland. You lucked out. They put me in Hoover Minimum for one week on my way out to California. I thought I'd died and gone to fucking heaven, man. I'd rather spend a week at Hoover than some fleabag hotel in Atlantic City. I shit you not."

"I didn't find the accommodations quite so pleasant. But it could've been worse, I suppose, yes."

"Could've been worse? You've got to be kidding me. I'd rather spend twenty-five years in Hoover than one afternoon in Victorville."

"All right, all right, you two," said Rosetti. "You sound like you're telling the kindergarten class how you spent your summer vacation. Joey and I need to talk about something. Joey, do you want these two *cafoni* in the meeting, or just you and me?"

"Just you and me, please," I said. I glanced at Carlo and Paulie to see if I'd offended them, but they didn't care. I guess they were used to being excluded from meetings. Everything in the Mafia, like the CIA, was conducted on a need-to-know basis.

"Mike, bring us two espressos and some donuts," said Rosetti.

"You got it, boss" said a voice from the kitchen.

Rosetti led me into the same conference room where we had planned the Columbus heist. We sat down and Rosetti said, "Well, what's your master plan, Mr. Dillinger?"

"Mr. Rosetti. Tony?"

He nodded to renew my first-name privileges. So I said, "I've got a confession to make."

"What kind of confession? I ain't no priest."

"I lied to you on the phone. I don't want to rob any more conventions."

For a fraction of a second, I thought I saw fear cross Rosetti's face. He managed it well and it was gone before I knew it. But for a millisecond, I could tell he was afraid.

"Joey. Don't even think about it. You'll never get out of here alive. You want to make your wife a widow? You want to make your kid an orphan?"

"No, no, no, Mr. Rosetti. Tony, please. I'm not here for revenge. I'm over it. I did my time. I'm ready to get on with my life."

"Then why *are* you here?"

"I need money. I need it bad."

"I don't have any money to give you, kid. I told you. I only made about twenty-five grand with that stupid caper in Columbus. Plus, things have been tight here recently. Our other businesses are slow, at least until football season starts."

After pleading poverty, and without any sense of irony whatsoever, he pulled a huge wad of hundred-dollar bills out of his pocket. He touched his thumb to his tongue and started peeling them off.

"Look, maybe I could give you one or two thousand. Maybe three thousand tops. That'll help you get your legs underneath you after getting out of prison. I guess I owe you that much. But that's all I can do."

"Honestly? I'd love to take the money, but I don't want charity. I have a business proposition for you."

"What kind of business proposition?"

"I had a lot of time to think in prison."

"And?"

"And I realized we went about it all wrong. It was a mistake to rob the convention. There's not enough money there to make it worth our while."

"That's what I've been trying to tell you, kid."

"What we should do is hold our *own* convention."

"What?"

"That's where the big money is, Mr. Rosetti. The sponsors of these conventions make millions of dollars. Most of it in cash. They're not trying to fence fake Rolexes. They're making it legally. They don't have to worry about going to prison because it's all on the up and up."

"Joey, look at my face."

I looked at him. The broken nose. The pitted skin. The nasty scar down his cheek.

"Do I look like an event planner to you?"

"Hear me out, Mr. Rosetti. I think you're going to like this idea. You see, when I was in prison, I realized there's an untapped niche in the market for Fan-Cons. It could be worth millions to the first person who exploits it. But nobody ever tried this before. Nobody's ever come up with this idea."

"What idea?"

I paused like an auctioneer at Sotheby's before unveiling the featured painting of the evening. Then I said it.

"Gangster-Con."

"What?"

"A convention just for gangsters."

"You mean like the Apalachin meeting? That got busted, you know. A lot of our guys went to jail."

"Nah, I'm not talking about real gangsters. I'm talking about television gangsters. Movie gangsters. I'm talking about a convention for fans of mob movies like *The Godfather* or *Goodfellas*. Or television shows like *The Sopranos* or *Button Men*. People who read books like *Honor Thy Father* or *Casino* or *Wiseguys*."

"I'm not a big reader, Joey."

"Yes, but other people are. You told me you're not a big television watcher either. Trust me, Mr. Rosetti, that's what ninety-nine percent of the population does with their free time. They watch this shit on television, and they get obsessed with it. I've known guys who couldn't talk for two minutes without quoting *The Godfather*. I mean, why do you think I can sign autographs for thirty-five bucks a pop?"

"I've wondered about that myself."

"People just want to get close to it, that's why. I wasn't even a big star. I had a few walk-on roles. It's fame by association, I guess. They want a little of that glitz and glitter to rub off on themselves. They go to Fan-Cons to get autographs, to get their picture taken with the stars, to get their silly little questions answered in the panel discussions. Don't ask me why they do it, but they do. We can make money off it."

"How much money?"

"More than a hundred thousand lousy dollars, that's for sure. More than a million. I'm talking about *millions* of dollars. I know a guy who sponsors these Fan-Cons. He's the richest man I ever met. He flies all over the world in his own jet. He has a hundred-foot yacht. He owns his own island in the Caribbean, for heaven's sake."

"Good for him," said Rosetti. "But I don't want to be in that business. It sounds too much like work. It sounds too—I don't know—*legal*. I like to make money the old-fashioned way. I like to steal it."

"One lawyer with a briefcase can steal more than a hundred men with guns."

"Who said that?"

"Mario Puzo. In *The Godfather*. The book, not the movie."

"I ain't no lawyer either. Thank God."

"It's a good idea, Mr. Rosetti. You have to admit it's a damn good idea."

"So go run with it. What do you need me for?"

"Mr. Rosetti, I don't have any money. I had to take the BoltBus to Philly. Hell, I had to take a city bus to Little Italy. I haven't got two pennies to rub together. I can't sign autographs anymore; I'm the guy who robbed the Columbus convention. I can't even get a regular job because I'm an ex-con. I need your help to get this idea off the ground."

"Why not ask your friend with the private jet for money?"

"I did! And he's interested, Tony, he's very interested. But he says he doesn't like to go into these things alone. He likes to share the risk, especially when it's a brand-new idea. He said he likes to use OPM."

"OPM?"

"Other people's money. It's a catchphrase they use on Wall Street. It just means that if you get a few other people to go in with you on an investment, you can spread the risk around. Guys like Mr. Beason aren't stupid. They like to minimize risk and maximize return."

"Me too."

"But Mr. Beason, the guy with the private jet, said to me, 'Joey, I like your idea. If you get an angel to back you on the initial investment, I'll take a closer look at it.'"

"I ain't no angel either."

"That's just another Wall Street term. It means the guy who puts up the seed money for a new business venture. The angel is the guy who takes the most risk, because it's an unproven idea. But the angel is also the guy who makes the most money if it works. He has the most shares in the business. You'd have to risk some money, sure, but the return could be in the millions."

"I don't know, Joey."

"Just do me this one little favor, Tony. Take a meeting with Mr. Beason. He's going to be in Philly tomorrow. He's willing to meet us for breakfast to talk this over. He suggested the Four Seasons over by the art museum."

"You told him I was going to meet him?"

"I told him I'd *try* to get you to come. He was glad to hear that. He said it would be even better if we had a real . . . a real . . ."

"A real what?"

"A real, I don't know how to say it, a real member of an orga- nized-crime family to take part in this venture. No offense, Mr. Rosetti. He said a man like you would bring more than just money to the table. You'd bring your expertise. Your experience. Your connections. He was excited about it."

Rosetti allowed a tiny smile to cross his lips. I could tell what I said flattered him. Either that or he was thinking that there might be some way to steal some money from Mr. Beason.

"Just breakfast, you say?"

"Just breakfast. That's all. You don't have to make any commitment. You don't even have to pay for breakfast. I'm sure Mr. Beason will pick up the check. Let's just talk about the idea with someone who knows what he's doing."

Rosetti let out a long sigh. Then he said, "Okay. I'll have breakfast with the guy. Why not? Nothing ventured nothing gained."

I'm sure he didn't know it, but Rosetti had quoted Benjamin Franklin while sitting less than a mile from old Ben's house.

29

The breakfast was set for 7:30 a.m. Which suited me fine because I couldn't afford a hotel and had to spend the night wandering around Center City, catching an occasional catnap on a park bench before some cop came along and rousted me.

My parents taught me that policemen were my friends. Since I got out of prison, I viewed them like flesh-eating zombies who wanted to kill me for no reason. Throughout the night, the mere sight of a cop car was enough to make me get up and walk to another park. I showed up at the Four Seasons Hotel in the morning looking like death warmed over.

Rosetti looked worse. Not because he was up all night wandering the streets, but because he wasn't used to wearing a coat and tie. He was wearing a plaid sport jacket, checkered shirt, and polka-dot tie. Even by the standards of the 1970s, it was a garish outfit, and that was probably the last time he wore it. Rosetti and I ran into each other outside the hotel.

"You look like shit," he said.

I resisted the temptation to say, "You too."

"Did you sleep in that outfit?"

"I didn't have money for a hotel."

"You should've taken the cash I offered you, kid. You could've stayed in *this* hotel."

Just then a stretch limousine pulled up to the porte cochere. Black and sleek, it looked as long as a city bus. The chauffeur popped out and ran to open the rear passenger door a few feet away from where Rosetti and I were standing. Out stepped the most elegant man I'd ever seen in my life.

He was wearing a dark blue pinstriped business suit, powder blue spread-collar shirt, and bright yellow tie with a subtle red pattern in it. A handkerchief in his suit coat pocket picked up the red in the tie. His cordovan shoes looked like they'd been custom-made on Saville Row. His socks were cashmere. It was an understated outfit, but he wore it so well, it draped on his thin body so elegantly, the effect was as if he'd stepped out of the limousine wearing a top hat, white tie, and tails.

"Keep the car nearby, Jimmy," he said to his chauffeur. "This will take less than an hour. And call the pilots to make sure they're fueled up and ready to roll. Have them file a flight plan for San Diego. I want to take off right after I'm finished here."

"Yes, sir," said the chauffeur.

I took a step toward the man in the suit and held out my hand.

"Hello, Mr. Beason. Good to see you again."

"Joey Volpe. How are you? You look . . ."

He paused to come up with a polite way to describe my appearance. I waited because I was curious to see what he'd come up with.

". . . like you've been working quite hard. I love to see diligence in a young man. And you must be Mr. Rosetti."

They shook hands.

"Joey has told me all about you, Mr. Rosetti. I must say it's an honor to meet a man of your stature in this great city."

"Likewise," said Rosetti.

"Well, gentlemen, shall we go inside and have some breakfast? I understand Joey has some ideas he wants to present to us, Mr. Rosetti, and I'm eager to hear them."

"Call me Tony," said Rosetti.

"Very well," said Beason, "and please reciprocate, I'm Jonathan."

As we walked from the lobby to the restaurant with Beason leading the way, Rosetti leaned over to me and whispered, "What does 'reciprocate' mean again?"

"It's like returning a favor. I do something for you. Then you do something for me."

"I know how that works," said Rosetti, chuckling.

When we sat down at the table, there was an awkward moment of silence. I saw Rosetti take note of the stark contrast between the way Mr. Beason and I were dressed—Douglas Fairbanks on his left and Charlie Chaplin's Tramp on his right. Like Fairbanks and Chaplin, we were business partners but not likely ones. He began by asking the obvious question, "How did you two meet?"

Beason and I glanced at each other.

"Shall I take this," he said, "or do you want to?"

"You go ahead."

"Well, as you know, Tony, I'm in the business of sponsoring popular-culture conventions, or what are widely known as Fan-Cons. I own the rights to Comic-Con in San Diego, for example, which is the granddaddy of them all. I also produce and sponsor about fifty smaller conventions around the country—around the world, actually. We have some in London, Paris, Berlin, and Sydney. Next year we'll be expanding to South America and Asia. Japan is a particularly promising market. The Japanese adore a certain kind of computerized cartoons called anime."

"The appeal of anime escapes me," I said.

"Well, some people might say the same about *Button Men*, Joey." He laughed. "*Chacun a son gout, n'est-ce pas?*"

Rosetti gave me a puzzled look.

"Each to his own taste," I translated.

"At any rate, gentlemen, I'm not a fan of anime either. But I'm not opposed to making money off of it, if you know what I mean."

Rosetti nodded. This much he understood.

"I'm not a fan of ninety-nine percent of the trash we promote in our conventions. Superheroes leave me utterly cold. As far as I'm concerned, fantasy novels like *The Hobbit* and *Harry Potter* comprise the most tedious genre of literature ever invented. Don't even get me started on zombies and vampires. I think it's among the most peculiar, and frankly disturbing, phenomena of the twenty-first century that we seem to be raising a generation obsessed with vampires. How in the world did that happen?"

"Perhaps because they combine romance with danger," I said.

"That's a good theory, Joey. You're a bright boy. But let me get back to the story of how we met. Even though I'm not a fan of most of the stuff and nonsense we promote in our conventions, I've always had a weakness for . . . a weakness for . . ."

"For what?" said Rosetti.

"Mr. Rosetti. Tony. I don't often find myself confused about the finer points of etiquette. But I must confess, with all due respect, I don't know the proper way to refer to your business. Is it permissible to say organized crime, or the mob, or Mafia, or what? Forgive my ignorance, please."

"We call it 'this thing of ours.' But I don't mind what you call it, Jonathan. If the question comes up in court, I'll plead the Fifth."

It wasn't a funny joke, but we all laughed anyway.

"Very well, then," said Beason. "I confess I've always been a big fan of the Mafia. Mafia movies like *The Godfather* and *Goodfellas*. Mafia television shows like *The Sopranos* and *Button Men*. Plus books, too, of course. I think I've read every book about the Mafia since *The Valachi Papers* came out back in the 1960s.

He mispronounced Valachi. Beason pronounced it the way most people did, the way Valachi himself probably did, like this: Valatchi. My father, the Italian professor, would've corrected him in a heartbeat. But I wasn't going to say anything. Rosetti, however, who'd been made to feel a little ignorant by the French phrase and the use of fancy words like *reciprocate*, jumped in to prove he was smarter than he looked.

"You said that wrong."

"What?"

"You pronounced it Valatchi. It's supposed to be pronounced Valacky."

"Oh, dear me," said Beason. "Thank you for letting me know, Tony. I've been saying it wrong for forty years. I'm sure you've spared me some dreadful embarrassment in the future."

"No problem," said Rosetti. "Valachi himself probably said it wrong. Some of these wiseguys can't speak Italian worth shit. The only words they know have to do with food."

"At any rate," said Beason. "Back to the story of how I met Joey. I was at the Fan-Con in St. Louis when I heard that one of the actors from *Button Men* was in the exhibit hall signing autographs. I was a huge fan of *Button Men*."

"So you were the one!" I said.

That line never failed to get a laugh. I wish I had more opportunities to use it.

"Yes, my dear boy, I'm afraid there were far too few of us, because it was a great show. To make a long story short, Tony, I went downstairs to meet Joey. I invited him to dinner that evening. We hit it off like a house on fire. The next day I gave him a lift back to New York City."

"In his private jet," I said.

"You have a private jet? What kind?" said Rosetti.

"Gulfstream Four. Don't be too impressed, though, Tony. It's old. But it's serviceable. I need to travel often in my business. The plane gets me from point A to point B without having to go through that dreadful security at the airports."

"They must have some security, though, don't they?" said Rosetti.

"Oh, yes, they do. But it's the difference between a tap on the shoulder and stop-and-frisk, if you know what I mean."

"Joey tells me you have your own Caribbean island, too."

"I'm afraid our young friend has a tendency to exaggerate, Tony. It's not an island. It's more like a peninsula. It's in the Turks and Caicos."

"The what?"

"Here I'll show you."

Beason pulled a smartphone out of his pocket and clicked on Google Maps. He typed a few words into the phone and a map of the Caribbean came up. He widened the map with his fingers until the Turks and Caicos archipelago filled the screen.

"There it is, right there. It's the area that looks like a little thumb jutting out into the ocean. That's my spread, as they say in Texas. It's about a thousand acres. I'd hardly call it owning my own Caribbean island, but it's lovely, I'll grant you that. When my airplane lands there, I turn off my cellphone, take off my clothes, and spend the whole weekend drinking margaritas and taking naps. If you'd ever like to go there on vacation, Tony, let me know and I'll arrange it for you. I'm so busy with work, the bloody place stays empty most of the time. I'd rather have somebody there enjoying it, even if it's not me."

"Thanks, I'll think about that," said Rosetti. "Are you British, Jonathan? I thought I heard an accent."

"No, not British. I'm American through and through. What you're hearing is that rather obnoxious accent one develops after suffering the misfortune of being educated at Groton and Harvard. I know it sounds horribly arrogant and aristocratic, but I'm afraid it's too late for me to change it."

"You remind me of a movie star," said Rosetti. "But I can't think of his name."

"George Clooney, of course," said Beason with a smile.

"No, no. An old-timer type movie star."

"Clark Gable, maybe."

"No, I'm thinking of somebody else, some guy who used to dress in a tuxedo all the time. It'll come to me. Anyway, maybe we should talk business. I've got to go soon."

This was my cue.

"Mr. Beason, I gave Mr. Rosetti the broad outline of the idea you and I discussed on the phone. To recap, I'm proposing the three of us produce a popular-culture convention called Gangster-Con. The idea is that we'll get all the actors we can find from every major mobster movie and television show from the past forty years, going all the way back to *The Godfather*. Some of those actors are dead, of course . . ."

"Natural causes and otherwise," said Rosetti, and all three of us laughed.

"True enough," I said. "But you'd be surprised how many of them are still alive. No, we won't get Al Pacino or Diane Keaton. But some of the bit players and the smaller character actors will jump at the chance because they haven't worked in years. We might even snag someone like James Caan. A ton of actors from *The Sopranos* will show up. Gandolfini is dead, of course. Edie Falco won't do it. But everybody else is fair game. Some of them we'll have to pay, of course, but some of them will come just for the autograph money. I can use my connections to get almost everyone from the *Button Men* cast. Plus, I think we can get some famous authors to come, too. Guys like Nicholas Pileggi, Gay

Talese—"

"Forgive me for interrupting, Joey," said Beason. "But I think I just had a brilliant idea, if I do say so myself. Before I reveal it, though, I must ask Mr. Rosetti a question to see if it's feasible. Tony, do people ever come *out* of the witness protection program?"

"Once in a while, yes."

"I thought so. Why do they do that? Isn't it dangerous?"

"Some of them just get tired of living like a citizen in some suburb of Sheboygan. They get bored. Or they run out of money because they can't hold down a regular job. Sometimes they even write a book and start doing book tours and TV interviews."

"So why don't they get killed?"

"Well, sometimes they do. But a lot of times the guys who want them dead are locked up in prison, or dead themselves. The guys who aren't in prison figure, well, it was a long time ago, it's water under the bridge, so why risk a murder rap just for killing a rat?"

"Excellent," said Beason. "That's what I thought. So here's my idea. What if we invited some real mobsters, or should I say ex-mobsters, to come to the convention, too."

"The fans would love that," I said. "Do you know of anybody in that situation, Mr. Rosetti?"

"I might."

"That's a fantastic idea, Mr. Beason. But to get back to the basic concept for this convention," I said, "here's the long and short of it. Until now most popular-culture conventions have featured science-fiction programs like *Star Trek* or *Star Wars*. Comic book superheroes like Spiderman or The X-Men. Or fantasy series like *Twilight*, *Hunger Games*, or *The Hobbit*. Gangster movies and TV shows have played a small role at these conventions. Usually, there are just one or two actors like me carrying the flag for the Mafia. But I believe there's a huge audience of Mafia fans out there who would flock to a convention called Gangster-Con. I'd bet my life on it."

"What does it cost to put on one of these things, Jonathan?" asked Rosetti.

"If you're talking about Comic-Con in San Diego next week, it's in the millions. But I would never spend that much on a new concept like this. I'd want to test it first in a smaller market like Denver or Cleveland. Then if it worked we could roll it out to the bigger venues."

"Las Vegas would seem like a no-brainer," said Rosetti. "I mean with the mob history and all."

"You know, Mr. Rosetti, you are absolutely correct. I hadn't thought of that. Las Vegas is a bigger market than I had in mind. But the venue is ideal when it comes to matching the theme."

Rosetti smiled.

"Plus, in Las Vegas, you have a wide range of different facilities. You can go with a smaller, cheaper hotel. Or you can go all the way up to a place like Bellagio. Which brings me back to your original question, Tony. As a test case, I would try to bring this convention in for under five hundred thousand in up-front cost."

"And how much could you expect to make in profit?" said Rosetti.

"If it doesn't work, we'll get our money back. So it's a low-risk proposition. Almost no risk. If it *does* work, well, the sky's the limit. Two million. Four million. Maybe as much as five million dollars."

"So that's a thousand percent return on my . . . on your money."

"Caribbean islands don't come cheap, Mr. Rosetti. Even if they're technically peninsulas."

"Can you really make that kind of money running conventions?"

"Have you ever heard of a man named Sheldon Adelson, Mr. Rosetti?"

"Sure. He's the guy who owns the Venetian Hotel in Vegas."

"The Venetian and many other casino properties in America and overseas. He's worth forty billion dollars, which makes him one of the richest people in the United States according to *Forbes* magazine. Do you know how he made his money, Tony?"

"In the casino business, of course."

"Well, you don't just waltz in and buy a casino with a home-equity loan, Tony. He got his start by doing what I do. He sponsored conventions. He started with one convention, in particular, called the Computer Dealers' Exhibition or COMDEX. It wasn't until he sold that business for a billion dollars that he started buying casinos like gumdrops."

"He sold the rights to a trade show for a billion dollars?"

"Almost a billion, yes. It's a lucrative business, Tony."

"One thing I don't understand."

"Yes?"

"If this business makes so much money, and you're so rich that you got your own airplane and island, why the fuck do you need help from someone like me?"

"Mr. Rosetti—" I started to say, but Beason interrupted me.

"No, Joey, let me answer. It's a fair question. More than fair, it's an important question and it deserves an answer. I don't *need* help from you, Tony, but I want it. And here's why."

Beason paused to gather his thoughts and Rosetti said, "Well?"

"You're correct when you say that I could afford to finance this myself. When I go to Las Vegas, I often drop five hundred thousand at the baccarat tables. Sometimes more. But I didn't get rich by being stupid, Tony. One of the things I've learned over the years is that in business you want to spread your risk around as much as possible. I believe in this idea of Joey's. I truly do. But I've had a lot of ideas I believed in that wound up going belly-up. If I'd suffered all the losses by myself, my vacation home would be a condo in Miami and my airplane would be a Cessna 152."

Rosetti nodded.

"Plus, and I'm not trying to butter you up here, we need your expertise. We need your connections. We need the wisdom and street smarts you've earned over the years by running a Mafia fam . . . an organization of your kind. I think your participation is crucial to the success of this venture. To be honest with you, Tony, I won't take part unless we have you on board. I've already told Joey as much."

"He has," I said. I don't know why I said that, I just felt like I hadn't said anything in a while.

"As I said earlier, we need five hundred thousand in investment capital. I will personally put up half of that. I'm asking you to put up the other half. If the convention does as well as I think it will, you'll get back two and a half million dollars, which, as you noted, is a thousand percent return on your investment. You can't get that kind of return on Wall Street, Tony. You probably can't even get it in your business."

"I don't know," said Rosetti, "it's really not my kinda thing. What do I know about putting on a convention?"

"You know more than you think you do," said Beason. "Look, I'll take this a step further. I hope I don't regret this, but I think it's the right thing to do."

Beason reached into his suit jacket pocket, and I thought I saw Rosetti flinch. I guessed Rosetti had been in some meetings where a sudden reach for the pocket was not a good thing. Beason pulled out his checkbook.

"I'm going to write a check out for twenty-five thousand and give it to Joey for seed money. That's ten percent of my total investment. I'm willing to lose every penny of that money if this thing doesn't get off the ground."

Beason pulled a Montblanc pen from his shirt pocket and began writing the check.

"I'm going to make this check out to Gangster-Con, LLC. That's the name of our venture from this day forward. Joey you need to file the papers of incorporation. It's easy, even for an actor. You can find the proper forms online. Then I want you to withdraw five thousand and buy two nonstop first-class tickets to San Diego. One for you and one for Tony."

"Why do you want us to go to San Diego?" said Rosetti.

"I want you to see my Comic-Con operation with your own eyes. I want you to see how big it is and how big Gangster-Con could be with your help. Trust me, Comic-Con will amaze you. I'll show you the exhibition floor, and then take you across the street to the Hyatt and show you our offices. You need to see how much cash we handle every day and how much of it . . . well, maybe I shouldn't say any more."

"No, go ahead," said Rosetti.

"Very well," Beason said. "I know I'm in the company of a man who understands how these things work." He glanced around him and continued sotto voce. "Frankly, Tony, I want you to see how much of that cash manages to find its way into our pockets without going through the books, if you know what I mean. That's another thing I've learned in business. The less you give to Uncle Sam, the better. Uncle Sam already owns plenty of islands. He owns Guam. He owns Puerto Rico. Hawaii. Why shouldn't you and I have an island, too? Just a little one."

All three of us laughed and when I looked up from my break-fast, I saw someone I recognized. Someone I knew from many years ago. The Four Seasons in Philadelphia is the kind of swanky hotel that when Hollywood stars come to town, they don't give a moment's thought to staying anywhere else.

Gwyneth Paltrow was seated five tables away from us. I'd worked with Gwyneth in summer theater twenty years ago. It was between my junior and senior years at Haverford and I got a job as an actor . . . well, more like an intern at the Williamstown Theater Festival in Massachusetts. Gwyneth was my age but light-years ahead of me in her career. She was playing leading roles at Williamstown while I was holding spears in crowd scenes. The cast and crew always partied a lot together, and I figured there was a chance she might remember me. Nothing ventured, nothing gained, as Ben Franklin and Tony Rosetti said. So I excused myself from the table and walked over to say hello.

"Pardon me for interrupting," I said to the two men seated with Paltrow. "Gwyneth, I doubt if you'll remember me, but I'm Joey Volpe. We worked together— "

"Of course I remember you, Joey." There was a touch of gold glitter on her eyelids. It made her eyes sparkle even more than I remembered.

I smiled and nodded at the two men, as if to say, yes, I belong here, too.

"You're the guy who embarrassed me to death by leading a drunken conga line through my living room in Williamstown."

The two men laughed.

It's not easy for an Italian with olive skin to blush, but I could feel the blood rush to my head and I assumed my face had taken on the color of a fire engine.

"Well, er, I . . ."

It was true, of course. Long story. Involving tequila shots. "Well, I just wanted to say it's good to see you again."

"It's good to see you again, Joey. Especially when you're sober. And dressed so elegantly, too."

The two men laughed again and I stumbled back to our table where Rosetti and Beason were watching the scene but weren't close enough to hear what was said.

On my way back to the table, I realized that from Beason and Rosetti's point of view, I had walked over to the table of a major movie star, someone who clearly recognized me, and I made her companions laugh with my charm and wit. So I decided to play it for all it was worth.

"Lovely girl, Gwynnie," I said as I picked up my napkin, shook it with a flourish, then laid it back on my lap, smoothing the wrinkles.

"Just as charming as she was twenty years ago when we had a little . . . well, I shouldn't kiss and tell, should I? Let's just say we had a great time together at the Williamstown Playhouse."

"I'm duly impressed," said Beason.

"What's that shit in your hair?" said Rosetti.

I reached up and found a dried chunk of vomit that was still stuck in my hair from the previous day's bus ride. I'd tried to wash it out in a public restroom the night before, but some of it was still stuck in there. Good Lord. As if the reunion with Gwyneth hadn't gone badly enough, I still had a chunk of puke in my hair?

Time to change the subject.

"Well, gentlemen," I said. "While I was chatting with Gwynnie, did you agree on a date and time to meet in San Diego?"

"I'm not sure about this," said Rosetti.

"Look, Tony," said Beason. "There's no risk in coming to San Diego. Consider it an all-expenses-paid vacation. The airline tickets are on me. The hotel is on me. Bring your wife if you want. Or maybe you don't. Those California girls can be very friendly, let me assure you. All I want you to do is take a look at Comic-Con, take a look at all the cash that's coming through our operation, then decide for yourself if Gangster-Con is something you want to invest in."

"Okay," said Rosetti. "I guess there's no harm in it."

"Excellent," said Beason. "Joey, you buy the first-class airline tickets out of the money I gave you, and I'll take care of everything else. Let's meet in the main exhibition hall of the convention center at high noon next Friday." He glanced at his watch. "And now, gentlemen, I'm afraid we must adjourn. I'm going to San Diego myself today to finalize my preparations for Comic-Con. Tony, I'm sure you have many important things to do. And Joey, you and Miss Paltrow may wish to rekindle your romance upstairs."

"I think she's married now."

"I'm just pulling your leg, Joey. Shall we go?"

We walked outside the hotel and the limo pulled up in front of us in a flash. All three of us shook hands and before I knew it Beason was gone. Rosetti and I stood there silently, still stunned by the presence of someone with such charm and charisma. A look of recognition crossed Rosetti's face and he almost shouted. "Douglas Fairbanks!"

"What?"

"That's who he reminded me of. Douglas Fairbanks. The silent movie star."

"You're right," I said. "He does look like Douglas Fairbanks. And guess what?"

"What?"

"I'm Charlie Chaplin."

I toddled off in the direction of the BoltBus stop in the bowlegged waddle that made Chaplin famous. I took one last look at Rosetti before I turned the corner. He was still standing in the same spot, looking both bemused and bewildered.

30

Bemused and bewildered.

That's was the look Rosetti had on his face as we stood in the middle of the main exhibition hall at Comic-Con in San Diego a week later. I would hasten to add another adjective—*awestruck*.

I assume I had the same expression on my face. As many times as I'd been to these Fan-Cons, this was the first time I'd seen the one that started this bizarre phenomenon.

Imagine you're in a cavernous hall ten times the size of the main concourse of Grand Central Station, or five hundred thousand square feet to be precise. Now imagine Grand Central during its busiest moment of the week. Let's say, Monday morning at 8:30 a.m. Can you picture the crowd of commuters in your mind? Good. Now multiply it by ten. No, multiply it by fifty. Multiply it by whatever number you need to get to one hundred thousand people. That's roughly how many people come to Comic-Con every year.

It's the same number of people who jam themselves like sardines into a modern NFL football stadium, although here they were in a single gigantic room. I couldn't move more than two feet in any direction without bumping into someone. I kept saying, "Excuse me . . . Pardon me . . . I'm sorry." Until I said it so often that I grew hoarse and stopped apologizing because. After all, nobody else was bothering to do so.

Do you remember the scene in *The Wizard of Oz* where Dorothy and the others were granted entrance into the Emerald City? With their eyes blinking in wonder and amazement, they walked into the town square and teaming crowds of peculiar people and bizarre sights surrounded them. It's the scene where the famous horse of a different color walks by, pulling a carriage. If the horse of a different color walked through the exhibition hall at Comic-Con, pulling a carriage while changing from purple to red to yellow, nobody would've noticed.

At Comic-Con it would've seemed normal.

At one point, I saw an entire Bat Family walk by me. The dad dressed up as Batman. Mom wore her Batgirl outfit. A teenage son dressed as Robin. And a tiny three-year-old toddler brought up the rear as Bat-Mite. As a parent myself, it appalled me. Would I have brought Bianca into a place like this? No way. I would've been afraid to lose her, which would've scared both of us half to death. I noticed a rope tied the Bat Family together. It made sure they wouldn't lose contact with one another, but also made it rather hard on Bat-Mite. He was the last person in a game of crack the whip. The little tyke was flailing from side to side like a water skier who'd lost a ski.

Hundreds of aisles, rows, booths, pavilions, and various crowd-control systems like velvet-roped stanchions and switch-backs divided the vast space. Thousands of people waited in long lines to get their hands on some swag. Something to buy. Or something to get free. Or both. I remembered Jerry telling me about the time he saw a sign that said, "Buy three *Star Trek* action figures, and get one Jeremiah Pennington free."

Here and there I saw huge pavilions devoted to the latest offer-ings of the major comic book publishers, like DC Comics or Marvel Comics, the big movie studios like Universal and Fox, and the hottest video game developers who had such colorful names as Naughty Dog, Black Isle Studios, and Insomniac Games. Then there were all the people whom this convention was intended to serve—comic-book dealers, retailers, independent publishers, artists, and writers. One lone comic-book artist might be at a tiny table with samples of his original drawings for sale, sitting under the shadow of the gigantic Paramount Pictures pavilion staffed by dozens of people promoting the corporation's latest movies, television shows, and video games.

I was so overwhelmed by all this I was literally speechless. I hadn't said a word to my companion for ten minutes. Finally, I broke my silence. "What do you think of all this, Mr. Rosetti?"

"It's fucking amazing."

"Just think of the amount of money changing hands here."

"Would Gangster-Con be this big?"

"Oh, no. Maybe half this size. Or even a third. But we're talking about the difference between making five million versus twenty million. It's still a pretty nice chunk of change, don't you think?"

He said nothing.

"Especially when you consider that your investment is only two hundred and fifty thousand."

"Easy for you to say. You're not putting up a penny."

"It was my idea, Mr. Rosetti."

"Yeah, I know. You're the idea man."

We stood there for a few more moments, taking it all in. You really couldn't take it *all* in, it was just too big. An eagle perched on the uppermost rafter couldn't see it all. My eyes turned up to the ceiling as if I could catch a glimpse of such a bird, and a fragment of Shakespeare popped into my mind. *This most excellent canopy, the air—look you, this brave o'erhanging firmament, this majestical roof fretted with fire. Hamlet*, Act II, Scene Two.

"Welcome to San Diego, gentlemen," said a familiar voice behind me. "And welcome to Comic-Con."

I turned and saw Jonathan Beason with a warm smile on his face.

His attire had changed from the smart sophistication of the East Coast to West Coast casual-style. He was wearing a cream-colored Armani silk suit with an open-collared patterned shirt. No necktie. A brown pocket square, puffed and folded, peeked out of his jacket pocket. Rich brown Gucci loafers adorned his smallish feet. No cashmere socks this time, his bare feet nestled into the soft leather shoes. He looked like a movie producer. No, better than that. I've met a few movie producers in my day and, frankly, they can't pull that look off, as hard as they may try. He looked like a wealthy Italian playboy sitting on the veranda of the Villa D'Este overlooking Lake Como, sipping a Campari and soda and smoking a cigarette. I don't believe I've ever seen a more sophisticated and stylish human being in my life.

The three of us shook hands.

"It's quite a sight, my dear boys, is it not?"

"Yes," I said. "Mr. Rosetti and I were just saying it's amazing."

"Let me show you around a bit before we go up to the offices."

Beason guided us out of the main exhibition hall and led us down another long hallway where there were a series of ballrooms, conference rooms, and meeting rooms ranging in size from cavernous to intimate. In each one, something interesting or unusual was going on. We poked our heads into a few of them and Beason explained what was happening or would be happening soon.

"This is a panel discussion of top comic book artists and writers," said Beason. "Stan Lee, Neil Gaiman, Allan Moore, and a few others whose names escape me." The room was filled with maybe five hundred people. Five middle-aged men were talking into microphones on the dais.

Beason showed us a somewhat larger room. "In about two hours we're going to have a panel discussion of *Star Trek* actors in this ballroom."

"All versions?" I said.

"All the way from *TOS* to *DS9*. Patrick Stewart and Bill Shatner won't be coming this year. Busy with other stuff. We're still expecting a packed house, though."

"Is Jeremiah Pennington coming?"

"Yes. Why do you ask? Are you a fan?"

"Personal friend."

I made a mental note to call Jerry on his cell phone. I wanted to figure out a way he could take part in Gangster-Con, even though he never played a gangster. I would feel better having him there.

"Next up is the big one," said Beason as we headed toward a grand ballroom. The line of people waiting to get inside stretched all the way down the hall and out the door.

"What are they lined up to see?" Rosetti asked.

"Tonight at nine o'clock, Steven Spielberg will be announcing his blockbuster film for the Christmas season. I can't remember the title. But I know that both Brad Pitt and Angelina Jolie will be starring in it. They'll be here tonight."

Nigel . . . oops, I mean *Jonathan* was doing such a great job acting like the CEO of Comic-Con he almost had me convinced. I wondered if he had taken the time to memorize the names of every star on these panel discussions, or if he was making this shit up.

"People are already lined up for it?" Rosetti asked. "It's still nine hours away."

"Oh, they've been lined up for much longer than that," said Beason.

I walked up to the teenage girl who was first in line. She was dressed casually in a T-shirt and jeans with holes in them, but her eyes were slathered with glitter makeup.

"How long have you been waiting on line, dear?"

She looked at her watch. "Twenty-six hours. We got here at ten in the morning yesterday. I think that's twenty-six. I'm not sure I'm adding it up right. I'm a little tired."

"You added it right," I said. "A little more than twenty-six hours, actually."

"Are you on television?" she said to me. "You look familiar."

"Well, I was once. A long time ago."

"Can I have your autograph?"

"Don't you want to know which show I was on?"

"It doesn't matter. Can I have your autograph, please?"

"I don't have a pen on me."

"I do," she said and she handed me a black Sharpie.

"Where should I sign?"

"On my back," she said as he pulled up her T-shirt.

I saw twenty other signatures there, but I didn't recognize any of the names. So I signed her back, above the bra strap and under her left shoulder blade.

"Thanks," she said. "What's your name again?"

"Joey Volpe of *The Sopranos*."

"Okay, cool. My grandpa loved that show. I can't wait to show it to him."

I guess I was a big hit with the senior citizen set. I could imagine the old guy's disappointment when he realized he had no idea who Joey Volpe was.

"Now that we've made this young lady's life complete," said Beason, "lets head over to our offices across the street and I'll show you the most important part of our operation."

"What's that?" said Rosetti.

"I'll show you the money."

31

We left the convention center and started walking northwest on Harbor Drive toward the Grand Hyatt Hotel where Beason had his "headquarters" for Comic-Con.

"Why don't you have your offices inside the convention center?" said Rosetti. "It would make things simpler."

"Having it in a nearby hotel is more secure," said Beason. "Quieter, too."

"But if you're moving cash from one location to the other, doesn't it make it less secure?"

"We have systems in place to make sure it's secure."

We kept walking along Harbor Drive past the Marriott Hotel. Like the convention center itself, the sidewalks and parking lots were filled with Wookies, Klingons, superheroes, vampires, and zombies. By now I barely noticed them.

"Why not put your office right here in the Marriott?" said Rosetti. "The Marriott is connected to the convention center. It looks like you don't even have to go outside to walk from one to the other."

"Well, the Hyatt is a nicer hotel, for one thing."

"That's a stupid reason," said Rosetti. "You're increasing your security risk."

"Trust me, Tony, the money is secure."

Rosetti shot me that nasty smile I'd come to know and hate. It meant he had something sneaky in mind. I could see the gears spinning in his brain. He thought he had an opportunity for a hijacking here. Rosetti had noticed something wrong with Beason's operation. But because of his greed he misinterpreted it.

We entered the Hyatt and walked to the elevators where Beason pressed the button for the ninth floor. As the doors were about to close, a short young man wearing a big fedora and pulling a large suitcase on rollers squeezed into the elevator.

"Good morning, Mr. Beason," he said in a high-pitched voice.

"Good morning, Mr. Ganymede. Everything going smoothly so far today?"

"Smooth as silk, sir."

Ganymede glanced in my direction, and our eyes met. I'd been looking into those eyes ever since my first year at Yale Drama School. I smiled. She did not. She was good at staying in character.

When the elevator doors opened on the ninth floor, all four of us walked down the hall until we got to room 917. Beason knocked on the door.

"Who is it?" said a female voice from the inside.

"It's Beason. Today's password: lighthouse."

When the door opened, I expected to see an ordinary hotel room because that's what it looked like from the outside. Instead, I saw a suite of several adjoining hotel rooms that had been transformed into a bustling office. Where there had been double beds, sofas, chairs, and dressers, now there were desks, filing cabinets, credenzas, fax machines, computers, and busy people scurrying here and there. Telephones throughout the suite were ringing constantly. Computers were making that distinctive *ding* announcing the arrival of a new email. A photocopier in the corner was running nonstop. The sound of fingertips tapping on keyboards never stopped.

The young man with the suitcase started walking toward one of the back rooms, but Beason stopped him.

"Ganymede, hang on a second, will you? I want to show my guests something."

"Sure, boss."

"Open the suitcase."

"You want me to open it out here in the reception room?" said Ganymede. "That's not procedure."

"It's okay, Ganny. We're going to break the rules this one time."

Ganymede did as Beason told him to. He unzipped the suitcase and pulled back the flap. When he did, Rosetti and I both sucked in our breath. Dozens of packets of crisp new twenty-dollar bills filled the suitcase. I've never seen so much cash in my life, so I couldn't tell you how much money was there. If I had to take a wild guess, I'd say it was at least fifty thousand.

"That's your fucking security?" said Rosetti. "One skinny, little unarmed guy with a suitcase?"

"I'm armed," said Ganymede, and he pulled back his suit jacket to reveal a shoulder holster.

"So you've got a peashooter on your tit, big deal." He turned and said, "I could knock this faggot over with a feather. No Brinks truck? No security guards? No machine guns? You're asking for trouble, Beason."

"That's the genius of it, Tony. Who'd notice a guy in a business suit rolling a suitcase down the sidewalk on Harbor Drive from the convention center to the Hyatt? A thousand guys do that every day. How would you know which one to hit? We use a different courier each day with a different suitcase at a different time. It couldn't be safer."

Again, Rosetti shot me a glance. I was sure he was planning a hijacking now.

"Okay, Ganny," said Beason. "Zip it back up and take it back to the count room, just like you normally would. Only this time we're going to follow you and watch what happens."

"Yes, sir," said Ganymede. He closed the suitcase and started rolling it back deep into the suite of offices. We passed room after room, each one filled with people doing various business tasks. They were so busy they barely looked up as we walked by.

As we followed the slight young man, Rosetti whispered to me, "That guy looks like half a fag. What the fuck kind of name is Ganymede anyway?"

"I don't know," I said. "He's the first Ganymede I've ever met. I think it comes from Greek mythology. Come to think of it, one of Jupiter's moons is named Ganymede."

"I don't like the name," said Rosetti.

"There was no thought of pleasing you when he was christened," I said. *As You Like It*, Act III, Scene Two.

"He doesn't even look like a man. He looks like some kind of transylvanian."

"A vampire?"

"No, a girl who dresses up like a guy. What are they called again?"

"Transvestite."

"Yeah, one of them."

Finally, we reached the last room in the suite. It was one of the most amazing sights I'd ever seen in my life.

The room was jam-packed with money.

Packets of cash were stacked from floor to ceiling wherever I looked. Most of them were packs of twenty-dollar bills. But there were plenty of fifties and hundreds, too. In the center of the room was a long table, where three people sat counting the money and making notes in ledgers.

"Welcome to the inner sanctum," said Beason. "This is the count room."

"Holy shit," said Rosetti.

"Wow," I said.

"But I don't understand something," said Rosetti.

"What's that, Tony?"

"Isn't most of your business done with credit cards nowadays? Even the guys selling stuff at little tables in the convention center were taking credit cards. I saw them."

"Very perceptive, Tony, and you're right. About seventy-five percent of our business nowadays is transacted with credit cards. This is the other twenty-five percent you're looking at. As you can tell, it's a considerable amount."

"Yes, I see." Rosetti was salivating.

"From my point of view, the cash business has a significant advantage."

"What advantage is that?"

"Until it reaches these three people you see sitting here, until they make a note in their ledgers, there's no record of it. As far as the IRS knows, all this cash doesn't exist. Ganny, why don't you open the suitcase again."

Ganymede laid the suitcase on its side, unzipped the zipper and pulled back the flap to reveal the packets of twenties. Beason reached inside the suitcase and pulled out as many packets as he could hold in one hand, maybe four or five of them. I guessed it was a thousand dollars' worth of cash. He handed the cash to Rosetti who, although surprised by the move, immediately held out two open hands to receive it.

"Here's a gift from Comic-Con to you, Mr. Rosetti," said Beason. "As a token of my personal respect and appreciation."

Rosetti didn't thank him. Instead, he nodded in the direction of the three people at the counting table and said, "What about them?"

"They're in on it," said Beason in a matter-of-fact tone. "They're well-compensated."

"It's the goddamn skim all over again."

"The what?" I asked.

"The skim. We used to do it back in the sixties when we owned most of the casinos in Vegas. Jesus, those were the days. Money was growing on fucking trees back then. Every month, my boss would send a guy out to Vegas with a big suitcase. He'd walk right into the count room, right past the security and everything. They wouldn't even bother to look up. He'd go into the back room and start stuffing the suitcase with cash. Nobody gave a shit. He'd walk out with five hundred grand, six hundred grand, you name it. Then the next month he'd come back and do it all over again."

"Did you ever do that?" I asked.

"Naaah, I was just a young punk back then. I was still robbing schoolgirls for their lunch money."

I wasn't sure he was kidding.

"After I made my bones, they let me go out to Vegas with the suitcase man. It was a reward for something good I'd done. When we got back to our room, the suitcase man—his name was Lorenzo, but we called him Zorro—he says to me:, 'Why don't we just take some of this cash down to the crap table. The boss won't mind.' I says, 'Zorro, the boss will mind—a lot.' He says, 'What the boss don't know won't hurt him.' So we pull about five grand out of the suitcase and take it down to the crap table. Then I go on the fucking roll of my *life*. I must've held the dice for an hour. When I finally sevened out, between the two of us, Zorro and me, we won about seventy-five grand. We put five thousand back in the suitcase for the boss and the rest of it was ours to play with. You wouldn't believe the shit we did the rest of that weekend. We upgraded to the presidential suite. We had hot-and-cold running hookers coming in and out of there. We got room service steaks and lobsters. Champagne. Hell, I filled the bathtub with champagne and fucked some girl in there. Jesus Christ, what a weekend that was."

Rosetti was lost in a reverie.

I looked at Beason, who gave me a thin smile. Rosetti had risen to the bait and taken the hook in his mouth. All we needed to do was reel him in. As long as Rosetti didn't spit the hook, we'd have our principal investor and Gangster-Con would become a reality.

"About this Gangster-Con thing," said Rosetti. "I'd like to talk with you about it some more."

"Fine," said Beason. "But not here. I know a nice restaurant nearby. It's about a ten-minute walk. Plus, I want someone else to join us."

"Who?" I said.

"My marketing guy, Charlie Scott. I briefed him on this and he's got some great ideas for promoting the event."

Beason turned to Ganymede and said, "Tell Charlie I want to introduce him to some people and take him to the Cape & Sword for lunch. He'll know what it's about."

"You've got it, boss," said Ganymede and left the room.

Charlie Scott was a genial, if somewhat nondescript, middle-aged guy. We shook hands all around. Then Beason said, "Let's head on over to the Cape & Sword and talk some more about Gangster-Con, shall we? I think you gentlemen will like the restaurant. The food is superb and the owner is a real character."

We left the Hyatt and headed north on First Avenue toward the Cape & Sword, whose owner, as Beason had promised, turned out to be an unusual guy.

32

When the four of us entered the Cape & Sword restaurant in the Gaslamp Quarter of San Diego, Beason did something out of character. He put his two index fingers up to his forehead like a bull and charged at the host standing in the reception area.

The host knew what was coming. He grabbed the nearest napkin and executed a perfect matador's pass, curving his lithe body into the shape of a C, while Beason's horns aimed for the napkin and passed harmlessly under the host's outstretched arm.

Charlie yelled "Olé!"

"You haven't lost your touch, Chris," said Beason.

"Well, it doesn't hurt that you're ten times slower and weigh ten times less than the real thing, Mr. Beason. Great to see you again."

"Chris Weston, I'd like to introduce you to some friends of mine. This is Mr. Tony Rosetti from Philadelphia. Mr. Joey Volpe from New York City. And Charlie Scott you already know."

"A pleasure, gentlemen," said Weston.

Beason turned to the rest of us and said, "Chris Weston is not only the owner of this fine restaurant, but he's the only American ever to work as a matador in Mexico."

"Well, I wasn't the *only* one," said Weston. "Just the best-looking. What brings you gentlemen here today?"

"I always come to the Cape & Sword for the moment of truth," said Beason. "Chris, I'm hoping you could kill a bull for me and give me one of your famous rib-eye steaks. Can you find a table for four without a reservation in the middle of Comic-Con?"

"For you I can, Mr. Beason," said Weston. "Follow me."

He led us upstairs to the second level. Along the way we had to dodge several waiters running up and down the stairs. After we took our seats, Beason said, "I rarely order for other people, but when I'm at the Cape & Sword I insist that everyone start with the mussel bisque en croute. It's the best soup you've ever had in your life."

Rosetti turned to me and said "En route to where?"

I had become Rosetti's official translator for foreign phrases and difficult vocabulary words.

"*En croute*," I said. "It means the soup has a layer of pastry baked on top. It's like *zuppa delle cozze in crosta*," I said, trying to think of some rough equivalent in Italian.

"Okay," said Rosetti. "When in Rome, I guess."

As we waited for the soups to arrive, Beason began the business meeting.

"I invited Charlie to join us today because he's the marketing genius behind Comic-Con. He's the reason you saw a hundred thousand people cramming the convention hall and flowing out into the streets and hotels. I briefed him about our Gangster-Con idea, and he seems excited about it."

"I'm very excited about it," said Charlie. "I think it'll be a big hit. I did a preliminary search on mailing lists and I believe we can find several million fans of mobster movies, television shows, and books. We can also have lots of fun with the website. Maybe a headline that says, 'We're going to make you an offer you can't refuse.' We've been talking about holding it at the Mirage Hotel in Vegas, where there's a shark tank behind the registration desk. So we can say this is your chance to 'sleep with the fishes.' Great opportunities for a Facebook page, Twitter account, and other social media."

"What about the financial side?" I asked.

"Well," said Charlie, "when you add up the out-of-town reservations to all the walk-in traffic we'd get in Las Vegas, I think we can attract at least ten thousand people per day, and maybe as many as twenty-five or thirty. If we charge just under two hundred bucks for a three-day pass, that's two million dollars right there. The one-day passes should go for just under fifty. Multiply that by twenty thousand people a day over three days, and you're talking about another three million dollars. So I think we're looking at a gross of about five million on an investment of five hundred grand."

"And if those numbers are too optimistic?" I said.

"That's the best part. Even if the event is a total bomb, I'm sure it will attract enough people to break even. So it's a no-lose proposition."

The waiter arrived with the mussel bisque en croute. It was a big puff pastry on top of a piping hot bowl of soup. Rosetti just stared at his for a minute, unsure how to attack it.

"Just take your spoon and break into it like you're digging a hole," I said.

"I know how to dig a fucking hole."

"Then keep swirling your spoon around until you find a mussel. It's like digging for buried treasure."

"Don't tell me how to eat, asshole."

But still he hesitated. When he broke the pastry crust with his spoon, a puff of vapor escaped from the bowl and the unmistakable scent of sherry wafted up to our noses. Nigel was right, it was an exquisite dish. I had the feeling that if I ever found myself with Nigel in Timbuktu, he'd know exactly where to go for food and what to order there.

After sipping his soup long enough to get the hang of it, Rosetti returned to the topic at hand. "So we're talking about a ten-to-one return on our money?"

"Exactly. Just like hitting a long shot at the track," said Charlie. "Even better, because if this horse loses you still get your money back."

"What if I wanted to invest *more* than that?"

I had to clench every muscle in my face to keep from breaking into a grin. Fortunately, keeping a straight face in a comedy was one of the acting tricks I'd mastered over the years.

"How much more?" said Beason.

"Let's say I put in four hundred grand and you put in a hundred."

"Absolutely not," Beason objected immediately. "You'd be cutting me out of the deal, and I was the one who brought it to you."

I said, "Well, technically, I was—"

"That's right," said Beason. "Joey came up with the idea. He shared it with me, and together we brought it to you. Now you want to run with it all by yourself? That's unacceptable, Mr. Rosetti. Besides, you need our expertise. I'm the one who knows how to produce this kind of event. Joey is the one who has all the connections with the actors. You need Charlie, too, the marketing guru who knows how to get bums in seats."

Rosetti turned to me for another translation. "Who's he calling a bum?"

"It just an expression that means to attract an audience," I said.

"How much do Charlie and Joey get out of this?" said Rosetti.

"Well, they're not putting up any investment capital, but they're putting in lots of sweat equity. So I think they should get about five percent each, don't you?"

Rosetti didn't answer. Instead, he made a counter offer.

"What if I put up three hundred and fifty grand and you put in one hundred and fifty? That means I'm taking most of the risk. If it's a hit, you still walk away with more than a million bucks. That's a nice haul."

Beason looked at the ceiling and thought about this for a moment.

"I'll accept on one condition."

"What condition?"

"If it's a hit, and we roll it out to other cities over the next few years, I want a more equitable distribution. I want to be fifty-fifty partners with you going forward."

"I've got a condition, too," said Rosetti.

"What's that?"

"I may ask some of my associates to invest in this thing out of my share. I'd like them to be able to come for free."

"Of course," said Beason. "Full room, food and beverage, as they say in the casino business. Plus free tickets to the convention."

"Good," said Rosetti.

"And just to show you I'm bargaining in good faith," said Beason. "I'm going to write a check out to Gangster-Con, LLC right now." He pulled a checkbook out of his sport jacket pocket. "And I suggest you do the same, Mr. Rosetti."

"I don't put my money in banks. It's not safe."

"Banks are extremely safe, Tony."

"Not the ones I've knocked off. They weren't so safe."

"So where do you keep your money?"

"Like I'm going to tell you."

"Suit yourself. But we're going to need your money right away. And I'd prefer it in the form of a check made out to Gangster-Con, LLC."

"What if I delivered the money in cash to Joey and he put it into the Gangster-Con account. Wouldn't that work?"

"I guess that would be acceptable. How long will it take you to put that kind of cash together?"

"Two or three weeks, tops. I know some people who might want to chip in. Subcontractors . . . wait, that's not the right word."

"Minority partners?" I suggested.

"No, these are all Italian guys. I don't want to team up with no *melanzane*."

"Well, what do you say, Tony? Do we have a deal?"

"Deal," said Rosetti.

All four of us shook hands and went back to eating. We were finishing up our entreés when Mr. Weston stopped by our table to say goodbye.

"So how was the meal, gentlemen? Everything to your liking?"

"I had the filet mignon," said Rosetti. "Did you kill that cow yourself?"

"I kill bulls, Mr. Rosetti, not cows. Bulls are more entertaining for the crowd. Cows like to stand there and chew their cud. It's not very sporting to kill them. Kind of like shooting a duck in the water."

"I've got to disagree with you on that," said Rosetti. "The less they struggle the better. Sneak up behind them and stick a shiv in back of their brain. They drop like a rock."

"Unfortunately, that's exactly what we're forced to do when the swords don't work," said the former matador. "If the bull is still standing after we've stuck the sword in him two or three times, the *presidente* says we've got to nail him in the back of the brain with a dagger in the spinal cord. And you're right, Mr. Rosetti, the bull always drops like a rock."

"What'd I tell you?"

"You see what I mean, gentlemen?" said Beason. "That's why I always come to the Cape & Sword for the moment of truth."

33

"Frank Vincent, please."

"This is Frank. Who's calling?"

Frank Vincent had one of the biggest roles on *The Sopranos*, although the bulk of it came in later episodes. He played one of the leaders of a rival gang of mobsters who sometimes worked with the Soprano family and sometimes battled them. He had one of the most visible recurring roles on the show until he was written off. And by written off, I mean he took a bullet in the brain. Then a car tire rolled over his head and squashed it like a pumpkin. Not a great way to go. I'd met Mr. Vincent during one of my brief appearances on *The Sopranos*. I was hoping this phone call might go a little easier than most of them had.

"It's Joey Volpe of *The Sopranos*."

"Joey who?"

"Volpe. We met on the set one day. We talked a little."

"What role did you play?

"Well . . ."

"Well what?"

He wasn't going to fall for the usual ploy. He knew the cast and guest stars on *The Sopranos* too well. I had to come clean about the role I played on the show.

"It was a scene at the Bada-Bing. I played one of the customers at the bar."

"There were a lot of scenes like that. Dozens of them."

"Anyway," I said, "it's great to talk to you again."

"What can I do for you Mr. . . . . what did you say your name was again?"

"Joey. Joey Volpe. Like a fox."

"What's like a fox?"

"*Volpe* is Italian for fox."

"I thought it was *lupo*."

"No, that's wolf."

"Oh, yeah. I knew that. What can I do for you? I'm kinda busy right now."

So I explained the whole Gangster-Con idea to him. I told him about the other actors and writers who had agreed to come. I told him it was the same sponsors who produced Comic-Con. I even said there would be some real gangsters there, some guys stepping out from the witness protection program, or who were too old to worry about appearing in public. When I finished my pitch, I could tell he was interested, though not exactly gung-ho.

"Maybe you should talk to my agent about this."

"I'd be happy to talk to your agent, Mr. Vincent, but most of our special guests are choosing to keep their agents out of this."

"Why?"

"Well, it's not really an acting job. Why give your agent fifteen percent of your money if you don't have to?"

"How much money are we talking about?"

Good question. I was trying to get some of these guys signed up for nothing at all—just whatever money they could make in the autograph line. But like I said before, Frank Vincent had a pretty big role on *The Sopranos*. Plus, he'd acted in *Casino*, *Goodfellas*— "Now go home and get your fucking shinebox!"—and dozens of other gangster movies and TV shows over the years. I needed him for a panel discussion in addition to the autograph room. It would be helpful to have his name and face on the promotions Charlie Scott was working on. I needed him to say yes.

"We can pay you a five-thousand-dollar appearance fee, plus whatever you can make in the autograph line."

"Which is how much?"

I had to stretch the truth a little.

"The sky's the limit, Frank. I've seen people walk away with ten, fifteen, even twenty thousand dollars. Cash."

Of course, those people were William Shatner, George Takei and Patrick Stewart. But Frank Vincent was a pretty big deal in the make-believe Mafia world, and he'd make some money.

"That's not too shabby," said Vincent. "All I need to do is sit there and sign autographs?"

"Well, some people are going to want to have their picture taken with you. You can charge more for that."

"How much more?"

"That's up to you. It's not unusual to charge thirty-five bucks for an autograph if they brought something for you to sign. If they didn't, you can charge another fifteen for your standard actor's headshot. Then if they want a picture taken with you on their cell phone, that's another twenty-five. We're talking up to seventy-five bucks for every person waiting on line to see you. If you've got a hundred people in line, that could be seventy-five hundred dollars . . ."

"You said more than that."

"I'm not finished. There are two autograph sessions each day and three days for the whole convention. You might make as much as forty-five thousand, not to mention the five thousand appearance fee. Fifty grand is a nice chunk of change for a week-end's work, don't you think?"

His chances of making fifty grand at this thing were about the same as me being elected head of the Gambino family. But I was painting the rosiest possible picture.

"When did you say the convention was again?"

"October fifteenth through the seventeenth."

"And where?"

"Las Vegas. At the Mirage."

"Expenses?"

"Full transportation, of course. Plus room, food and beverage. It's all covered."

"Let me check my calendar. I'm going to put the phone down for a minute. Hang on."

I hummed the theme to *The Godfather* while I waited for him to come back.

"Yeah, I'm free then. I'll do it."

"Great! I'll send you the paperwork today."

We spent a few more minutes on the phone working out the details. I hung up and looked at the next name on my list. Tony Sirico. He wasn't going to be so easy. First of all, he had one of the biggest roles on *The Sopranos*. Second, he was known to be a little gruff. Rumor had it that Tony Sirico really *was* a mobster before he went into acting.

I reached for the phone, but it rang before I could pick it up.

"Joey Volpe here."

"It's me."

The hair on the back of my neck stood on end, as it always did when I talked to Rosetti.

"I got the money together. You want to come to Philly or should I go to New York?"

"I wouldn't feel safe carrying that much cash on the BoltBus, Mr. Rosetti. Or even the Acela train."

"Good point. I'll bring it to you. No problem."

"You put that money together fast, Mr. Rosetti."

"People loved the idea."

"What people?"

"I got some of my friends to invest in this thing. I only had to put in about fifty grand myself. They're all excited about it. They can't wait to come to Vegas. They think it's going to make them rich."

I thought I heard him chuckling. "What's so funny?"

"I might've gotten my figures wrong. I'm not good with math."

"What do you mean?"

"Well, I sold a fifty percent share to one guy. And a seventy-five percent share to another guy. And thirty percent to somebody else. It adds up to more than a hundred percent, if you know what I mean."

"Mr. Rosetti . . ."

"It's okay. They'll never find out. I swore them all to secrecy. We take secrecy seriously in our business, Joey."

"Mr. Rosetti, isn't that how Bugsy Siegel came up with the money for the Flamingo?"

"Where do you think I got the idea from?"

"Bugsy Siegel took a bullet in the eyeball for doing that."

"Yeah, well, I'm smarter than Bugsy Siegel. I got it all figured out. I've got an accountant who can make it look on paper like we didn't make much money from this thing. I'll give them their money back plus a few thousand bucks in profit and they'll walk away happy. Don't be such a pussy, kid. You gotta take your shots in life."

"That's what I'm afraid of, Mr. Rosetti, you taking a shot. If they take a shot at you, they'll probably take one at me, too. I don't think oversubscribing your investors is such a good idea."

I didn't know if "oversubscribing" was the word to use, but I knew it was a risky strategy under the best of circumstances—even riskier when your investors carried guns.

"You worry too much," said Rosetti. "Look, kid, let me give you some advice that might be helpful to you as you go through life. You know, Joey, I look at you as sort of a prodigy of mine."

Prodigy?

"Everything you've heard about loyalty, friendship, fidelity. That's all bullshit. In this world, everybody is out for themselves. You may have a wife. You may have a business partner. You may have so-called friends. You may have loyal employees—or employees you *think* are loyal. But the truth is that everyone is looking out for his own self-interest. You live alone, and you die alone. Maybe your wife holds your hand while you're dying, but you know what she's thinking? She's thinking, I wish this guy would hurry up and die so I can get out of this shitty hospital room and grab a cheeseburger. You're alone in life, Joey, all alone. That's why you gotta get what's yours, and you gotta get it any way you can. Fuck your friends. Fuck your employees. Fuck your business partners. Given the chance, they'd fuck you, too. In the end, money is the only thing that matters. Money is the only thing that's gonna take care of you when you're sick. Money is the only friend who won't desert you when the going gets rough. Don't let anybody try to tell you any different. You know what I'm saying?"

"I guess so."

"Good. I'll come to your apartment tomorrow afternoon. Make sure you're there. And Joey?"

"Yes?"

"Don't be thinking about doing something stupid with that cash."

"Like what?"

"Like stealing it."

"I wouldn't do that, Mr. Rosetti. I'm not a crook."

"You're a convicted felon, Joey. Armed robbery."

I wanted to say, "Thanks to you." But I bit my tongue.

"Well, technically it was a RICO violation."

"I know. I can't believe they charged an actor with RICO. I'm still laughing about that. Who were you using for a lawyer? Moe, Larry, or Curly?"

"I'm glad you think it's so funny."

He got serious. "Don't even take a penny of it, Joey. Put it right in the Gangster-Con account. If I find out some of that money is missing, it's not going to be good for you."

"I understand."

"Or your wife. Or your daughter. Or your little dog. *Capisci?*"

"*Si, capisco.*"

"*Va bene.*"

And the line went dead.

ACT THREE
THE SWITCH

34

"Welcome, Gangsters!" said the marquee in front of the Mirage Hotel and Casino. The two-word message appeared in the same famous type font used in the Godfather book jacket and movie posters.

"Can you see the sign?" I said to Rosetti who sat with me in the back of a stretch limousine. "Pretty cool, huh?"

"Yeah, I guess so."

"We got top billing over the Beatles show and Terry Fator."

"The Beatles broke up, didn't they?" said Rosetti. "Two of them are dead, for chrissakes."

"Well, it's more of a tribute to the Beatles. It's a retrospective of their music, along with dancing and acrobatics by Cirque du Soleil."

"Sounds like a boring piece of shit. Who the fuck is Terry Fator?"

"He's a ventriloquist."

"Like Edgar Bergen and Charlie McCarthy?"

"Yes. But more up-to-date. Racier. He's really funny. I saw his show last night. Hey, guess what? He made a joke about Gangster-Con."

"What joke?"

"Terry Fator said, 'Did you know the hotel is filled with mobsters this weekend for Gangster-Con?' His little dummy says, 'Yeah, I had dinner with one of the gangsters last night.' Fator says, 'What did you have for dinner?' And the dummy said, '*Testa del cavallo.*' Fator says, 'What's that?' The dummy says, 'It's Italian for horse's head.'"

Rosetti didn't laugh. "I'm sick of *Godfather* jokes, to tell you the truth."

"Yeah, well, I thought it was funny. But the sign looks great, doesn't it? I paid through the nose for that sign, let me tell you. At first the hotel didn't want to put it up at all."

"Why not?"

"They gave me some song and dance about how Las Vegas has spent the last forty years trying to downplay its reputation as a Mafia town. They said nowadays, the city was trying to cultivate the image of a fun place to go for the whole family . . . blah, blah, blah."

"How did you get them to change their mind?"

"I made them an offer they couldn't refuse."

"You threatened them?"

"No, I just offered them more money."

"You're spending too much money on expenses, Joey. You're cutting into our profits. You didn't need to pick me up at the airport in a limo. I could've taken a cab."

"Maybe so. But all the actors and special guests expect to have limousines. So we made a package deal with the livery company. We've got five limos at our beck and call for the whole weekend. More if we need them. It's all one price, so it didn't cost me extra to pick you up at the airport."

"Still, you're spending too much on frills. I need to take some profit out of this thing. I've got investors, you know. I can't tell them it lost money. Guys in my line of work, they don't understand the concept of losses in business. They say, 'You lost money? Tough shit. Pay me back anyway.'"

"Speaking of your investors, are they coming to the VIP dinner tonight? They've all been invited. All the actors are coming."

"They'll be there, don't worry. They're looking forward to it."

"Me too," I said.

I didn't know if I was looking forward to it or not. The dinner was Charlie Scott's idea. He said, "Why don't we invite all the special guests to a private dinner the night before the convention begins? We'll have it at the steakhouse restaurant in the Mirage. It's perfect because the chef is Italian. His name is Tom Colicchio. The restaurant specializes in free-range beef. Grass-fed and organic."

"I'm not sure these guys are into organic food," I said.

But Jonathan Beason loved the idea. So we set it up. I invited all the actors from mob movies and TV shows who would be at the convention. The writers, too: Nicholas Pileggi, Gay Talese, and a few others whose names you probably wouldn't know. When I sent the invitation to Rosetti, he insisted that all the wiseguys he was bringing to the convention should be invited, too. First and foremost his investors, who were all big wheels in the Philadelphia, New Jersey, and New York mobs. Then a couple of other low-level soldiers and hangers-on. Paulie and Carlo would be there, of course. Plus, Rosetti wanted the refugees from witness protection program to come. We still weren't sure how many of those guys would show up; none of them had RSVP'd. I reserved four seats at the table for them anyway.

It struck me as a rather volatile group. I didn't want any fights to break out the night before the convention. But Beason and Charlie outvoted me. So the VIP dinner at Tom Colicchio's Heritage Steakhouse was on. We headed there as soon as we got out of the limo and checked Rosetti's luggage with the bellman. Rosetti's flight from Philly had been late and we were cutting it close. By the time we entered the private room at the restaurant, nearly everyone else had taken their seats.

I say nearly everyone else, because two seats were empty. Since I had reserved four seats for members of the witness protection program, it meant two showed up. Which surprised and delighted me, despite my lingering concerns that these guys might not fit in and play nicely with the rest of the group.

And what a group it was!

Charlie and I decided to use place cards at the dinner and alternate the real mobsters with the make-believe mobsters. We had Frank Vincent of *The Sopranos* seated next to Bruno "Fat Bernie" Bianchi of the Philadelphia mob. Angelo "The Little Angel" Santoro seated next to Gianni Russo who played Carlo, Connie Corleone's husband in *The Godfather*. Gay Talese, the famous author of *Honor Thy Father* was in the far corner chatting with the two gangsters on either side of him, Anthony "The

Killer" Moretti and Alfonso "No Nickname" Mancini. So it went all the way down one side of the table and up the other.

When Rosetti and I walked into the room, Jonathan Beason stood up, clinked his wineglass with a spoon, and said, "Gentlemen, may I introduce the man of the hour. The man who made all this possible. My partner and principal investor, Tony Rosetti of Philadelphia."

There was a smattering of applause and two or three guys at the table yelled, "Speech! Speech!"

I saw a look of fear cross Rosetti's face.

I'd seen that look many times before—stage fright. I'd seen it on amateur actors who spent months learning their lines and rehearsing a play, only to learn at the last moment that performing in front of a live audience is a different experience from rehearsal. I'd seen it on professional actors when they've forgotten their lines or made some other critical mistake. I'm sure that look has appeared on my own face a few times, too. A good actor is someone who can face the fear, work through it, and come out the other side in one piece.

One time when I was doing summer theater in Camden, Maine, I was playing a guy hosting a small dinner party with his wife and another couple. I had to open a wine bottle with a corkscrew and pour four glasses of wine. I wasn't a big wine drinker at the time and I had little experience with using a corkscrew. I managed to push the cork down into the neck of the bottle so no wine would come out. That wouldn't have been so bad if this had been a big proscenium stage where I could turn my back on the audience and fake it. But it was a tiny arena-style theater where nearly every member of the audience could see what happened. I heard one sympathetic member of the audience gasp, and two other (less sympathetic) members chuckle. Someone actually said out loud, "Uh-oh."

Then I had an idea.

I began miming the action of pouring the wine into everyone's glasses with a flourish. Everyone in the audience could see that no wine came out of the bottle and the glasses remained empty.

I ad-libbed, "Be careful now, my friends, and don't drink too fast. This is a very *dry* wine."

The audience burst into laughter and gave me a standing ovation.

Unfortunately, the speech that Tony Rosetti improvised didn't work quite so well.

35

"Oh, no," said Rosetti. "No speeches. I don't like giving speeches."

He wasn't acting humble and hoping everyone would insist he speak. I could tell he didn't want to do it. But the little audience of mobsters and actors wouldn't give up. They kept shouting, "Speech! Speech!" They applauded. They whistled. They stomped their feet.

I'm not sure why they were so insistent. My own feeling was, if a man doesn't want to give a speech he shouldn't have to do it. As I surveyed the little crowd their motivations became clear. The mobsters realized Rosetti was shy and unaccustomed to giving speeches. They wanted him to make a fool of himself. (I had to keep reminding myself these weren't the nicest people in the world.) The actors, on the other hand, loved speeches at events like this. They figured if people started giving speeches, it would only be a matter of time before they could give one.

Rosetti dragged himself to his feet like a ninety-year-old man at the dog track in Florida reluctantly standing for a recording of "The Star Spangled Banner." When he did, everyone cheered. They fell silent to hear what he would say.

As Rosetti stood, I could tell from the blank look on his face he had no idea what to say. He stared at the group for what seemed like a full minute, which is almost an eternity when a performer is facing an audience alone. He started to mumble something. I was surprised to hear my own name was the first thing that came out of his mouth.

"Joey Volpe, I want to thank you for organizing this meeting here today. And also the other associates. We have with us Angelo Santoro from New York. Anthony Moretti from Atlantic City. Alfonso Mancini from north Jersey. And Mario Spagnuola from my own hometown of Philadelphia. And all the other associates and actors who came from as far away as Kansas City, California, and all the other territories of the United States. Thank you for coming."

This was starting to sound familiar.

"How did things ever get so far? It was so unfortunate. So unnecessary. Tattaglia lost a son. And I lost a son. We're quits."

At this point, a burst of laughter drowned out Rosetti. He was quoting Vito Corleone from *The Godfather*. It's the scene where the heads of the five families came together to call a truce. This from a guy who fifteen minutes ago had told me he was sick of *Godfather* jokes.

The mobsters and actors at the table ate it up. In fact, they ate it up too much. They started shouting famous lines from the scene at Rosetti.

"Hey, Tony," said Frank Vincent from *The Sopranos*. "You can present us with a bill for the dinner. After all, we are not communists!"

Big laugh.

"Of course we'll pay the bill," said Jonathan Beason. "We don't have to make assurances to each other as if we were lawyers!"

Another laugh. I was surprised that Mr. Beason had seen *The Godfather*, much less memorized it. He struck me as the kind of person who would prefer *The Sting*.

"We're all grateful to Don Rosetti for calling this meeting," said Alfonso Mancini from Jersey. "He's a modest man. He'll always listen to reason."

"He's too modest," said Gianni Russo, who was actually *in* the movie. "He had all the judges and politicians in his pocket. He refused to share them."

From that point forward, the whole thing devolved into chaos. Rosetti lost control of his audience.

As every actor knows, an audience is a mercurial thing. On the one hand, they're all rooting for you and want you to succeed. But they have a nose for blood and sweat that would put a hyena to shame. They can smell weakness, uncertainty, and fear before the actor himself feels it. And they *will* turn on you. It's like the crowd at a bullfight. They want to see beautifully executed passes and shout, "Olé!" They want to see the sword go into the bull's back like a knife through butter and watch it drop dead in an instant. But as soon as the first sword bounces off the bull's shoulder blade, they turn on the matador like a fickle girlfriend. They boo. They whistle. They make catcalls. Now they're rooting for the bull and hoping he gores the matador to death. All they want to see is blood and they don't care whose it is. Every audience is like the crowd at a bullfight, a prizefight, or a cockfight—even if they're dressed in tuxedos and attending the ballet or an opera at the Met. Yes, they want to see excellence, talent, and artistry on display. But they're just as happy to see blood, guts, and tears. That's what makes acting such an exhilarating profession. It's also why opinion polls say most people fear speaking in front of an audience more than they fear death itself.

While the group around the dinner table continued to laugh and shout quotations from *The Godfather*, Rosetti sat down next to me, deflated. He said nothing for a long time. Then he turned to me and whispered, "I'm worried, Joey."

"Don't worry about it, Mr. Rosetti. You thanked them for coming and welcomed them. That's all you need to do in a speech like that. Heck, you even made them laugh. They're having a good time. You did great."

"No, not about that. I'm worried about the convention."

"Worried about what exactly?"

"I'm worried nobody's going to come tomorrow."

"Ah, please don't worry about that. Charlie tells me the advance reservations have exceeded our goals by a mile. The hotel is filled with gangster fans. If the foot traffic is even *half* what we expect, we're going to make out like bandits." (Perhaps an unfortunate choice of words on my part.)

"That's just it, Joey. When we walked through the lobby and the casino on the way to the restaurant, I didn't see a single fan. I didn't see anybody dressed up like Spiderman, or Superman, or Captain Marvel. I didn't even see anybody in *Star Trek* uniforms. It didn't look anything like Comic-Con in San Diego, Joey. I don't think there's anybody here. I think it's going to be a big bomb."

"Mr. Rosetti, Tony, listen to me. This is Gangster-Con, not Comic-Con. It's a *gangster* convention. Remember the big sign outside that said, 'Welcome, Gangsters.' Of course nobody here is dressed up in *Star Trek* uniforms or superhero outfits. The people are fans of gangster movies."

"So how come they're not dressed up like gangsters?"

"They're not into that kind of thing, Mr. Rosetti. They're older, for the most part, in their forties or fifties. They've got their wives with them. Not the type to slather their faces with greasepaint and glitter. They've got beer bellies. They dress in cargo pants and golf shirts and big white running shoes."

"Well, I did see a lot of fat guys dressed in cargo pants and golf shirts."

"See what I mean? The hotel is filled with them. After dinner, go outside and look around. You'll see thousands of them. Tens of thousands. And most of them are coming to Gangster-Con tomorrow. We're all going to be rich by this time tomorrow night, Mr. Rosetti. Relax this evening and have a good time."

Rosetti sat to the right of me, and my old friend Jeremiah Pennington was at my left. You may be wondering on what pretext I invited the *Star Trek* actor to this gangster convention. Well, there was a computerized device on the later versions of *Star Trek* called the holodeck. It was a virtual-reality game that crew members on the starship used for recreation and entertainment. They could program the holodeck to put themselves into any scenario they could imagine. If they wanted to take part in the shootout at the OK Corral, they'd give the holodeck a few instructions and—*poof!*—they were holding a six-shooter and staring Wyatt Earp in the face. In one episode, Jeremiah Pennington's character wanted to go back to the Prohibition era in Chicago and play a gangster who had a violent confrontation with Al Capone. I never saw the episode myself. The truth is, I wanted Jerry to be there for moral support.

Steven Dubois had never played a gangster, not even in the holodeck. But believe it or not, I invited him to Gangster-Con, too. Amazingly, he accepted. Despite the fact that I was responsible for him getting shot in the foot. He was either a very forgiving guy, or he couldn't pass up one of these Fan-Cons. *Why did I invite him?* Well, it wouldn't be a real Fan-Con without him. At the moment, he was sitting between two mobsters and talking to them about the relative merits of Bruno Magli versus Salvatore Ferragamo shoes.

I turned to Rosetti and said, "Mr. Rosetti, have you met my old friend, Jeremiah Pennington of *Star Trek* fame?"

"No, I haven't," said Rosetti, and he reached across me to shake Jerry's hand.

"An honor to meet you, sir," said Pennington. "Joey's been telling me all about you."

"Jerry, Mr. Rosetti is worried because nobody in the hotel is dressed up in costumes."

"Don't worry about that, Mr. Rosetti" said Jerry. "Only sci-fi and superhero fans engage in that kind of foolishness. Gangster fans have more class."

"Yeah, that's what Joey just told me. I hope he's right."

"Oh, he's right, Mr. Rosetti. Trust me, I've been to a million of these conventions over the years."

After a few minutes, Rosetti started talking to the guy on the other side of him, so Jerry and I had a moment to speak in private. "Are you ready for tomorrow?"

"Yep. All set."

"You know exactly what to do?"

"I do."

"When I give you the sign, that's when you start talking to the other actors. But not before I give you the sign."

"I know, Joey, I know."

"I hope you don't mind the way I keep going over this business."

"No, not at all."

"It's an old habit. I spent my whole life trying not to be careless."

"Now *you're* quoting from *The Godfather.*"

I didn't realize it, but I was. I was quoting from the scene where Michael and his father are talking in the garden. So we both laughed.

Rosetti touched me on the shoulder, and I felt a chill go down my spine. Had he heard what Jerry and I were talking about?

Fortunately, no.

"Joey, I want to introduce you to somebody. An associate of mine from Philadelphia. Mario Spagnuola. On the street, they call him Spags."

I reached in front of Rosetti and shook hands with the mobster on his right.

"Pleased to meet you, sir," I said.

I hadn't seen Spags since the day I left the Hoover Federal Correctional Complex. But I'd talked to him over the phone several times. He was helping me and Nigel on this caper. Not so much for the money, although we were cutting him in for a nice piece of the action. I think he liked the idea of screwing Rosetti.

"Likewise. What did you say your last name was?"

"Volpe. Like a fox."

"You know, Spags, Joey lives in New York City now," said Rosetti. "But he's from Philly originally. Maybe you two have met before."

"Where in Philly are you from?" said Spagnuola.

"Gladwyne."

"Gladwyne. Ha! The only time I ever got to Gladwyne was to crack a safe in some rich guy's house. I live in Little Italy, near the cheesesteak restaurants."

"That's ironic," I said. "The only time I ever got to Little Italy was to have a wooder ice."

"A wooder ice?" Spagnuola laughed and turned to Rosetti. "You're right, this guy really is from Philly."

"Come to think of it," said Rosetti. "You two might have met in the joint. Spags, weren't you at Hoover in Arizona for a few months?"

"Yeah, I was there until my lawyer sprung me on a technicality."

"Joey was there, too. Two years. He got mixed up in some armed robbery deal. Not his fault. Lousy lawyer. Did you two ever run into each other out there?"

"I don't think so," I said. "Which building were you in at Hoover, Mr. Spagnuola?"

"Call me Spags. Everybody does. I was in max."

"Oh, well, that explains it. I was in minimum."

"You were in minimum? Lucky son of a bitch. I heard that was like doing your time at the Rittenhouse Hotel."

"Well, it wasn't quite that nice. It could've been worse, I guess."

"It's like old home week here," said Rosetti. "Hey, Joey, could you do me a favor?"

Another chill went down my spine. There was nothing like having a gangster ask you for a favor. The only thing worse was having a gangster *do* you a favor.

"After dinner is over, can we take a peek at the ballroom?"

"Well, Mr. Rosetti, they're still working on it, you know. The construction crews and volunteers are going to be working all night. We'll be lucky if it's finished by the time we open the doors tomorrow morning."

I didn't know what to expect to find in the grand ballroom at the Mirage. Beason was in charge of all the preparations there. When I poked my nose in the ballroom after I arrived at the hotel that morning, it was empty except for some cardboard boxes and folding tables. I wasn't sure how much Beason was able to do, or planned to do, in the meantime. If Rosetti saw an empty ballroom a few hours before the opening of the convention, he'd shoot me on the spot.

"I still want to see it," said Rosetti. "It'll make the whole thing seem more real to me."

"Okay."

"Right now, it seems like a mirage."

"It *is* a mirage," said Spagnuola. "The Mirage Hotel and Casino." Rosetti laughed.

I didn't.

36

The rest of the dinner party went well. The actors and mobsters got along famously. The mobsters were fascinated by the actors. No surprise there. What surprised me was that the actors paid some attention to the mobsters, too.

Actors usually don't show the slightest interest in what someone outside of show business does—unless they're paid to follow somebody to prepare for a role. Even then, they only pretend to be interested. Sometimes they ask a reporter or a publicist to follow *them* around, saying, in effect: "Watch me while I watch this person."

At Collicchio's Steakhouse, both the real gangsters and the fake gangsters seemed to enjoy one another's company. That is, until I overheard one of the Atlantic City gangsters come up to Rosetti and say, "Tony, can I speak with you man-to-man?"

"Sure, go ahead."

"Why did you sit me next to a fanook?"

"What fanook?"

"The little French faggot over there." He pointed to Steven Dubois.

"How do you know he's a fanook?"

"I saw him on *Oprah*, that's how."

"Look, Pete, it's not fanook. It's *finocchio*. If you're going to say these words, learn how to speak Italian for chrissakes."

"I didn't say he was a puppet. I said he was a queer."

"Not Pinocchio. Finocchio!"

"Pinocchio, finocchio, what difference does it make? He's a fag and I don't want to sit next to him."

"If you're watching *Oprah* in the middle of the day, maybe you're the fanook. Did you ever think about that? If it bugs you so much, talk to the guy on the other side of you."

"The guy on the other side is a rat. He sold out Sonny Corleone. He beat up his wife just so Sonny would leave the compound and take the causeway into Manhattan."

He was talking about Gianni Russo, who played Carlo in *The Godfather*.

"It's a movie for chrissakes," said Rosetti. "Sit down and shut the fuck up. Eat your cannoli or I'll stick it in your face."

We were four hours into the evening at this point, and I think we were all suffering from the barbershop-mirror effect. Or maybe it was the funhouse-mirror effect. Nobody could tell what was real and what wasn't. Was this an actor? Or a mobster? Or an actor playing a mobster? Or a mobster playing an actor who was playing a mobster? What with the infinitely receding reflections of reality, plus all the red wine we were drinking, not to mention my anxiety, I was getting a headache and wanted to wrap it up.

Then one of the waiters spilled a few drops of wine on Dennis Farina's cashmere sport coat. The waiter got so scared I thought he was going to shit his pants. He kept saying, "I'm sorry, sir, I'm so sorry, send me the bill, I'll make it up to you. I'll get it dry-cleaned. No, I'll buy you a new one."

Dennis was a bit of a clothes horse, and I could tell the accident had annoyed him. But he was gracious and said, "Don't worry about it, kid." The waiter, however, broke down in tears. He got down on his hands and knees and begged for forgiveness. He thought Dennis was going to whack him. I had to call him over and reassure him that Dennis Farina was just an actor. I said, "The worst thing he can do to you is stiff you on the tip."

Then I turned to Rosetti and said, "I think we should call it a night."

"*D'accordo.*"

"Don't worry about the bill," I said. "I already paid it from the Gangster-Con account."

"What did I tell you about keeping the expenses down, Joey?"

"What do you want me to do, Mr. Rosetti? Ask the waiter to write separate checks for twenty-five actors and twenty-five Mafiosi?"

"We didn't even need to have dinner at such a fancy place. We coulda took them all to McDonald's."

"It's expected, Mr. Rosetti. It's one of the perks. It's one of the ways you get actors to come to these conventions. They'll do anything for a free meal."

"*Alora*," said Rosetti, which was the Italian equivalent of *whatever*.

Then he said, "*Andiamo*. I want you to show me the ballroom, remember?"

"Don't you want to say anything to our guests before we go?"

"Hell no. No more speeches. When they run out of wine they'll go up to their rooms. We're going to see them in the morning anyway. Let's go."

The ballroom was located on the other side of the casino. Which was typical of every hotel in Las Vegas. No matter where you wanted to go, it was always on the other side of the casino. If you got up in the middle of the night to take a piss, you had to go through the casino to get to your toilet.

In the case of the Mirage, however, the meeting rooms all the way at the other end of the resort, perhaps a quarter mile away. After getting up from the dinner table and saying a few quick goodbyes, Rosetti and I began the long journey on foot—a journey I wanted to make as slowly as possible.

"You see what I mean when I say most of these gangster fans wear cargo pants and golf shirts?" I said, as we sauntered through the vast casino with its tropical jungle theme.

"You're telling me all of these assholes in golf shirts are coming to the convention tomorrow?"

"Most of them, yes, I'm sure."

"Charlie says we're sold out?"

"Well, not exactly sold out, because there's no limit on attendance when it comes to something like this. You can always squeeze in a few more fans. But he's thrilled with the results, let me put it that way. We've exceeded all of our goals."

"So we're going to make money?"

"No question about it. Exactly how *much* money will depend on how much foot traffic we see this weekend."

"Foot traffic?"

"Folks who drop in for the day without making a reservation. Charlie's optimistic about that, too. The Facebook page and Twitter feeds have been buzzing like crazy."

"So when am I going to see some of it?"

"Some of what?"

"Some of the money."

"I'm glad you asked that question, Mr. Rosetti. Mr. Beason has a suitcase full of cash he wants to give you tomorrow morning. It's just the first installment. But it's a bundle."

Rosetti smiled.

By this time we were passing the Terry Fator Theater and on our way to the small complex of meeting rooms named after tropical islands. I walked Rosetti by each one of them and we poked our noses in to take a look.

"This is the Martinique Room," I said. "This is where we're going to have our *Godfather* panel discussion."

"With the guy who fingered Sonny?"

"Yes, Gianni Russo will be there. We tried to get Al Pacino and Diane Keaton, but they were busy making movies."

"So who did you wind up getting?"

"You wouldn't know their names, but you'll recognize their faces. Over here is the Barbados Room. That's where we're going to have our panel discussion of writers. Nicholas Pileggi. Gay Talese. A few others."

"Where's the ballroom?"

"We're getting there."

I was hoping I could stall him long enough for him to grow tired and decide to go up to his room. So far it wasn't working.

"Here's the St. Croix Room."

"What's in there?"

"That's where we're going to have our *Sopranos* panel. We got Frank Pellegrino, the FBI agent. We got Robert Loggia, who played Feech LaManna. Remember the guy who got out of prison on parole and caused Tony all sorts of problems? We got—"

"How many times do I have to tell you I never watched the show? Now show me the goddamn ballroom."

"Just one more, Mr. Rosetti. This is St. Kitts Room, where we'll be having the *Button Men* panel. I'll be doing that one myself with some of my friends from the show."

"Well, goodie-goodie for you. Which way is the ballroom?"

"Are you sure you don't want to call it a night, Mr. Rosetti? It's getting late and we've got to get up at the crack of dawn tomorrow."

"No, I want to see it now."

"Remember, this is a work in progress. The construction crews and volunteers are going to stay up all night working on this."

"I know. But let's take a peek and see how it looks now."

"Okay," I said. I walked toward the main doors of the grand ballroom like a prisoner on his way to the death chamber. I held my breath and opened the door to the ballroom. And what I saw was . . .

Not bad. Not bad at all. Better than I expected, in fact.

"Where is everybody?" said Rosetti.

"I guess they're finished already."

As I looked around the room, the little booths and pavilions were set up and ready to go. There was a booth with Jeremiah Pennington's name on it. One for Gianni Russo. There were autograph tables set up for Robert Loggia, Frank Pellegrino, and even Joey Volpe. The witness protection program guys had their own section. It was set up so the fans could meet and talk with the mobsters without seeing their faces. Ingenious. That must've been Beason's idea. There were tables for the "retired" Mafiosi that Rosetti had invited to attend. Everywhere you looked were giant posters—murals, really—showing famous scenes from mobster movies and television shows. One showed Marlon Brando with the orange peel in his mouth, frightening his little grandson in the garden. One had James Gandolfini strangling Michael Imperioli to death in the car. Speaking of cars, there were three antique cars om the 1930s parked around the room—a 1932 Duesenberg, big Buick sedan like the one in *The Untouchables*, and a 1931 Studebaker President like the one from the classic Edward G. Robinson film, *Little Caesar*. Everything looked fabulous.

The room impressed the hell out of me. Rosetti not so much. "It ain't no Comic-Con."

"We told you this wasn't going to be anything like Comic-Con. This convention is going to be one-tenth the size of Comic-Con. But that doesn't mean it won't make money."

"Where are all the big movie studio companies and video-game companies? How come they don't have pavilions here like at Comic-Con?"

"It's not appropriate in this case, Mr. Rosetti. The studios aren't making gangster movies anymore. This convention is all about nostalgia. Besides, you told me to keep the expenses down. Hell, you've told me twice *tonight* to keep the expenses down. This is what you get when you keep the expenses down."

"I don't know about this."

"Don't worry, Mr. Rosetti. Wait 'til tomorrow. It's going to be a big success. This room is going to be packed with fans. You're going to be rolling in money."

"I hope so."

"Remember the time you skimmed all that cash from the casino count room and took it down to the crap table? Remember the champagne bath with the hot-and-cold running hookers?"

He smiled. "Yeah, I remember."

"Well, multiply that by a hundred and that's how you're going to be feeling tomorrow, okay?"

"Okay."

"I'll bring the hookers and champagne up to your room myself."

He smiled.

"Let's meet down here tomorrow at eight o'clock sharp," I said. "That's one hour before the doors open to the fans at nine. Mr. Beason wants to give you your first suitcase stuffed with cash. Sound good?"

"Yeah, sounds good."

"Let's go up to our rooms now and get some sleep. What you say?"

"No, you go up. I want to stay down here and look around bit."

"Okay, fine," I said. "*Buona notte.*"

"*Buona notte.*"

I began the long journey back to the hotel elevators. Along the way, one thought kept going through my head:

Tomorrow I'm going to be a wealthy man . . . or a dead one.

37

When we met in the grand ballroom at eight the next morning, the place was buzzing. All the actors had taken their places in the booths and were getting ready to sign autographs. The guys from the witness protection program settled into their special booths where they could talk to the fans without revealing their identities. Even Rosetti's senior-citizen mobsters were eager to get the convention started. Rosetti took a moment to introduce me to the ones I hadn't met the night before.

"Joey, I'd like you to meet Frank 'The Maytag Repairman' Bruno. He's retired now, but he was one of the greats. You didn't want to cross this guy back in the day, right, Frank?"

"Don't believe anything he says, kid, I was a pussycat. Nice to meet you. What did you say your name was again?"

"Joey Volpe."

"Well, thanks for inviting me to this shindig. It looks like it's going to be fun."

"Mr. Bruno, if you don't mind me asking, how did you get your . . . er, unusual nickname?"

"The Maytag Repairman? Oh, that goes back a million years. We had a guy who wasn't giving us the information we needed from him, if you know what I mean. He was just a little guy, and one of the legitimate businesses I owned at the time was an industrial laundry. We had these giant washing machines and dryers in our plant. So I says to him, I says, 'Look, Tommy, if you don't tell us what we want to know, I'm going to stuff you in this washing machine and set the dial on heavy load.'"

"Did he give you the information?"

"Not at first, no."

"So did you put him in the washing machine?"

"Yeah, but just for one or two cycles. The rinse cycle and the spin cycle."

"Did he drown?"

"No, he was okay. We knew he was alive because we could ⌐ him screaming in there. After the spin cycle was over, we pu⌐ him out and asked him again for the information we wante⌐ He's choking and puking and bleeding from his nose. His face i⌐ all black and blue. But he still won't spill the beans."

"So what did you do then?"

"We put him in the dryer. We set it on permanent press. Five minutes and he still won't talk. So we turned it up to durable fabrics. Gave him about ten minutes of that. It must've been hot as hell in there. He's going round and round, screaming the whole time, and finally we hear him yelling 'I'll talk! I'll talk!'"

"So did he talk?"

"Oh, yeah, he sang like a canary."

"Then what did you do with him?"

"You don't want to know. It wasn't pretty."

"Well, thanks for coming to Gangster-Con," I said in a quavering voice. Listening to this horrifying tale made me feel dizzy and sweaty. "We're glad to have you here."

"My pleasure, Joey, my pleasure. Thanks for inviting me."

As we walked away, Rosetti said to me, "What a sweet old guy. I never get tired of hearing that story."

Rosetti and I walked through the entire ballroom and stopped to chat with each of the special guests. Wherever we went, Rosetti's gaggle of investors followed. Spags . . . Fat Bernie . . . Little Angel . . . The Killer . . . Alfonso "No Nickname" Mancini. Plus three or four others whose names and monikers escape me at the moment. There were ten of them altogether. I wondered how much their shares in Gangster-Con would add up to. Three hundred percent? Five hundred? Rosetti was playing a dangerous game with that investment scheme, especially if Gangster-Con wound up losing money.

Speaking of losing money, Rosetti popped a question I wasn't expecting. "Where's the line?"

"What line?"

√hat do you mean what line? The line of customers waiting
.et in." He looked at his watch. "We're only thirty minutes away
ɔm opening. There should be a long line of fans out there."

"You didn't see it?"

"No, I didn't. Where is it?"

"I saw the line," I said. "It's huge. It almost goes all the way
out the building. I can't believe you missed it. Where were you
looking?"

"Outside the main doors to the ballroom, of course, where
else?"

"Oh, well, that explains it," I said. "We couldn't put them right
up against the main doors to the ballroom. Hotel security told us
it was too dangerous to make people line up there. They said if
we did that, they could break down the doors and cause a stampede. People could get trampled. We set the line up along the
northeast wall of the casino. Didn't you see it? There were thousands of people in line."

"I thought that was the line for the breakfast buffet."

"No, that was our line."

Rosetti was right, of course. It was the line for the breakfast
buffet.

"It really looked to me like it was the line for the breakfast—"

Fortunately, at that moment, Mr. Beason came up to rescue me
from this conversation.

"Gentlemen, we need to go upstairs to the business office for
a moment. I need Mr. Rosetti to sign some papers. And I want
to give him his suitcase"—Beason looked to make sure no one
could hear him—"the first cut of the cash from this morning's
ticket sales. It turns out Charlie Scott was right. The walk-in
traffic is huge. Better than we expected. Gangster-Con is a big
success, gentlemen, and it hasn't even started yet."

At the mention of the word *cash*, Rosetti forgot his concern
with the line of fans. Fortunately, the buffet line was still there as
the three of us walked through casino. I pointed it out to Rosetti.

"Do you see the line now, Mr. Rosetti? See how long it is?"

"Yeah, you're right. It's pretty long."

"The plan is that when the doors open at nine, the hotel's security guards are going to let a hundred people come into the room every five minutes. That way there won't be a stampede.

"Good idea. We don't want anybody to get hurt. Liability issues."

I wondered what the liability issues were when it came to stuffing a human being inside a washing machine and turning on the rinse cycle.

We took the elevator up to the seventh floor. Like last night when I showed Rosetti the ballroom, I wasn't sure what to expect when we opened the door to the offices. Beason had been in charge of everything at the Mirage except for the VIP dinner. I assumed it would look like the phony suite of offices Beason had set up at Hyatt in San Diego for Comic-Con. So I was as surprised as Rosetti when Beason opened the door to reveal . . .

An ordinary hotel room.

Two double beds. Twin nightstands. A desk. An easy chair and coffee table. Just a standard Las Vegas hotel room.

"Where is everybody?" said Rosetti.

"Where is who?" said Beason.

"The secretaries. The clerks. The telephones. The fax machines. Where's all the stuff you had in your offices in San Diego?"

Beason sighed. "If we've told you once, Tony, we've told you a thousand times. This is a much smaller operation than Comic-Con. But that doesn't mean you're not going to make a lot of money. In fact, come with me and I'll show you."

"But this is just a plain old hotel room."

"No, it's not. As a matter of fact, it's a suite." He pointed to an open door that led to the adjoining hotel room. "Come into the other room with me and I'll show you."

So we walked through the door and found another hotel room exactly like the first one. Two twin beds. Nightstands. Desk. Chair.

"This is just another fucking hotel room like the first one."

₁at's where you're wrong, Tony," said Beason. "Because this
₁n has a suitcase on the bed. And I've filled that suitcase with
sh."

"Oh, okay," said Rosetti, mollified by this. "Can I take a look at
the cash now?"

"Absolutely," said Beason. "Why don't you take a moment to
count it. I think you'll find it comes to four hundred thousand
dollars. You've already made a nice profit, and that's just the first
installment. Joey and I have to run downstairs to take care of
some last-minute details. We'll meet you down there in twenty
minutes, okay?"

"Okay," said Rosetti as he sat down on the bed and unzipped
the suitcase.

Beason and I started to back out of the room. I wanted to leave
as fast as possible, but Beason held me back for a moment. "Hold
on just a second, Joey. I want to see the look on Mr. Rosetti's face
when he sees the money."

The look on Rosetti's face was priceless.

The suitcase was stuffed with Monopoly money.

38

"What the fuck is this?" said Rosetti. "What the FUCK is t.
This is fake. Fake money. You motherfuckers. Do you know w.
the fuck you're dealing with?"

Nigel and I had backed out the door and into the adjoining room. Nigel took out a key and locked the door from the outside. Immediately, Rosetti started banging on the door, but we were safe for the time being.

"What if he starts shooting, Nigel?"

"He doesn't have a gun."

"How do you know he doesn't have a gun?"

"Because I borrowed it from him this morning when I shook his hand. I gave him a man hug and came away with a handgun." He pulled the pistol out of his pocket and showed me.

"Got his Rolex, too. Couldn't help myself. Old habits."

"That was risky."

"Life is risky, my dear boy. That's what makes it interesting."

Rosetti was still banging on the door and screaming. "You two cocksuckers are dead men. Do you hear me? Dead! I'm not going to make it easy for you either. I'm going to make you suffer. Do you *hear* me, assholes?"

From the day I first met him at Hoover, Nigel was the coolest customer I'd ever known in my life. He tapped on the door with his knuckles.

"Listen to me, dear boy. Please do calm down a bit. Everything's going to turn out fine. Just relax and you'll be out of there soon enough."

"You're a fucking dead man, Beason!" came Rosetti's muffled scream from inside.

"What about his telephone?" I asked.

"Cell phone or hotel phone?"

"I didn't even think about his cell phone."

said Nigel, and he pulled Rosetti's cell phone out of his

…at about the hotel phone?"

"…isconnected," said Nigel.

"The other door to that room?"

"I locked it from the outside. Tricky, but it can be done."

"Shouldn't we put the Do Not Disturb signs on the doors so the maids don't let him out?"

"The maids haven't even started work yet, Joey. Too early. They won't find him for another hour. By that time we'll be long gone. It doesn't matter if they let him out. We *want* them to let him out before too long."

With Rosetti still screaming and banging on the door, Nigel and I left the room and took the elevator downstairs. By the time we got to the grand ballroom, it was 9:15 am. Theoretically, Gangster-Con had been open for fifteen minutes. But nobody—and I mean *nobody*—was there. Not a single fan. Not even a curious bystander.

The actors, writers, and retired gangsters all sat there playing their parts, waiting for the hordes of fans to arrive. Rosetti's little group of investors looked dumbfounded and disappointed. But there was *another* look on their faces, and it became evident with each passing minute: They were angry.

After a while, I looked at my watch. It was almost nine thirty. I caught Jeremiah Pennington's eye and nodded. He took his cue like the pro he was.

Jerry stood up and, loud enough for everyone in the ballroom to hear, shouted "What the fuck is this? Where is everybody? I was promised thousands of fans."

Some of the other actors started mumbling in agreement.

"Hey, you," said Jerry, pointing to me. "What's your name again?"

"Joey Volpe."

"You're one of the guys who organized this thing, right?"

"Well, I'm really just an actor."

"But this was your bright idea, right? You put this together, am I right?"

"I guess so."

"Well?"

"Well what?"

"Where the hell is everybody? You told me we'd have ten thousand fans here this morning. You told me I'd walk away with fifty thousand bucks in autograph fees."

"He told me that, too" said Frank Vincent of *The Sopranos*.

"You fucking *lied* to us, man," said Jerry. "This thing is a total bomb. I'm a big star, for chrissakes. I don't have to put up with this shit."

"Well, like I said, I'm just an—"

"I don't even know who you are," said Jerry. "What show were you on?"

"I was on *The Sopranos* and . . ."

"He wasn't on *The Sopranos*," said Frank Vincent. "I can tell you that for damn sure."

". . . and *Button Men*."

"*Button Men*? Who ever saw that show?" said Jerry. "It was canceled after the first commercial. You know what I think? I think you're a con man. I think this whole thing is a fake and a fraud. And I'm getting out of here right now."

"Don't leave, Mr. Pennington, please."

He ignored me and spoke to all the other actors in the room. "How many people here are members of SAG-AFTRA?"

Two dozen hands went up.

"How about Actors' Equity?

Most of the hands stayed up.

"Well, listen to me, my union brothers. I've been active in the Screen Actors Guild ever since I first came to Hollywood. Even before I got into television, I was the Equity deputy in the plays I did in New York. I take our unions very seriously, gentlemen. Without unions, producers would still be paying actors with room and board. Without unions, there would be no residuals. No catering on the set. No mandatory five-minute breaks fifteen minutes. Life as we know it would not be the same, ~emen. I'm declaring a wildcat strike right here and now. I ~we walk out of here. Who's coming with me?"

"I am," said Frank Vincent.

"Brotherhood!" said Dennis Farina.

Nigel nudged me and whispered into my ear. "Did your friend Jerry ever do *Hank Cinq*?"

"*Henry the Fifth*? I don't think so."

"What a pity. He'd be perfect for it."

Every actor in the ballroom cheered and started to follow Jerry out the door. The writers followed suit in solidarity, although the writers weren't unionized. Good thing, too, or you'd be paying as much for a book as a Broadway show. You'd pay a hundred bucks for the next John Grisham novel. (Even a far-fetched story about gangsters and actors would run you seventy-five.) The retired mobsters joined the walkout, too. After all, many of them were union workers themselves—albeit of the no-show variety.

"Wait a second," I said to them as they filed past me. "This isn't even a union production."

They ignored me and before I knew it, they were gone. Nigel and I were standing in the middle of the grand ballroom of the Mirage Hotel, surrounded by a group of Rosetti's investors, some of whom were starting to get mad as hell.

"I think we'd better get going, too," said Nigel. "The natives are starting to look restless."

"Good idea," I said.

By the time Nigel and I got to the taxi stand, the last group of actors took the cab in front of us.

"Follow that cab," Nigel ordered the driver. He turned to me with a smile. "I've always wanted to say that."

I laughed. "Maybe we should tell the driver where we're going anyway in case they shake our tail."

"You're absolutely right, dear boy," said Nigel. "Follow that cab, my good man, and take us to Bellagio."

Bellagio was a half mile from the Mirage, but the cabbie didn't complain. Las Vegas taxi drivers were used to taking these short

hops from one casino to another. The sad thing is that m
them have to wait in line for an hour to pick up one of these
fares. I was sure Nigel would give him a big tip. He tipped
wherever he went.

When we got to Bellagio two minutes later, I saw the giant
marquee. I was happy to see we got top billing again. The flashing
digital sign said, "WELCOME, GANGSTERS!"

39

saw the line as soon as we turned into the Bellagio's long driveway. "That can't be the line waiting for a taxi. Not at nine thirty in the morning."

"No, they're not waiting for a taxi," said Nigel.

"It can't be the breakfast buffet line either. Can it?"

"The breakfast buffet at Bellagio is lovely," said Nigel, "but I don't think the line ever extends out the front door."

As I got out of the cab, I went up to one of the first people in line. "What are all these people waiting for?"

"Are you kidding me?" said the guy dressed in a golf shirt, cargo pants, and big white running shoes.

"No, I'm not kidding. What's the line about?"

"Gangster-Con! Have you been living in a cave?"

I ran inside, pushing the revolving door too fast for Nigel to follow me. I took a hard right at the Dale Chihuly glass sculpture and started jogging past tourists toward the grand ballroom and meeting rooms. They were located—surprise, surprise—on the other side of the casino. I ran past the blackjack tables until I came to a T at the crap pit. I hung a left and kept running. I was almost in the meeting room area now. I was bumping into so many people along the way I hardly noticed when I plowed into one whom I knew.

"Excuse me, ma'am," I said. "I'm in a hurry." I started to run again, but she grabbed me by the sleeve.

"Do you not know me, my lord?"

"Oh, my God."

We hugged and I gave her a long kiss on the lips.

"Are you Ganymede or Rosalind today?" I said.

"Neither one."

"If there be truth in sight," I said, "you are my wife."

"I'll have no husband if you not be he," she said. *As Yc*
Act V, Scene Four. "Come into the ballroom, Joey," she sar
won't believe your eyes."

Caitlin was right. I didn't believe them. Even though I wa.
one in charge of the Bellagio version of Gangster-Con. (Nr
handled the Mirage.) Caitlin and I had made all the arrange
ments for set decoration, pavilions, booths, posters, flats, and
props. Charlie had told me that it was a big hit, bigger than
anything we had ever imagined. He told me the advance reservations were twice what we expected. Judging by the long line
outside the door, the walk-in traffic was going to exceed our
expectations, too.

The grand ballroom was like the one at the Mirage, but much
more so. While Nigel had spent ten thousand dollars of Rosetti's
money to set up the mirage at the Mirage, Caitlin and I had spent
a hundred thousand decorating and outfitting the Bellagio ballroom.

Gigantic movie posters on huge flats were fifty feet tall. We
parked dozens of antique gangster cars around the room. We had
a replica of an electric chair set up, so fans could experience the
thrill of capital punishment, and a replica of a prison cell, too. I
lied to Rosetti about the movie studios and video-game companies not doing gangster stuff anymore. Sony PlayStation had a
new gangster game coming out in a few months. They paid us
two million dollars for a pavilion promoting it at Gangster-Con.
Fox Searchlight was releasing a new gangster film, too, and they
gave us three million for a pavilion in the grand ballroom It was
an absurd amount of money to spend on promotion but—what
can I say?—that's Hollywood for you.

The greatest sight of all was the crowd. Thousands of people.
Maybe ten thousand—all of them wandering through the ballroom, gawking at the exhibits, lining up for autographs from
the actors, writers, and retired mobsters. There must've been
a hundred people waiting in line to get Jeremiah Pennington's
autograph. I circled the line and came up behind him. I put my

und his neck while he signed an autograph for a fan and
m a hug.

ink where man's glory most begins and ends," I said. "And
ny glory was that I had such friends."

Shakespeare?" he said.

"No. William Butler Yeats."

"I always get those two mixed up," said Jerry, and he gave me one of his famous winks.

I moved down the autograph area from behind the tables and thanked the actors, writers, and retired mobsters for being so cooperative this morning.

"What was that dog-and-pony show at the Mirage about anyway, Joey?" said Frank Vincent.

"Oh, just a practical joke on a friend is all. I really appreciate you playing along."

"I appreciate the extra thousand for doing it," said Frank.

That's an actor for you. Tell them to do this, do that, stand here, move there, stay, sit, beg, roll over. They'll do it. The only question they'll ever ask is, "How much extra do I get for this?" Most of the time they won't ask that. They'll get their agents to do it for them.

Before long, Nigel caught up to me and put his arm around my shoulder.

"It's even better than we hoped, isn't it, dear boy?"

"It's amazing."

"It's enough to make me think about going straight," said Nigel. "Maybe I have some talent as an event planner. When you stop and think about it, it's not all that different from running the long con."

"You'd really quit?"

"Not a chance," said Nigel with a chuckle. "Once a criminal, always a criminal."

Speaking of criminals, I felt a tap on the shoulder. I turned and saw the man I was expecting. But I wasn't expecting him so soon. I glanced at my watch. It was half past ten. "You're here already?"

"It went down quicker than we expected," said Spags.

"How did it go?"

"Maybe the three of us should go to a bar and talk it over"

"Can we find a bar open this early in the morning?"

"This is Vegas, Joey. The drunks show up at five in the morn. and ask the bartender to drop two eggs in their beer for break fast."

"I guess you're right. Can my wife come along?"

"I don't think that's a good idea. This is man talk, if you know what I mean."

I found Caitlin and told her that Nigel, Spags, and I had to work out some last-minute details. I asked her to keep an eye on things in the ballroom until we got back. The three of us walked to one of the bars in the casino. We sat down and ordered three screwdrivers—the breakfast of champions.

"So how did it go?" I said.

"Like a wet dream."

"Tell us about it."

"I figured he might be up there for an hour or two before the maids found him. Somehow he managed to break out and come downstairs ten minutes after you left. It worked out better that way."

"Dare I ask what kind of a mood the poor chap was in?" said Nigel.

"Pissed."

"What did he do?"

"He came running up to me and the other investors. Most of those guys were already mad at him. They got even madder when they heard what he had to say."

"What was that?" I asked.

"He said he'd been set up. Conned. He said he needed to borrow a gun, because Beason had stolen his pistol. He was going to the airport and sending Paulie to the train station and Carlo to the bus station. He said you two guys were going to try to leave town with the money, but he was going to find you and kill you. And if he couldn't find you, he knew where your wife and daughter lived. "

at did you say?" I asked.

first, I played along with him. I said, 'Yeah, we gotta grab e guys before they get away. I want my money back. I've got eventy-five percent share of this thing."

Nigel chuckled.

"Then Bruno Bianchi looks at me like I just farted at a funeral. He says to me, 'What do you mean you've got a seventy-five percent share? I've got a fifty percent share.'"

"It's Bugsy Siegel all over again," I said.

"Then Little Angel Santoro chimes in. 'What the fuck are you talking about?' he says. 'I have a sixty percent share.' 'Me too,' says Al Mancini."

"You mean No Nose?"

"No, No Nickname."

"Oh, that's right," I said. "I forgot. I don't know how you guys remember all these names. It's like reading a Russian novel."

"We don't use the nicknames much ourselves. The newspapers come up with that shit. We use them when we want to break some guy's balls."

By breaking balls, I wasn't sure whether Spags meant pulling someone's leg or literally rupturing their testicles. I let it go. "What did you say then?"

"I didn't have to say much after that. The other guys started closing in on him, asking questions. He couldn't answer most of them. Everybody knew that you and him did that heist in Columbus together. They knew you were partners in crime, so to speak. They put two and two together and assumed you planned this whole con to rip them off."

"Perfect," said Nigel. "In my business, Joey, the role Spags played is called The Fixer. His job is to come in at the end and make sure the mark doesn't go to the cops, or start shooting, or come up with some other way to spoil the job."

"So what happened to Rosetti?"

"Well, all of us investors had a meeting of the minds. We decided it was time for Rosetti to resign from our organization, if you know what I mean."

"I thought nobody resigns from the Mafia," I said.

"They don't."

"They made an exception in Rosetti's case?"

"They did not."

"What happened?"

"Let's just say that Tony Rosetti sleeps with the cactuses. *Buon anima*."

"Oh, I see," said Nigel. "What a pity. He was such a charming fellow."

"What about the others?" I asked. "Are they going to come after Nigel and me?"

"I doubt it. Tony Moretti said something about looking for you guys to get their money back. I volunteered for the job. I told them I'd hunt you guys down. And guess what? I found you!"

"Are you going to kill us now?" I said, half joking.

"Naaah, don't sweat it. Lay low for a while. Go on vacation. It'll blow over. If this convention makes a profit, we can give their front money back to them. But it doesn't matter. They blame Rosetti for this mess, and he paid for it."

"'Thus the whirligig of time brings in his revenges,'" I said. *Twelfth Night*, Act V, Scene One.

"Apt quote," said Nigel.

"What does it mean?" said Spags. Ever since the first day I met him in prison, he always asked for a modern translation of my Shakespearean quotes.

I thought about it for a moment and said, "What goes around comes around."

"Hell," he said, "that could be the fuckin' *motto* of the mob."

We were quiet for a long time after that We sipped our screwdrivers, lost in our own thoughts. I was feeling a little guilty, to tell you the truth. I assumed that Nigel and Spags were not. If I knew them as well as I thought I did, Nigel was thinking about all the money he was making and Spags was wondering how Rosetti's death changed the balance of power in the Philadelphia mob. These are the lives they have chosen, I thought. I felt someone

ıy neck from behind and for a moment I thought Rosetti
ome back to life to strangle me.

Wherefore art thou, Romeo?"

ı I assume I don't have to provide the attribution for that quota-
on.)

"Ah, my old friend, Ganymede," said Nigel. "I haven't seen you
since we set up those phony offices in San Diego."

"Good to see you again, Nigel."

Spags held out his hand and said, "We haven't met."

"Oh, I'm sorry," I said. "Mario Spagnuola, this is my wife,
Caitlin Volpe."

"Pleased to meet you, Mr. Spagnuola."

"Call me Spags. Everybody does."

Then another old friend showed up.

"What the fuck are all you guys doing in the bar for chrissakes?
We've got a convention to run out there. There are ten thousand
people on the ballroom floor. I could use a little help. It's eleven
in the morning and you're hitting the bar already?"

"We're coming, Charlie, we're coming. Hey, Caitlin," I said, "do
you have your cell phone with you?"

"Yes."

"Good, I want you to take a picture."

"Of what?"

"Of Nigel, Charlie, Spags, and me in the prison cell," I said.
"Just for old times sake."

40

We made eight million dollars altogether on Gangster-C
after expenses. We split it four ways. Two million each for Nig
Charlie, Spags, and me. Nobody complained or asked for more
Who says there isn't honor among thieves?

Then again, we made that money legally and on an investment of 350,000 dollars OPM—courtesy of Rosetti and partners.
In the end, we made good on Spags's promise to the partners
and paid back the front money, minus the fifty thousand dollars
Rosetti put up. Neither Spags nor Nigel had the slightest inten-
tion of paying taxes on their profit. They were career criminals,
after all. Charlie, Caitlin, and I—good upstanding citizens all—
gave Uncle Sam his share of the take.

That left me and Caitlin with a little more than 1.3 million
dollars. More than enough money to do what we should've done
twenty years earlier after we graduated from Yale. We moved
to Los Angeles where actors can find some decent work. I told
Caitlin, "Let's focus on *your* career for a while, and I'll take care
of Bianca this time."

Sure enough, she started gaining traction as an actress within
a few weeks after we arrived in Los Angeles. She had the perfect
look for commercials. Even though she was over forty, she still
looked young enough to play a mother with small children.
(Heck, she *was* a mother with a small child!) She was pretty, but
not too pretty, if you know what I mean. Commercial casting
directors love that look. In her first year in LA, she shot commercials for Pampers, McDonald's, and Cascade dishwashing liquid.
The money started rolling in. So did the attention from casting
directors who specialized in film and television.

She started landing some day-player roles on sitcoms and
hour-long TV dramas. It was like I'd always heard: When success
finally comes, it comes *fast*.

ay, she got a call from her agent for an audition for a
This wasn't a day-player or a guest-star role. She was up
e of the biggest recurring roles on the show. Not the star
e show, but the star's next-door neighbor. Yes, she was the
com neighbor," the best role in television: You don't have to
emorize as many lines as the star but you usually get most of
the good ones.

Our little family was rolling in money and as happy as a family
of three could be. Or maybe I should say a family of five. Because
the best part was that we repaid my parents all the money we'd
borrowed over the years. With interest. Or vigorish, as we call it
in the Mafia. Plus, we gave them a Mercedes for Christmas. Even
better, they got the chance to see their granddaughter more often
than they could when we weren't speaking to each other.

As Bianca got older and we could afford a nanny for her, I
tried to get back into acting. But my heart wasn't in it. I landed
a few walk-on jobs. They seemed so dull compared to the things
I'd done with Nigel, Charlie, and Spags. Even the heist I pulled
off with Rosetti. That was life on the edge. That was real life.
Pretending to be somebody in front of a television camera didn't
seem so exciting anymore.

For the time being, I was content with being a house husband
and a Mr. Mom. What is fame and fortune, after all, compared to
the love of a beautiful daughter and a wonderful wife? And hey,
it doesn't hurt if that wife happens to be rich and famous, too.

While Caitlin went off to work at the television studio every
day, I made the most of the time I had with Bianca while she
was still young enough to think her daddy walked on water. One
Saturday morning, she wanted go to the Cosmopolitan Studios
theme park. I was happy to oblige, even though I hated the place.
Bianca, on the other hand, thought it was heaven on earth.

After stopping at the bank near our house in Beverly Hills
to load up on cash, we headed off to the amusement park. The
studio where Caitlin shot her television show was nearby, so I
told Bianca we could stop and see Mommy at work afterward.
Bianca got a kick out of that because the other actors and tech-

nicians on the set treated her like a visiting princess. C
loved having her there, too, although Saturday was a busy
for her. She'd be doing a final dress rehearsal in the morning a
shooting in front of a live audience that evening. But I knew s.
could spare a few minutes for me and Bianca.

Have you ever been to Cosmopolitan Studios theme park? If
not, don't bother. If you have, you know what it's like. It's a tourist
trap with a phony bus tour of movie sets, lots of lousy restaurants,
and several other cheesy attractions and dopey rides. There was
one kiddie ride, in particular, that Bianca couldn't get enough of.
I was sick of it. So I bought one ticket and gave it to her.

"You're old enough to go on the ride by yourself now," I said.
"Daddy will be right here waiting for you when you get off, okay?"

"Okay," she said with a big smile. I think she was happy to be
ditching her dad. She was reaching the age where it was more fun
to do stuff like that alone.

As I stood along the fence line watching Bianca go up and
down on the ride, I nodded to another single father standing
next to me.

"Daddy's day out with his little girl, huh?" he said.

"Yeah, she loves it here," I said. "Heaven knows why."

"My boy does, too. I keep trying to take him to Santa Anita
instead, but he insists on the amusement park."

I laughed. "Which one is your son?"

"He's the one with the Dodgers baseball cap. The divorce agreement says I get him two weekends a month. I try to do whatever
he wants. I spoil him, I guess. But what the hell. Have you got the
same deal with your ex?"

"No, we're still married. My wife works on Saturdays. I like to
let Bianca choose whatever she wants to do on that day."

"Bianca? That's a pretty name."

"We thought so. It's from Shakespeare. *The Taming of the Shrew*.
Of the two sisters, Bianca is the pretty one. Not the mean one."

He was no longer listening to me. He had that glaze in his eyes
that people sometimes get when I'm quoting Shakespeare. I realized he wasn't bored, he was looking at something.

e my eyes playing tricks on me, or do you see something
ering underneath that bench over there?"

looked where he was pointing. "Yeah, I see it."

"What the heck is it? A bracelet?"

"Let's take a look."

So we walked over to the bench, and I picked it up.

"Wow," I said. "It's a Rolex watch."

"Let me look at it," he said. He studied it for a minute. "This isn't just any Rolex watch, my friend. I happen to know a little about fine timepieces. It's a gold Rolex Presidential Limited Edition. It's got diamond studs in the numerals and platinum bars in the band. Day and date. Self-winding. Sweep second hand. Even a moon-phase indicator. That's rare as hell, dude. This watch is worth fifty grand if it's worth a penny."

"I wonder who it belongs to?"

He was quiet for a long time.

"I guess it belongs to us now," he said.

"Finders keepers, losers weepers?"

"That's the rule I've always played by. But we both found it."

"You're right," I said. "We both found it. I'm not trying to cheat you."

"We can't both wear it, though, can we?"

"No, we can't."

"Look, I'll tell you what," he said. "I know a pawnshop about thirty minutes from here. An hour at the most if there's traffic on the freeway. The guy there is honest. He won't give us the full fifty thousand for it. No pawnshop will do that—the watch is used and they're in business to make a profit. But he might give us twenty-five grand for it. Fifteen at least."

"I don't have time to go to a pawnshop," I said. "My kid would go nuts if I tried to drag her out of here now."

"Yeah, mine, too."

We stood there for several minutes trying to come up with a fair solution to the problem.

"Tell you what," he said. "I've already got plenty of nice v
The Lord has been good to me. If we can agree on a fair pr
sell you my share."

I smiled. For some reason, I really wanted that watch. Des
all the money I made on Gangster-Con—and all the mon
Caitlin was making as an actress—I never got around to buying
myself a nice watch. I remembered Rosetti making a nasty
comment about my Timex on the day he kidnapped Gizmo. How
ironic, I thought. I could have a gangster-style Rolex like Rosetti
himself used to wear and get it on the cheap.

"How much cash do you have on you right now?" asked the
man.

"I just stopped at the bank on my way here," I said. "I've got a
thousand bucks on me. But that's all I'm afraid."

"Well, this is your lucky day, dude. I'm going to make you a
deal. I'll sell you my share of the watch for a thousand bucks. You
can pawn it if you want. You can put it in your safety-deposit box
to help pay for your retirement. Or you can wear it and let your
friends think you won the lottery."

"Just a thousand bucks? Really?"

"You're making out like a bandit, man. Have we got a deal?"

"You better believe it." I pulled out my wallet and gave him all
the cash I'd taken out of the bank.

"Wear it in good health, my friend," he said. And he started
backing away.

"Where are you going?" I asked.

"I've got to hit the men's room. Watch my kid for me until I get
back, will you? The one in the Dodgers cap."

"Okay."

I wouldn't have left my child alone under those circumstances,
but there are all kinds of parents in the world. I didn't give it
much thought, though, because I was distracted by my new
watch. I strapped the gold band on my wrist, and it fit perfectly.
The diamond numerals glittered in the Southern California sun.

I noticed something strange.

second hand was jumping from one second to the next. *click, click.* I didn't know a lot about watches, but I knew wasn't typical of a Rolex. That's what cheap quartz watches .. The sweep of the second hand on a fine Swiss watch like a olex is supposed to move smoothly around the dial. I didn't .hink Rolex even *made* a quartz watch. This knockoff on my wrist was probably worth about twenty-five bucks, tops.

"Hey, wait a second! Come back here!"

The man was a hundred yards from me now and walking fast. I thought about chasing him, but the kiddie ride was coming to an end and I promised Bianca I'd be waiting for her when she got off. Sure enough, the kid in the Dodgers cap ran up to his mother and father and asked them if he could go on the ride again.

"Why are you crying, Daddy?" said Bianca when she came up to me.

"I'm not crying, honey. I'm laughing."

I was laughing so hard I could barely speak. Tears were pouring out of my eyes. Like I said before, tears were *always* coming out of my eyes for one reason or another.

"What's so funny, Daddy?"

"Oh, nothing, sweetheart," I said. "Daddy just realized his life is a comedy after all. So I started laughing."

"Can I go on the ride again?"

"Sure, honey, but I need to find a cash machine. Then we'll come back here and you can ride as many times as you want."

Do you feel sorry for me that I got ripped off by a con man? Forget about it. I learned an important lesson in life. All it cost me was a thousand bucks, two years in jail, and twenty years trying to make it as an actor.

Merchant of Venice, Act II, Scene Seven:

"All that glitters is not gold."

Acknowledgments

Shakespeare actually wrote "All that *glisters* is not gold," when Juliet says "Wherefore art thou, Romeo," she means are you Romeo, not *where* are you, Romeo. Please forgive me taking those liberties with the Bard's immortal words.

I also owe an apology to Trekkies (or Trekkers, if you prefer, for taking many liberties with the plots, characters, episodes, and versions of *Star Trek*. In my defense, I can only offer the weak excuse that it's much more difficult to master the intricacies of *Star Trek* than the thirty-seven (thirty-eight?) plays of William Shakespeare.

I am indebted to Rob Salkowitz's excellent book *Comic-Con and the Business of Pop Culture* for teaching me what I needed to know about fan conventions in general and Comic-Con in particular. The image of the Bat Family on the convention floor was borrowed directly from Mr. Salkowitz's book.

Anybody who writes a book on con artists stands on the shoulders of the late David W. Mauer, whose classic book *The Big Con* lays out step-by-step how confidence men work, think, and talk. Mr. Mauer was the Herodotus--and the Margaret Mead—of the underground world of con artistry.

I'm glad to say that everything I know about prison comes from surfing the internet. So I'm grateful to Justin Paperny and Walt Pavlo, who talk about life inside a minimum security federal prison with great insight, compassion, and sensitivity in a series of short online videos available on YouTube.

Speaking of prison, the character of Charlie Scott, Joey Volpe's cubie, is a wholly fictional character. But I owe a tip of the hat to the late, great copywriter Gary Halbert for giving me the idea of a prisoner writing a book about marketing to his two children. Bond and Kevin Halbert, all grown up now, still offer Gary's excellent book, *The Boron Letters*, for sale on Amazon.

There really is a restaurant in the Gaslamp Quarter of San Diego owned by a former matador. His name is Paul Dobson and

.nt is called Dobson's. And it really does serve the best
up en croute in the world. But that's where the simi-
the Cape & Sword ends. Of course, Mr. Dobson played
: whatsoever in the shenanigans portrayed in this fictional
:. (Neither did Gwyneth Paltrow!)

m deeply grateful to all the people who read the book in
 manuscript form and offered advice, guidance, and encour-
agement. They include Dorinne Armstrong, Carl Scott, Deke
Castleman, Justine Walp, Renee James, Louis Wasser, Gretchen
Archer, Donna Baier Stein, Ann Bauer, Alexa Stark and Ellen
Levine of the Trident Media Group, the late Beverly Swerling,
Michael Willis, Lori Willis, Jane Brookstein, the late Max Busetti,
Bill Mueller, John Bullion, and especially my wife, Sharon
Armstrong, who continues to believe in my ability as a writer
despite mounting evidence to the contrary.

Many thanks to all the people at Linden/Pace for being thoroughly professional and utterly delightful to work with—especially my editor Kent Sorsky and my publicist Jaguar Bennett, as
well as my personal publicist Claire McKinney. Special thanks to
my friend Bob Bly, author of nearly one hundred books and an
expert on the publishing world, who encouraged me to send the
manuscript to Linden.

This book never would've come into being if my wife and I
hadn't had dinner one night in Maine with my dear friend of
forty-plus years, Jonathan Frakes, who played Commander Riker
on *Star Trek: The Next Generation*. He regaled us with funny
stories about fan conventions. Until that moment, I never knew
such a thing existed. Thanks also to Jonathan for inviting me to
join him for a magical evening at the Louisville SuperCon where
we had dinner and drinks with William Shatner, LeVar Burton,
and Henry Winkler. Meeting Captain Kirk, Kunta Kinte, and The
Fonz was like hitting the trifecta of iconic television stars.

Finally, to all the actors out there, the extras and the stars, the
wannabes and the washed-ups, the has-beens and never-weres,
I salute you! Don't forget—and never regret—what you did for
love.

ALSO BY RICHARD ARMSTRONG

Leaving the Nest

(with Dorinne Armstrong)

The Next Hurrah

God Doesn't Shoot Craps

ABOUT THE AUTHOR

Richard Armstrong's first book, *Leaving the Nest* (coauthored with his mother, Dorinne Armstrong), was published by William Morrow & Co. in 1986 and had five printings. His second book, *The Next Hurrah*, was published by Morrow in 1988. It was praised by the *Los Angeles Times* as "captivating and complete" and by *Kirkus Reviews* as "One of the best books on the ramifications of the electronic political process since Joe McGinniss's *The Selling of a President*." His first novel, *God Doesn't Shoot Craps*, was published by Sourcebooks in 2006 and optioned for film by the producers of the Broadway show *Xanadu*. A 1974 graduate of Carleton College, he works as a freelance advertising copywriter and lives with his wife Sharon in the Glover Park neighborhood of Washington, DC. If you'd like to contact Richard Armstrong with questions or comments, or about interview or book club requests, please visit www.TheDonCon.com.